P9-DVO-722

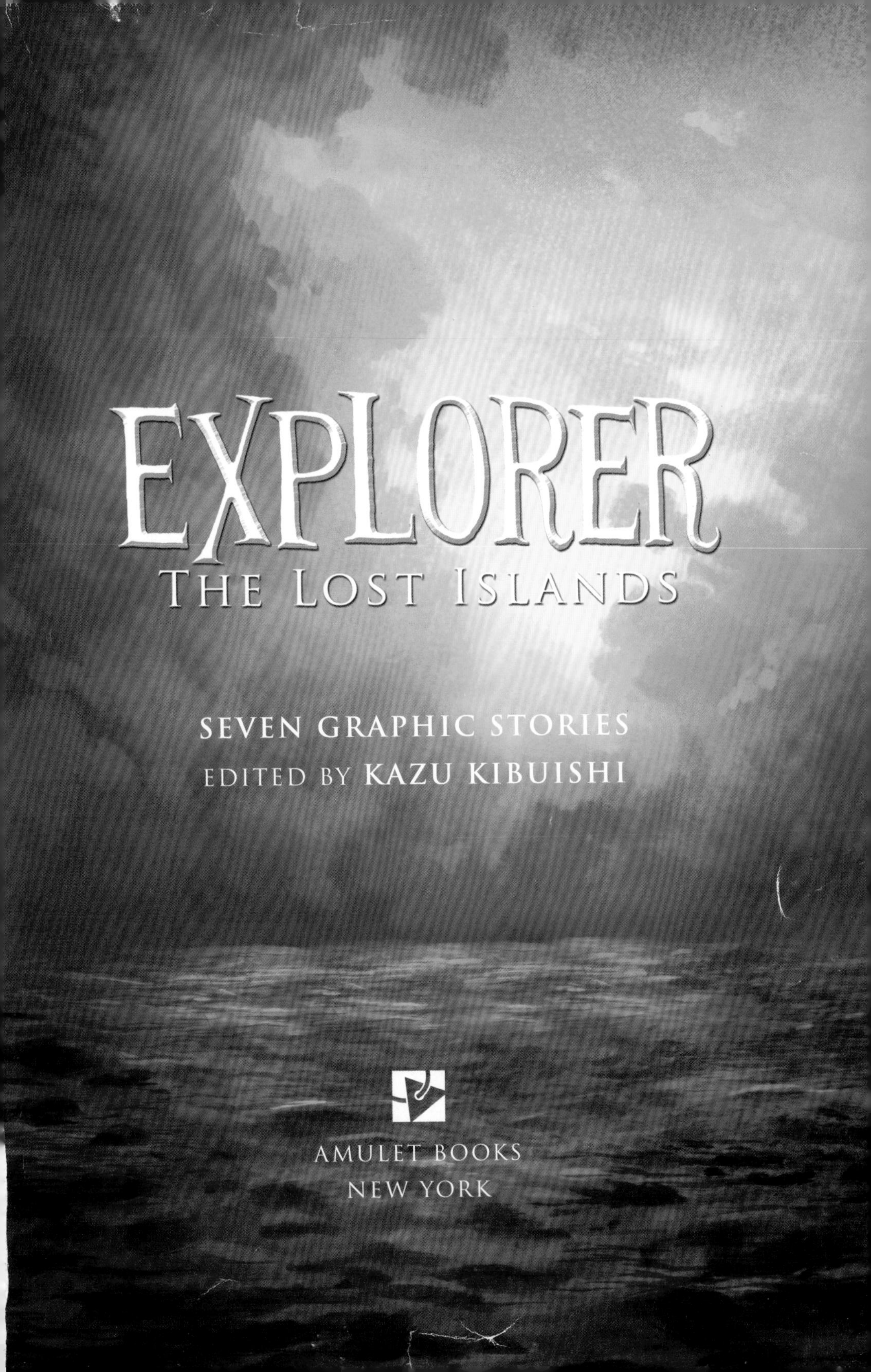

EXPLORER
THE LOST ISLANDS

SEVEN GRAPHIC STORIES

EDITED BY KAZU KIBUISHI

AMULET BOOKS
NEW YORK

THANKS TO MY COEDITOR, SHEILA KEENAN
—K.K.

Publisher's Note

This is a work of fiction. Names, characters, places, and incidents are either the product of the author's imagination or are used fictitiously, and any resemblances to actual person, living or dead, business establishments, events, or locales is entirely coincidental.

Library of Congress Control Number: 2013935794

Paperback ISBN 978-1-4197-0883-1
Hardcover ISBN 978-1-4197-0881-7

Cover art © 2013 Kazu Kibuishi
Book design by Chad W. Beckerman

Text and illustrations © 2013 by the individual artists as follows:
"Rabbit Island," pages 4–19, © 2013 Jake Parker
"The Mask Dance," pages 20–37, © 2013 Chrystin Garland
"Carapace," pages 38–55, © 2013 Jason Caffoe
"Desert Island Playlist," pages 56–73, text © 2013 Dave Roman;
illustrations © 2013 Raina Telgemeier
"Loah," pages 74–91, © 2013 Michel Gagné
"Radio Adrift," pages 92–109, text © 2013 Steven Shanahan;
illustrations © 2013 Katie Shanahan
"The Fishermen," pages 110–127, © 2013 Kazu Kibuishi

Printed and bound in China
10 9 8 7 6 5 4 3 2 1

Amulet Books are available at special discounts when purchased in quantity for premiums and promotions as well as fundraising or educational use. For details, contact specialmarkets@abramsbooks.com, or the address below.

ABRAMS
THE ART OF BOOKS SINCE 1949

115 West 18th Street
New York, NY 10011
www.abramsbooks.com

CONTENTS

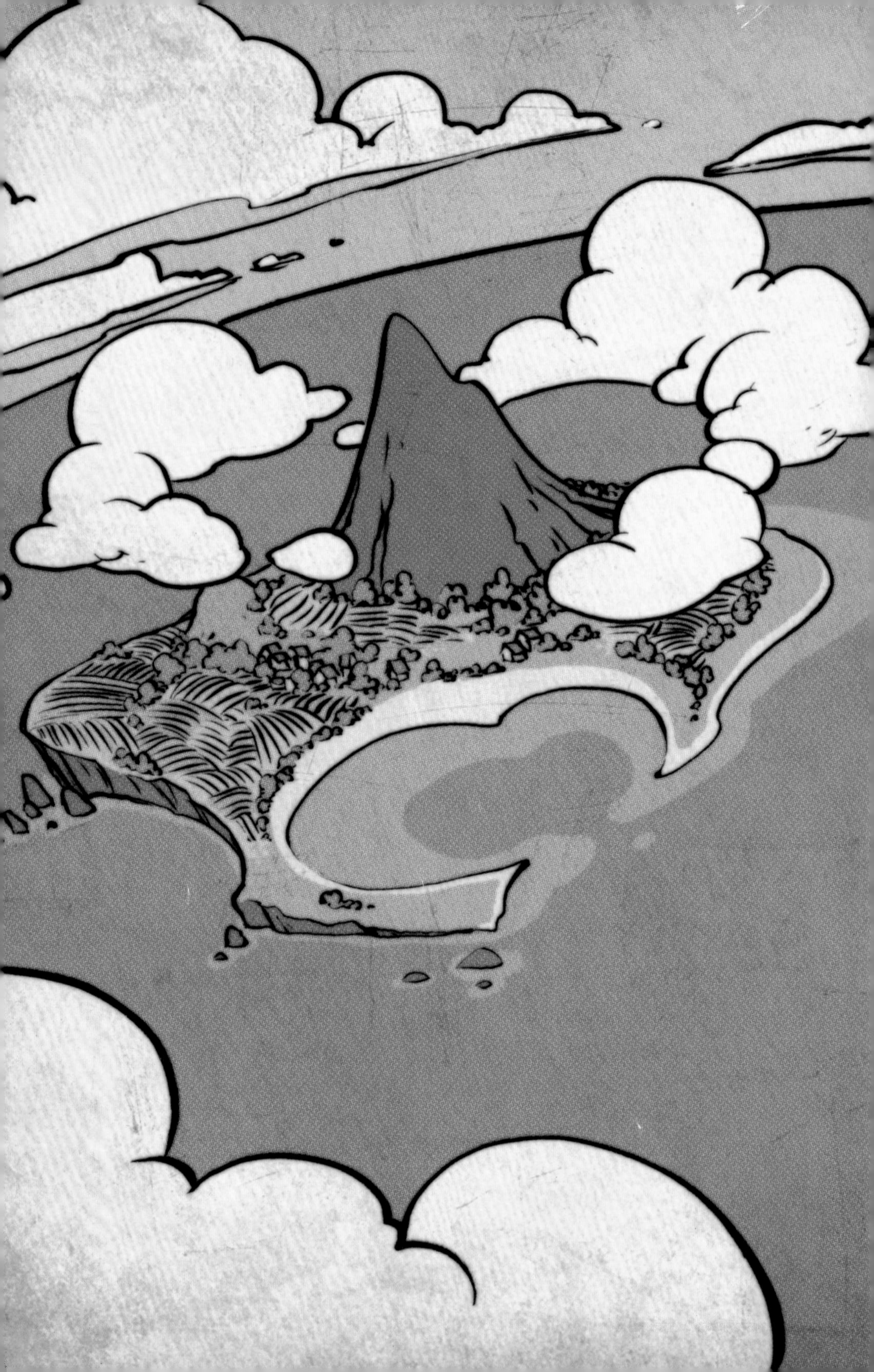

RABBIT ISLAND

BY JAKE PARKER

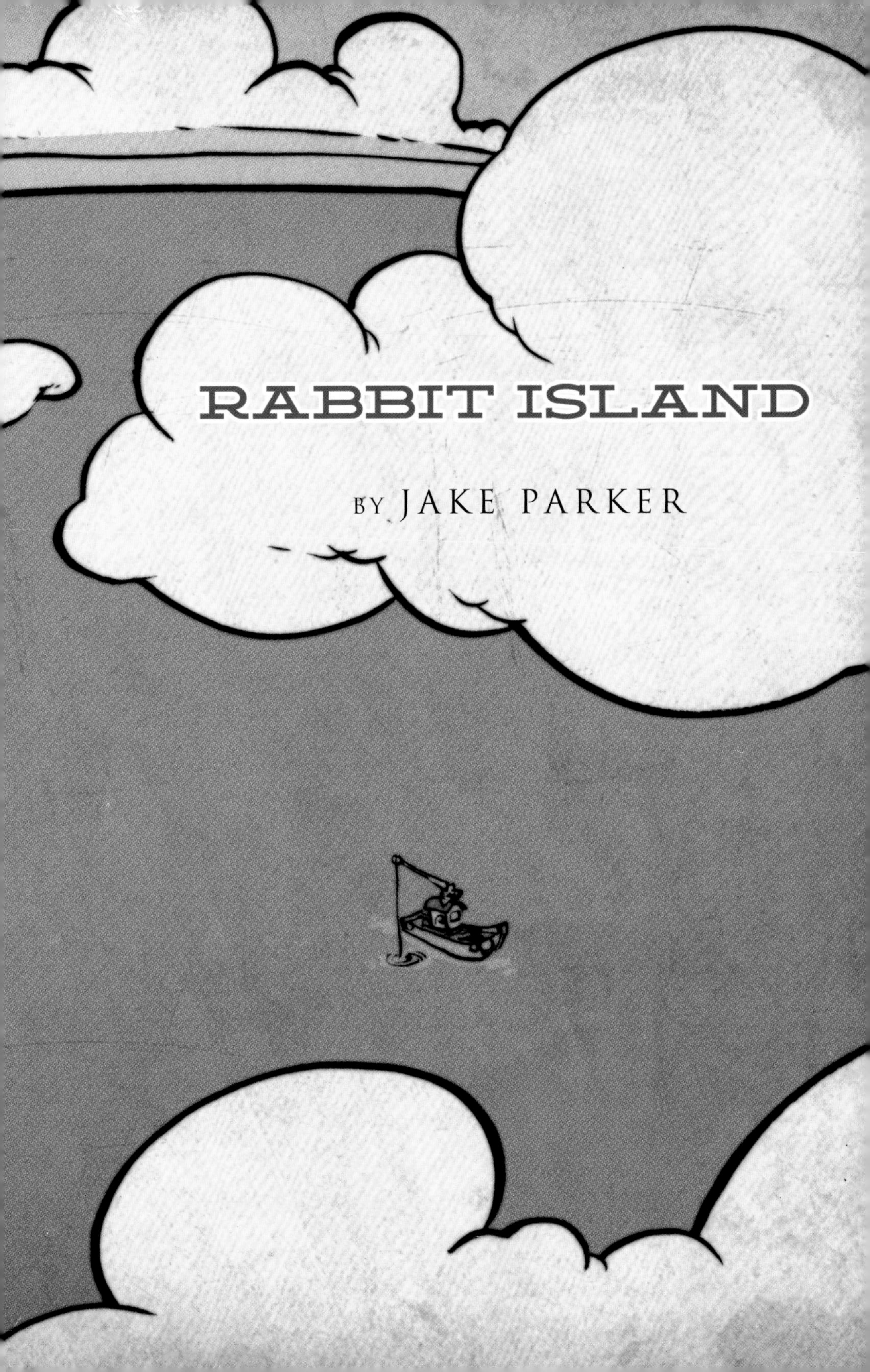

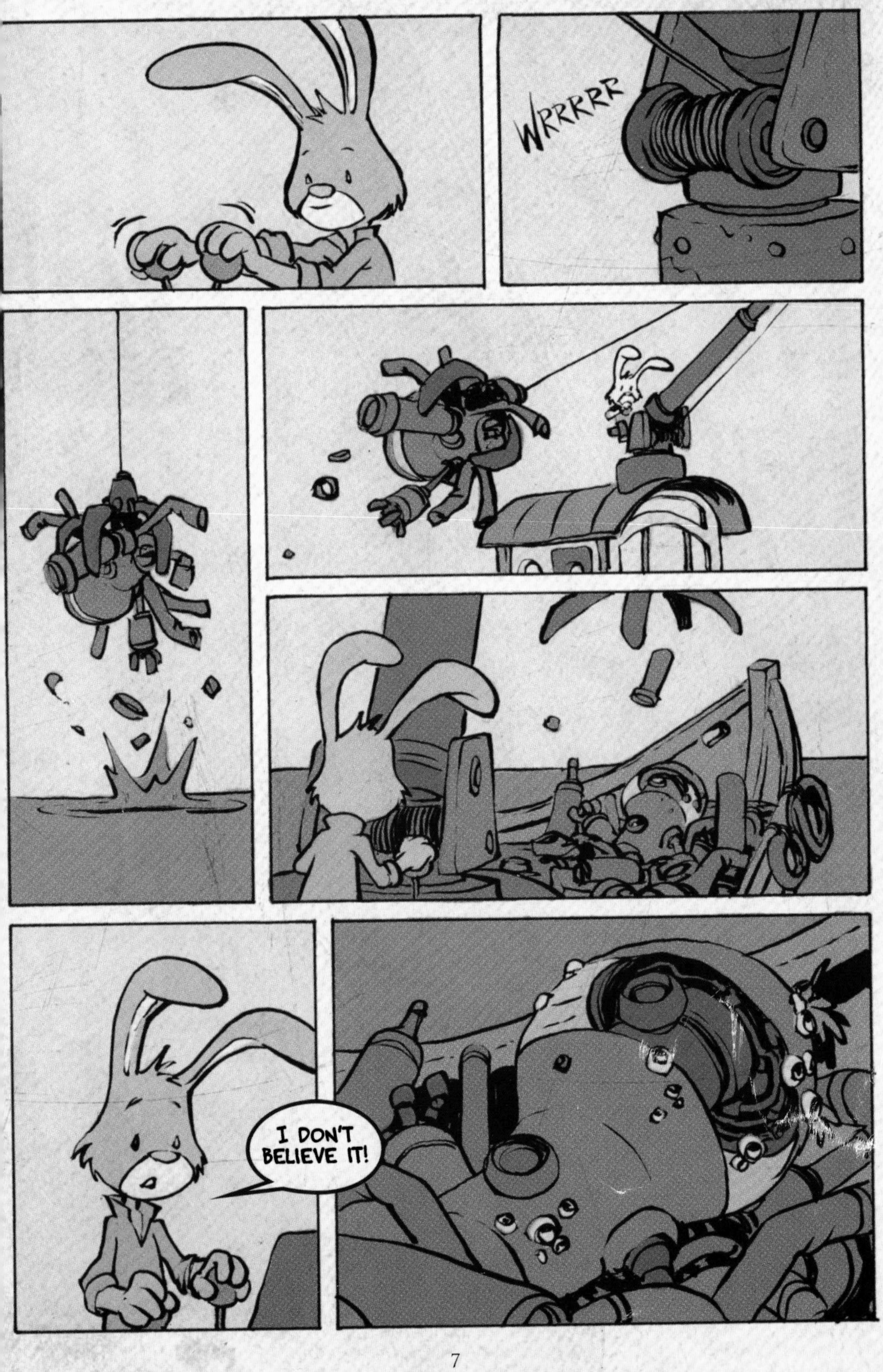
WRRRRR
I DON'T BELIEVE IT!

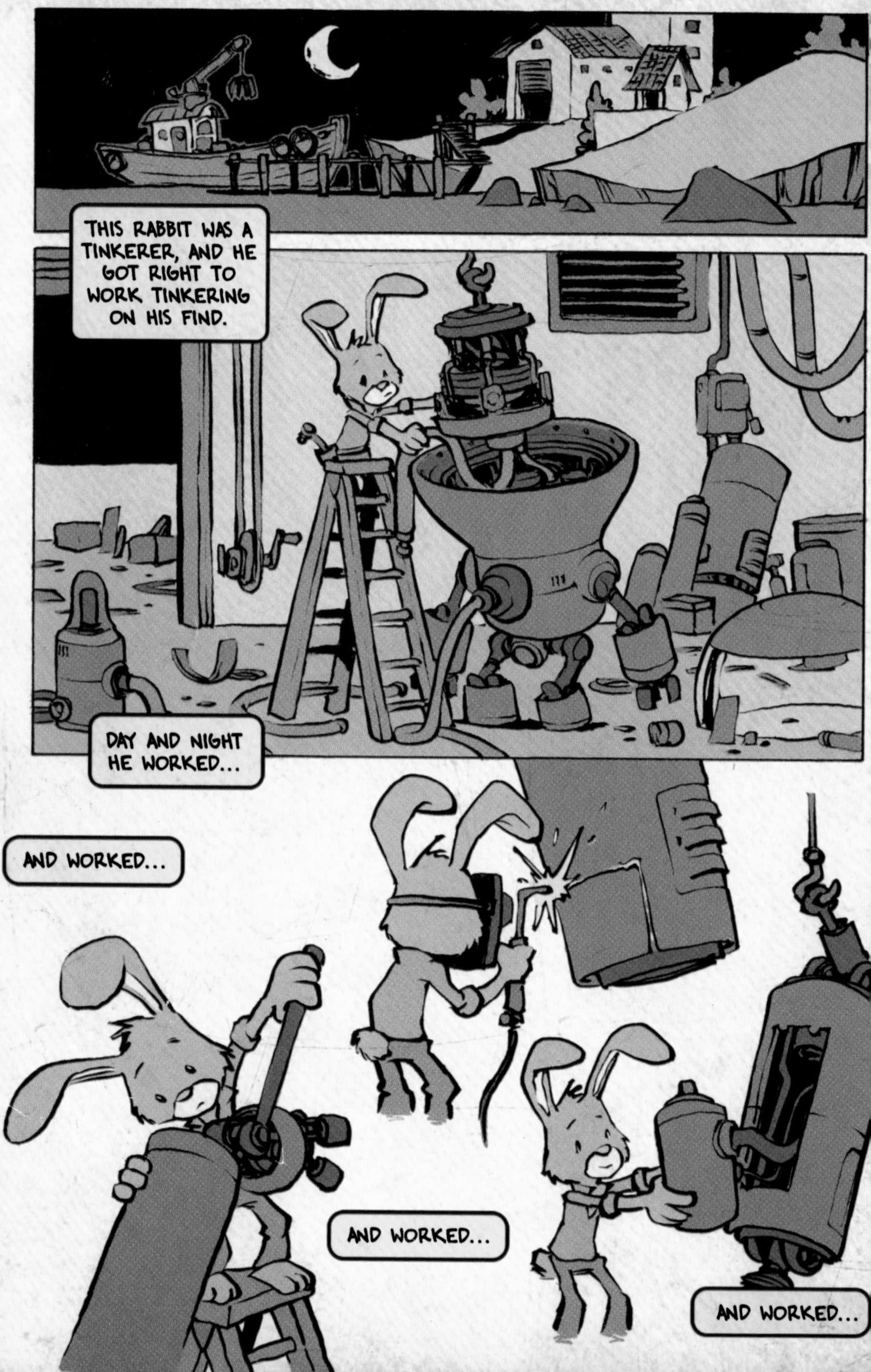
THIS RABBIT WAS A TINKERER, AND HE GOT RIGHT TO WORK TINKERING ON HIS FIND.
DAY AND NIGHT HE WORKED...
AND WORKED...
AND WORKED...
AND WORKED...

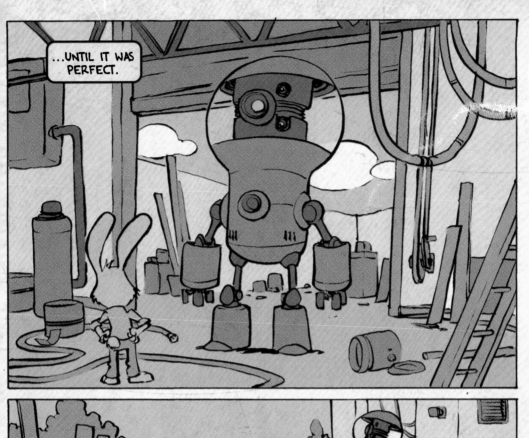

...UNTIL IT WAS PERFECT.

ALL RIGHT, ROBOT, THIS PLACE NEEDS CLEANING.

YOU START OVER HERE AND I'LL START OVER THERE.

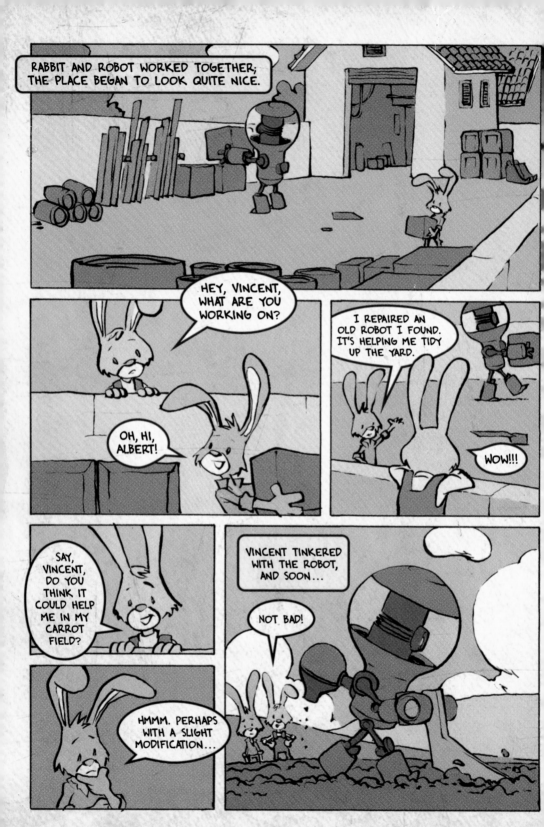

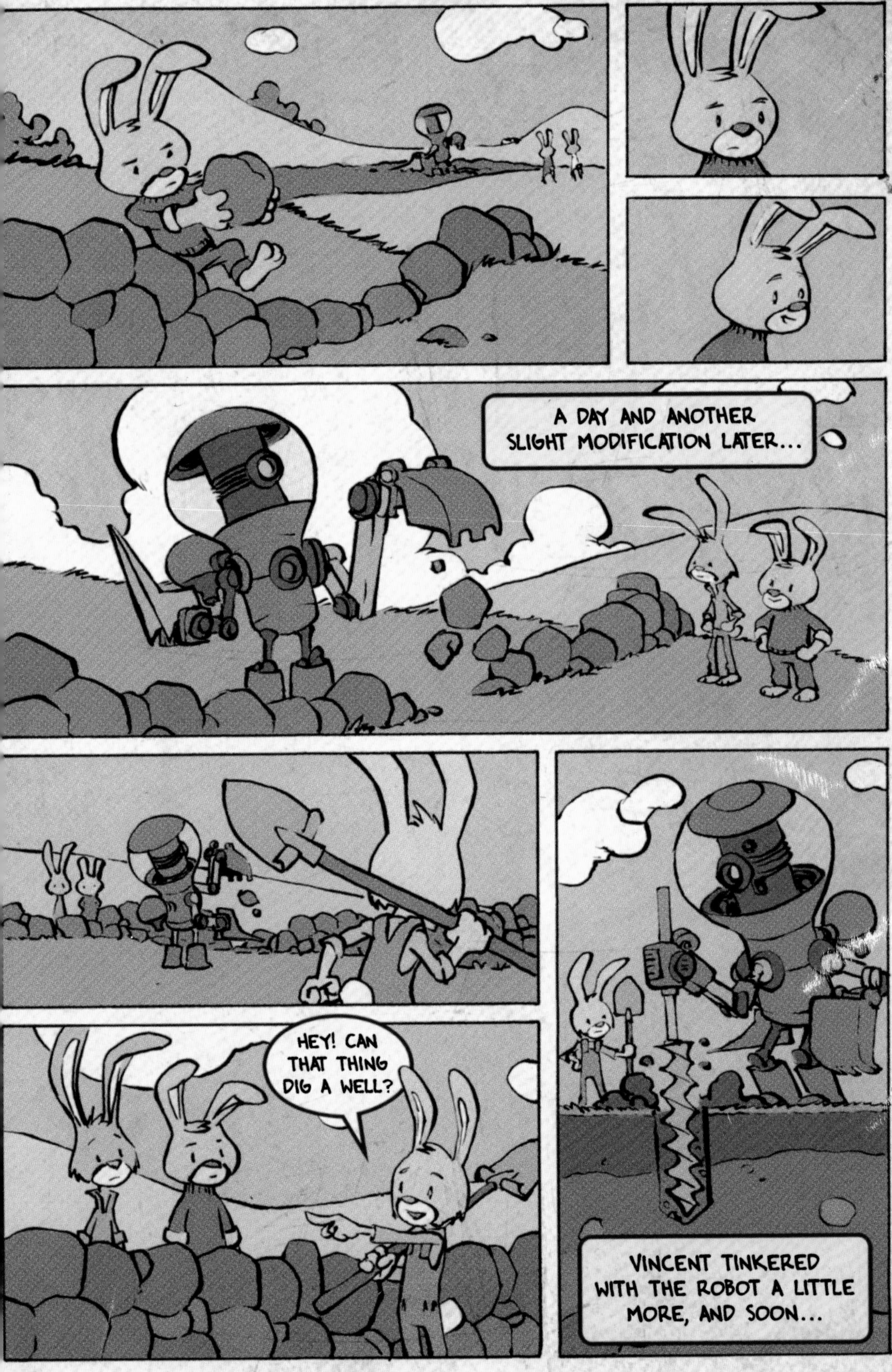
A DAY AND ANOTHER SLIGHT MODIFICATION LATER...
HEY! CAN THAT THING DIG A WELL?
VINCENT TINKERED WITH THE ROBOT A LITTLE MORE, AND SOON...

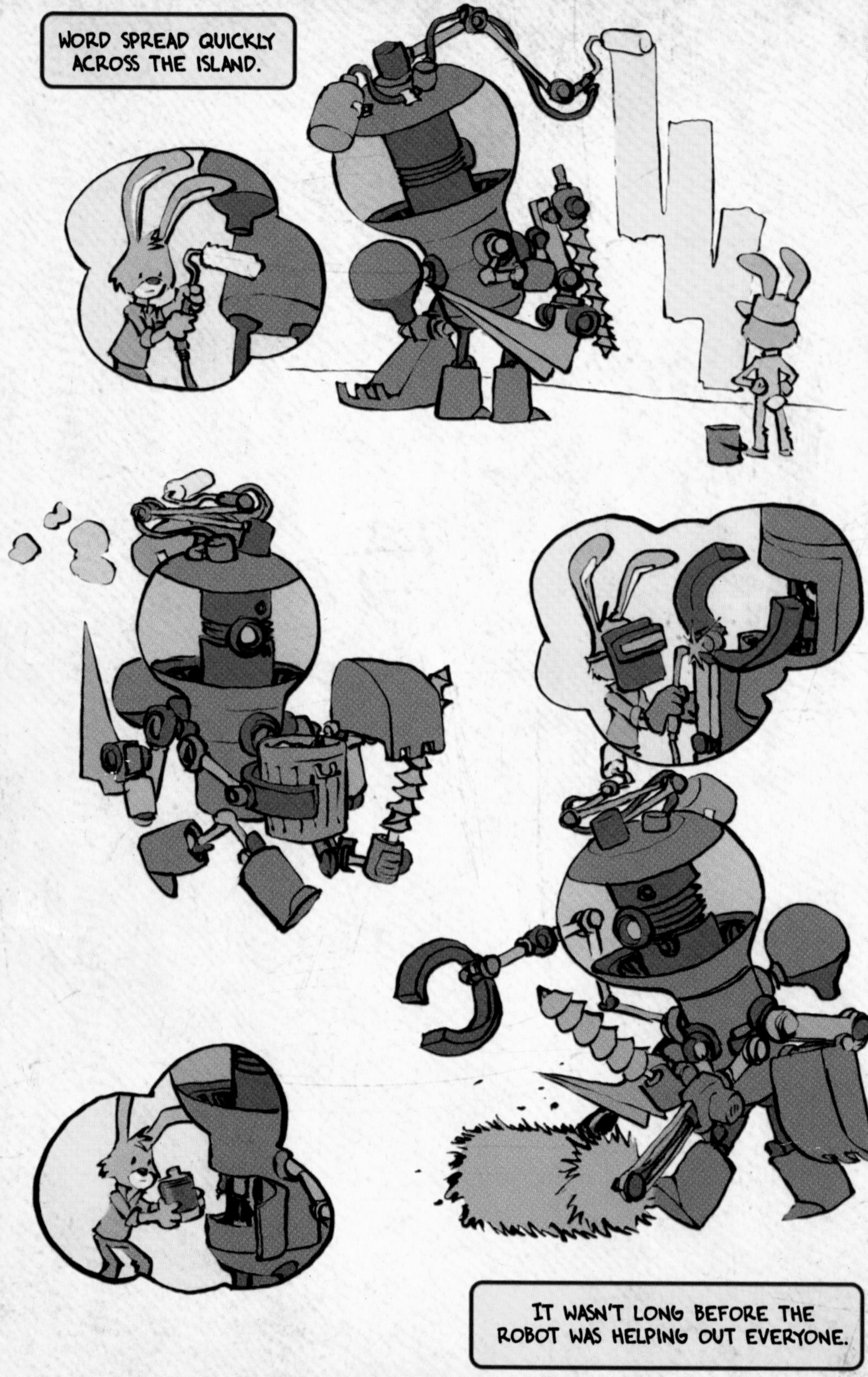
WORD SPREAD QUICKLY ACROSS THE ISLAND.
IT WASN'T LONG BEFORE THE ROBOT WAS HELPING OUT EVERYONE.

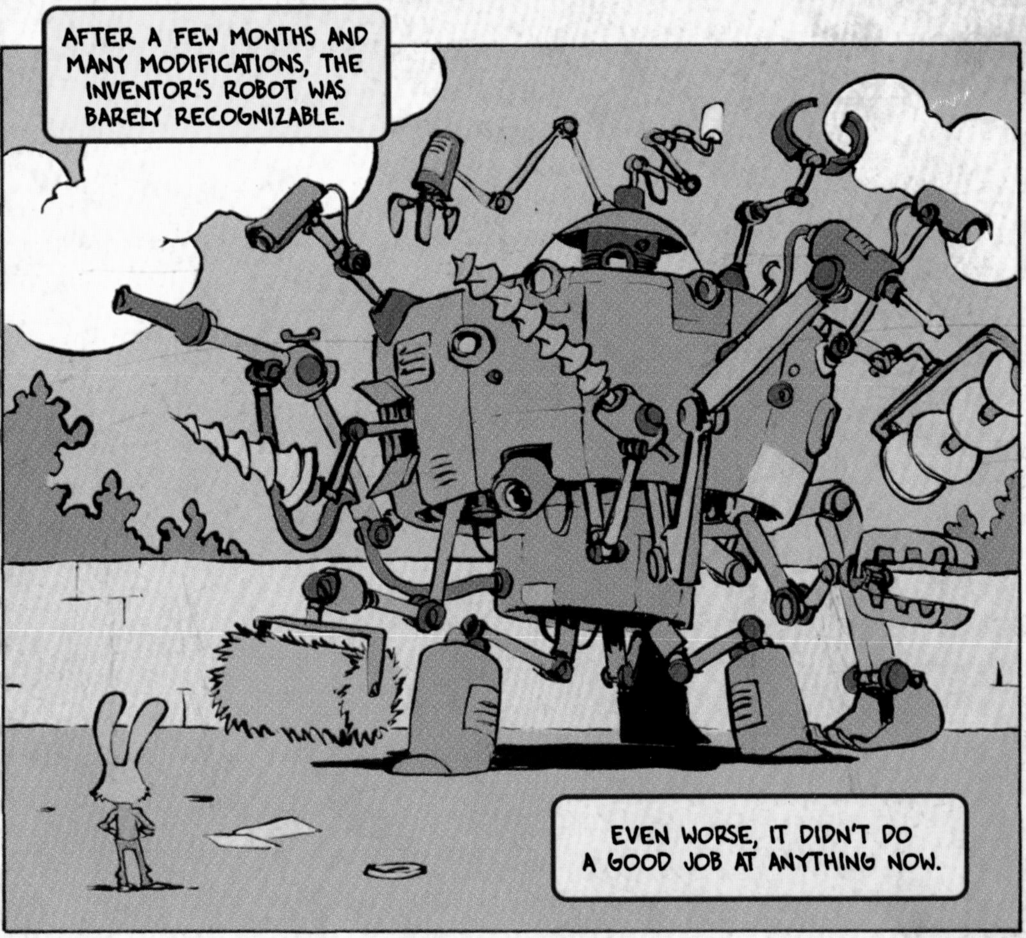
AFTER A FEW MONTHS AND MANY MODIFICATIONS, THE INVENTOR'S ROBOT WAS BARELY RECOGNIZABLE.
EVEN WORSE, IT DIDN'T DO A GOOD JOB AT ANYTHING NOW.

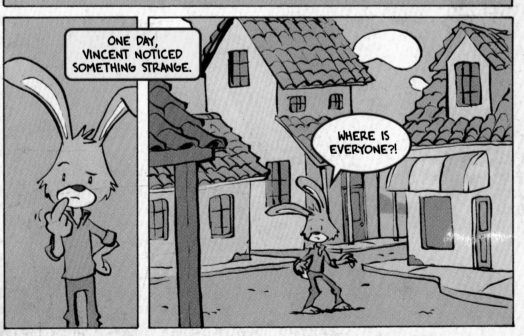

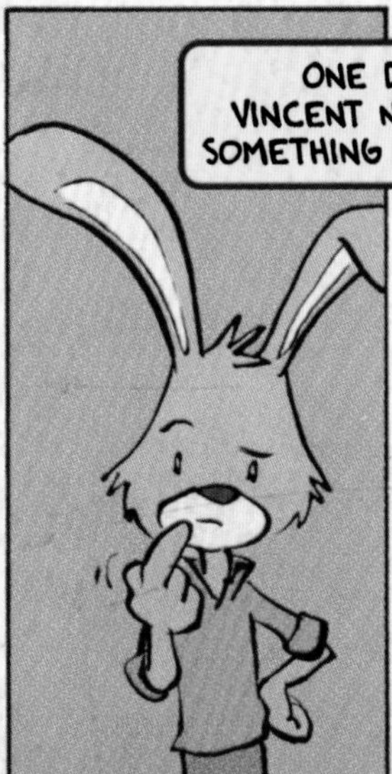
ONE DAY, VINCENT NOTICED SOMETHING STRANGE.

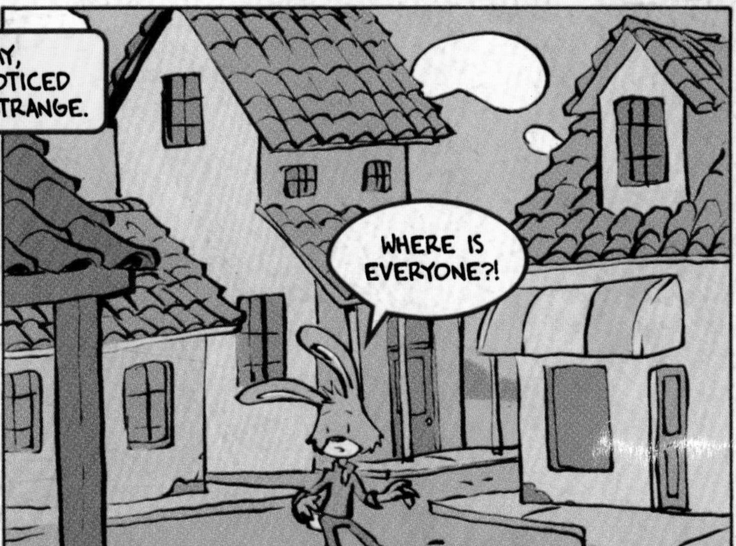
WHERE IS EVERYONE?!

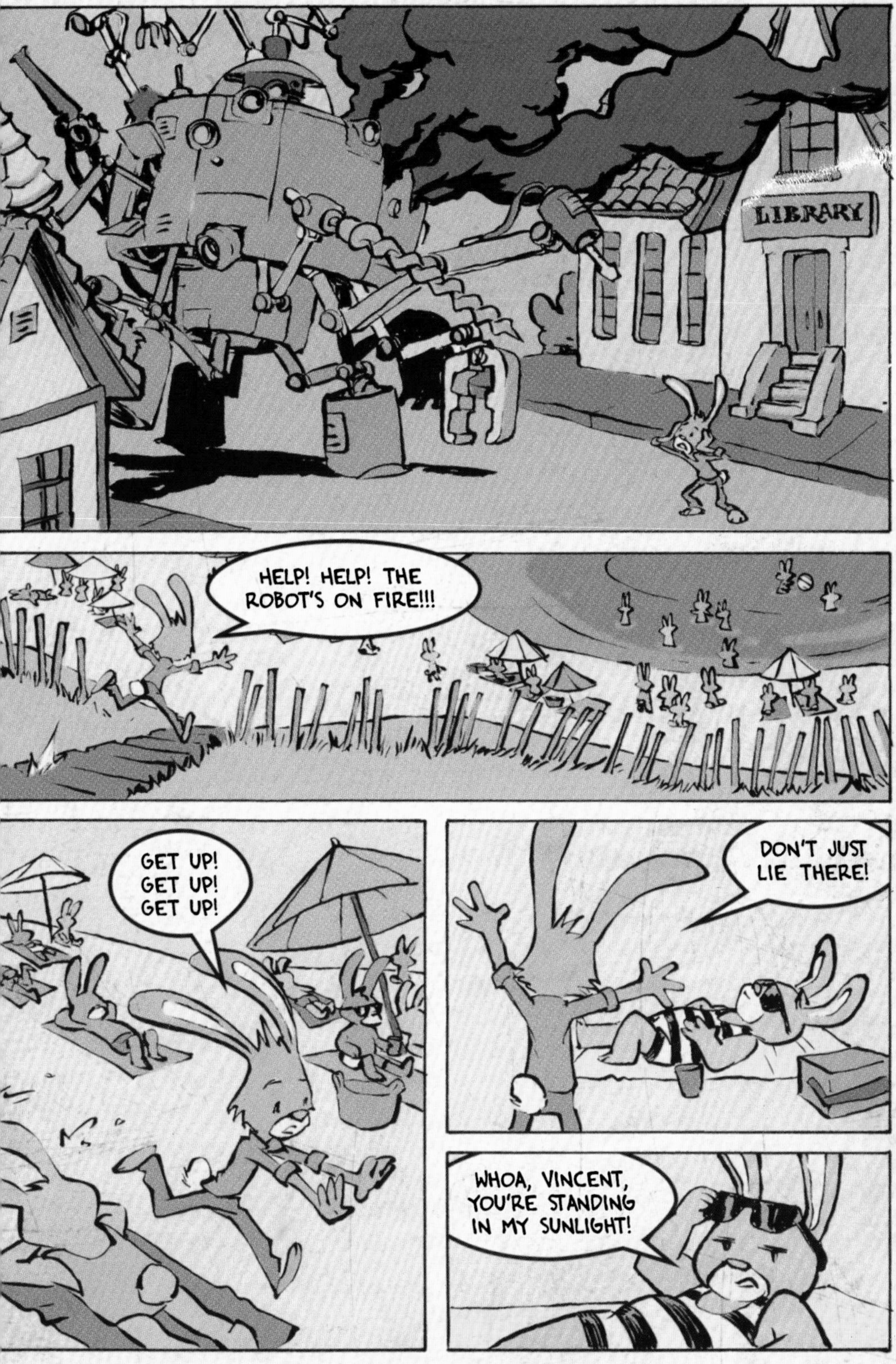
LIBRARY
HELP! HELP! THE ROBOT'S ON FIRE!!!
GET UP! GET UP! GET UP!
DON'T JUST LIE THERE!
WHOA, VINCENT, YOU'RE STANDING IN MY SUNLIGHT!

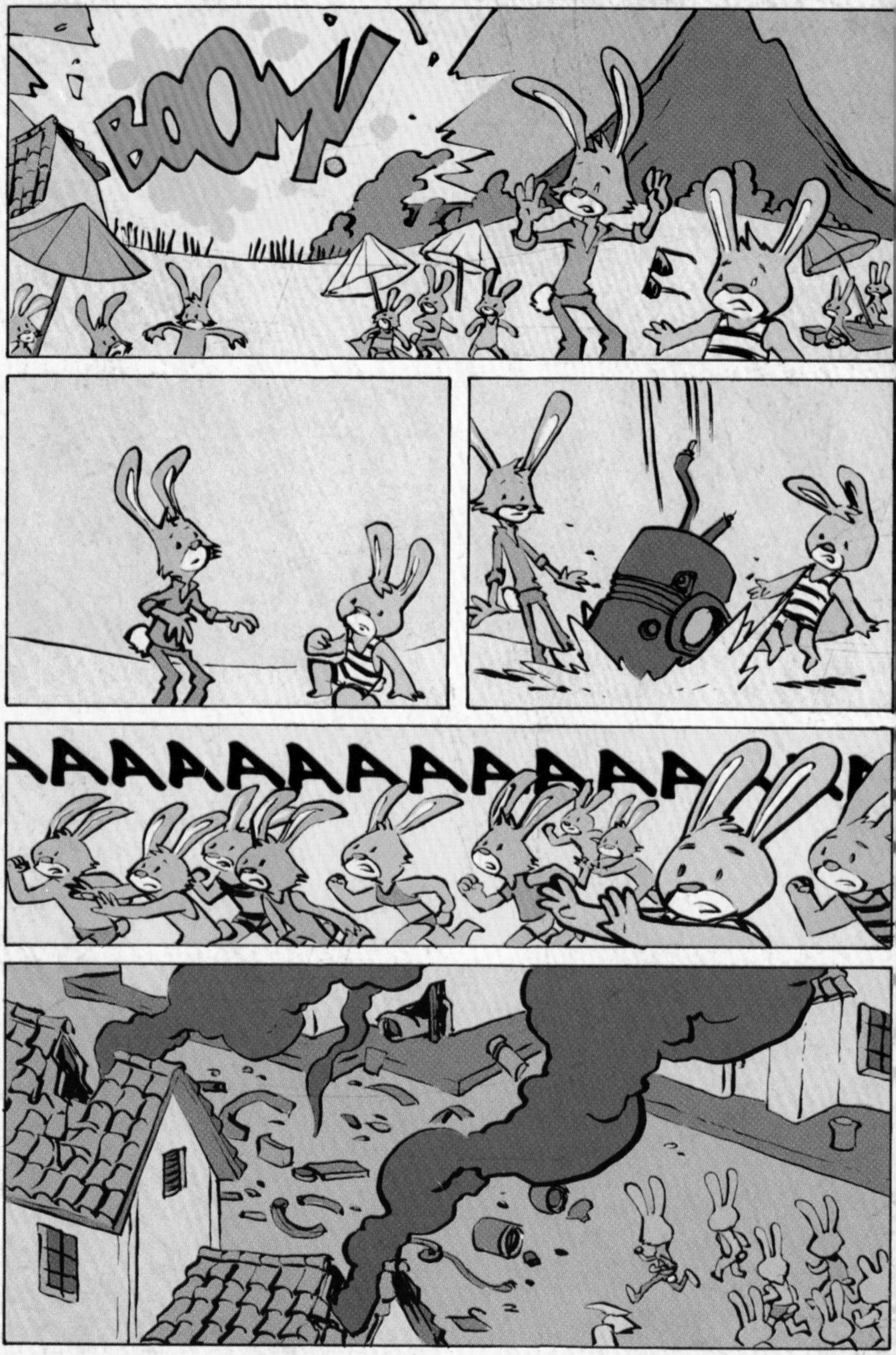
BOOM!
AAAAAAAAAAAAA

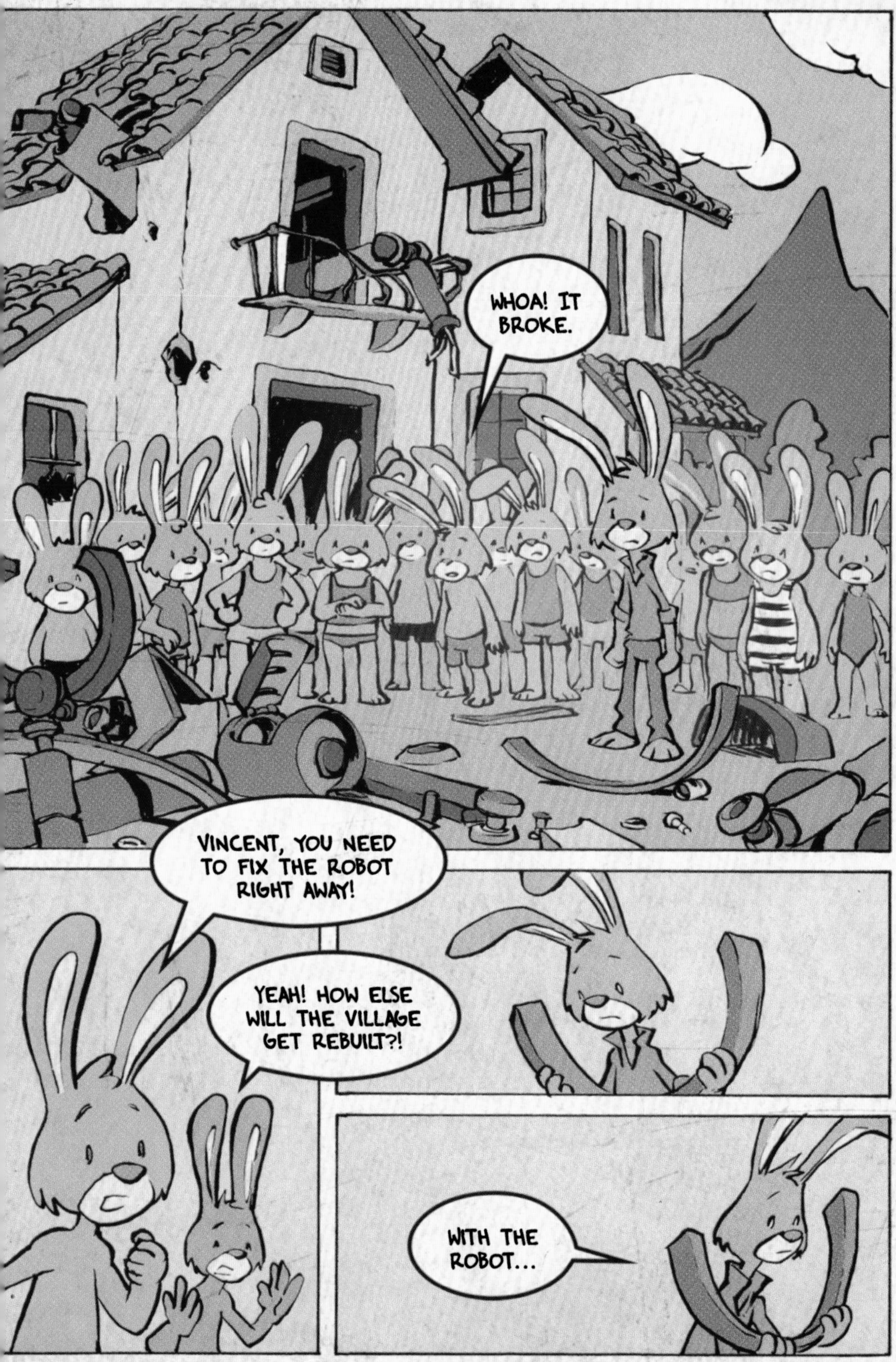
WHOA! IT BROKE.
VINCENT, YOU NEED TO FIX THE ROBOT RIGHT AWAY!
YEAH! HOW ELSE WILL THE VILLAGE GET REBUILT?!
WITH THE ROBOT...

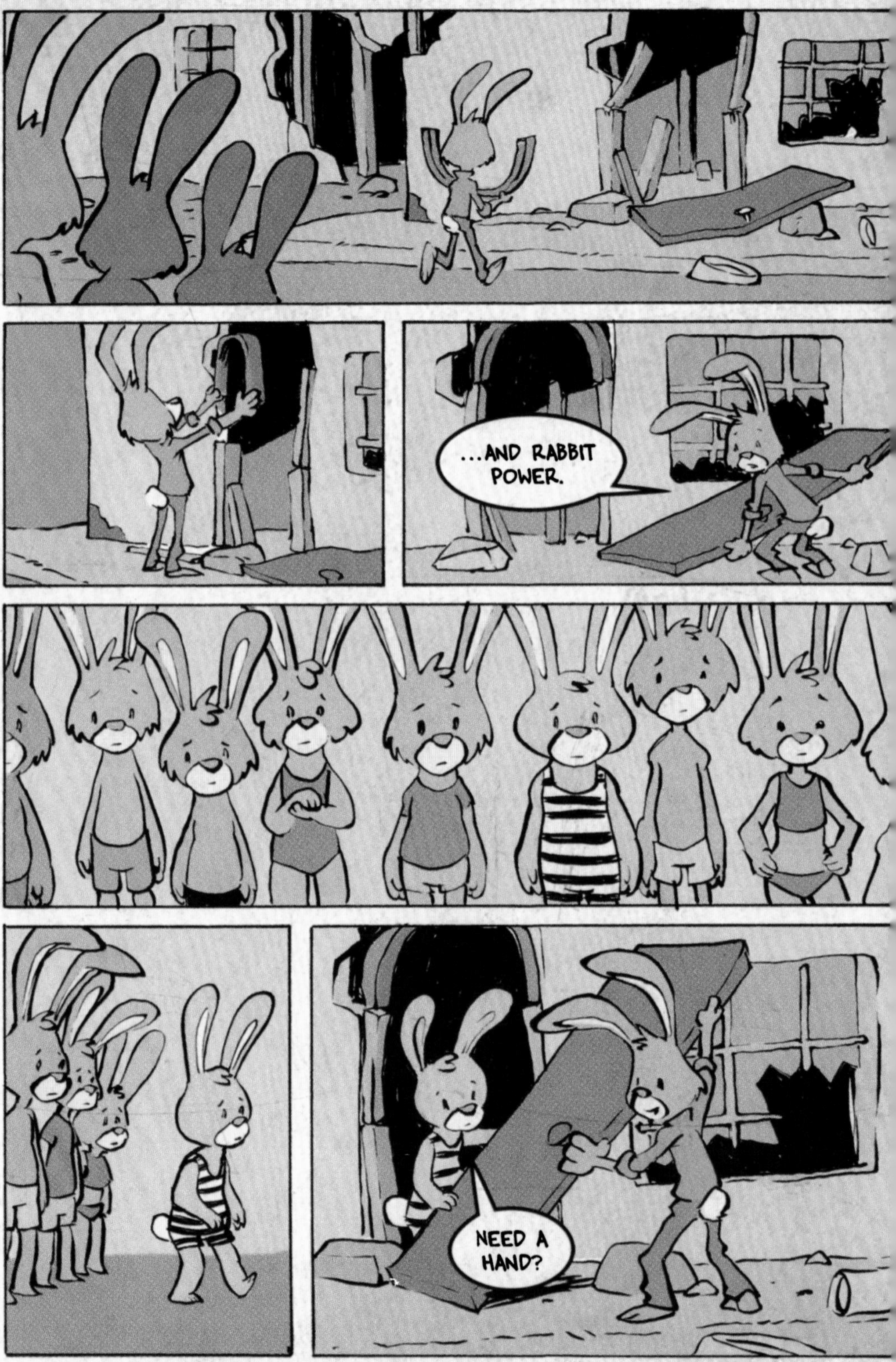
...AND RABBIT POWER.
NEED A HAND?

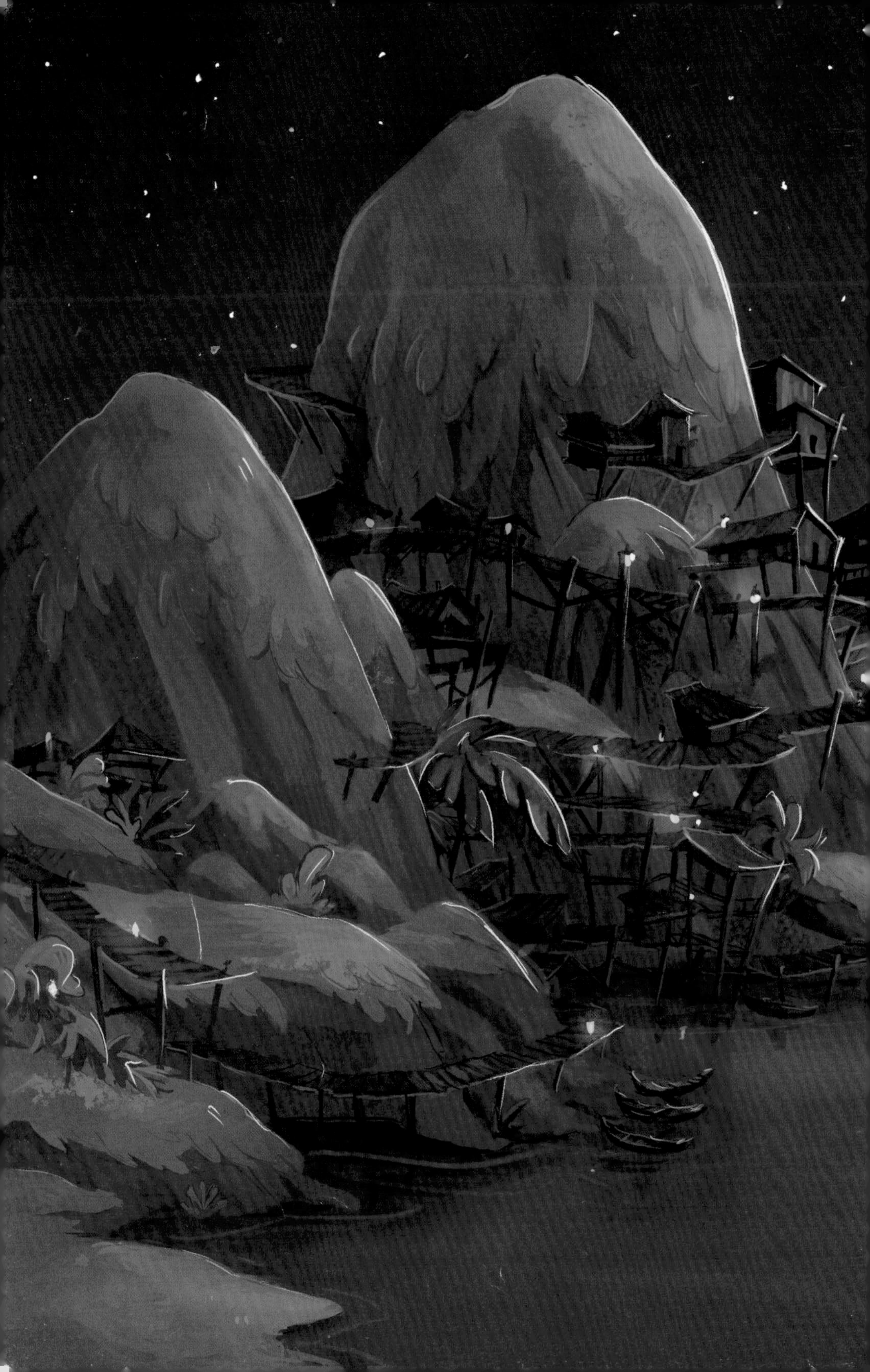

THE MASK DANCE

BY CHRYSTIN GARLAND

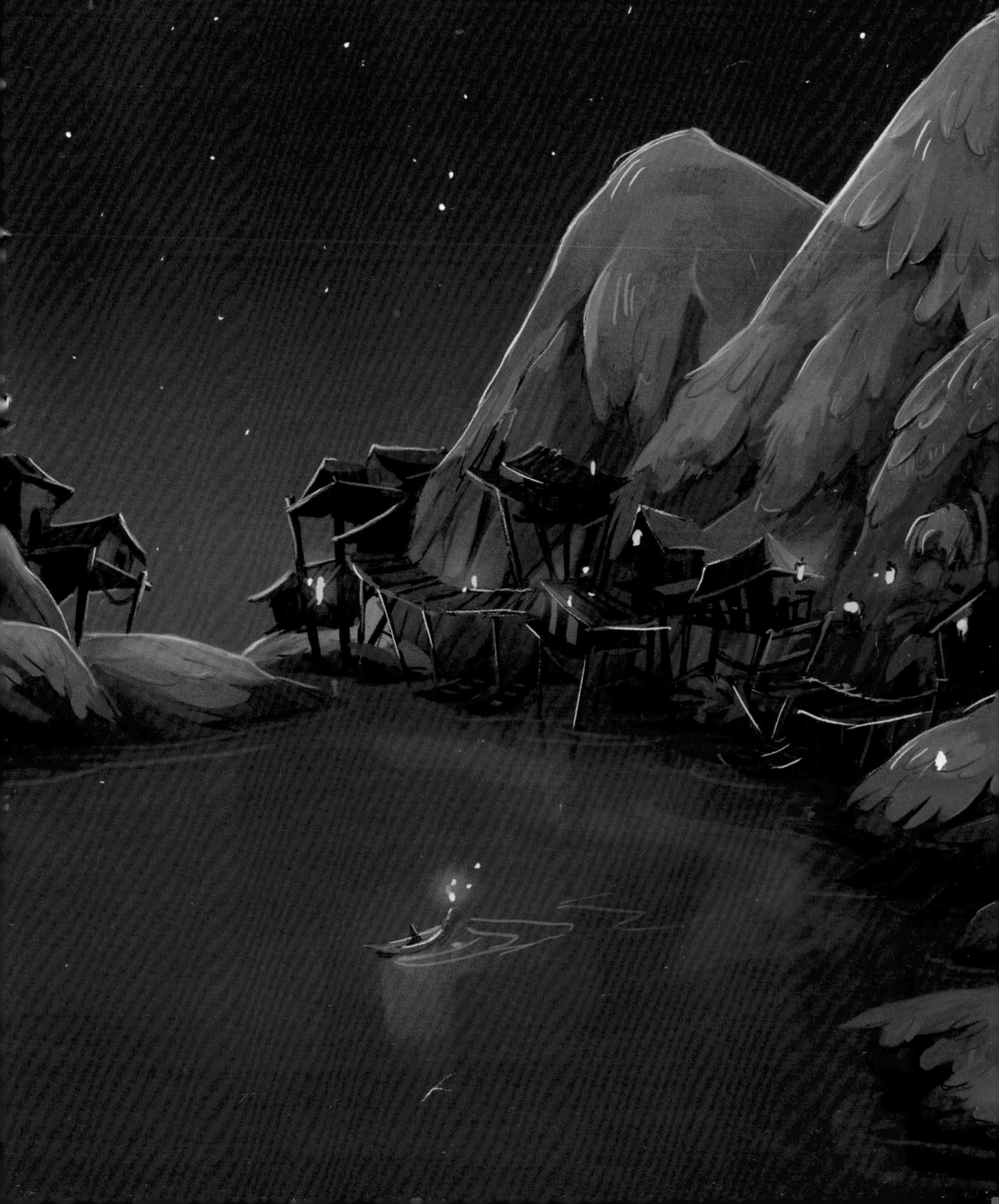

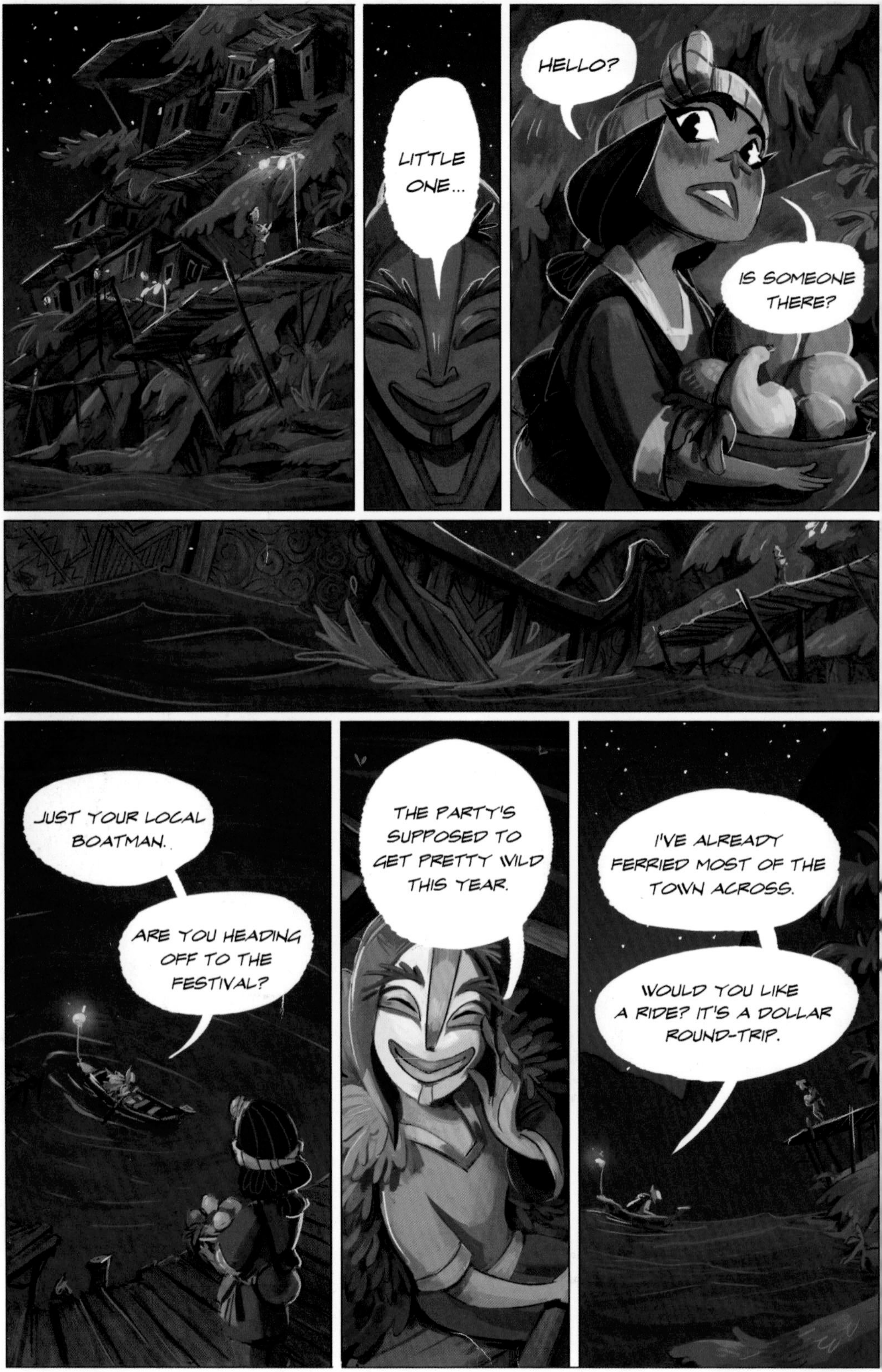
LITTLE ONE...
HELLO?
IS SOMEONE THERE?
JUST YOUR LOCAL BOATMAN.
ARE YOU HEADING OFF TO THE FESTIVAL?
THE PARTY'S SUPPOSED TO GET PRETTY WILD THIS YEAR.
I'VE ALREADY FERRIED MOST OF THE TOWN ACROSS.
WOULD YOU LIKE A RIDE? IT'S A DOLLAR ROUND-TRIP.

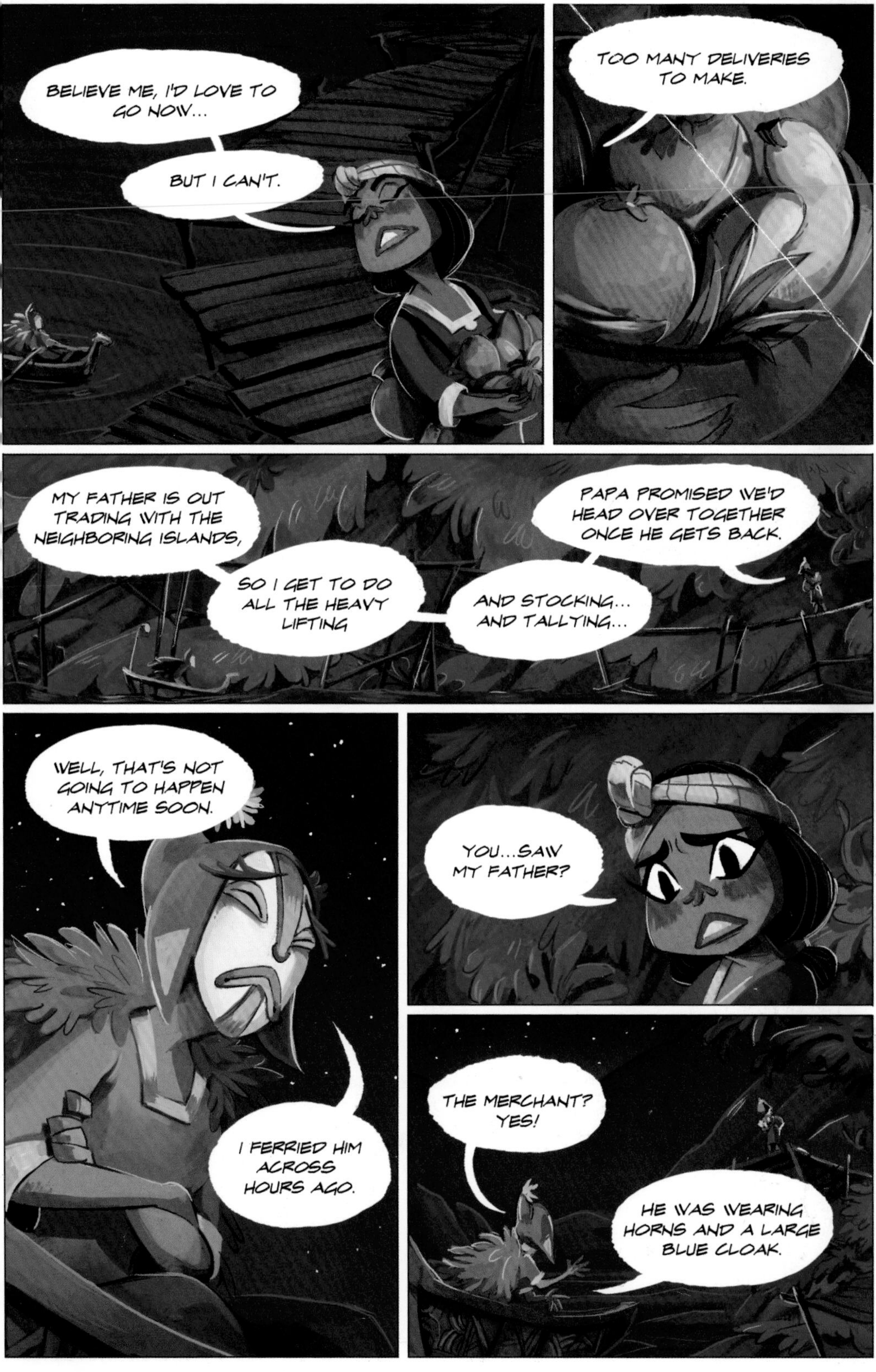
BELIEVE ME, I'D LOVE TO GO NOW...
BUT I CAN'T.
TOO MANY DELIVERIES TO MAKE.
MY FATHER IS OUT TRADING WITH THE NEIGHBORING ISLANDS,
SO I GET TO DO ALL THE HEAVY LIFTING
AND STOCKING... AND TALLYING...
PAPA PROMISED WE'D HEAD OVER TOGETHER ONCE HE GETS BACK.
WELL, THAT'S NOT GOING TO HAPPEN ANYTIME SOON.
I FERRIED HIM ACROSS HOURS AGO.
YOU...SAW MY FATHER?
THE MERCHANT? YES!
HE WAS WEARING HORNS AND A LARGE BLUE CLOAK.

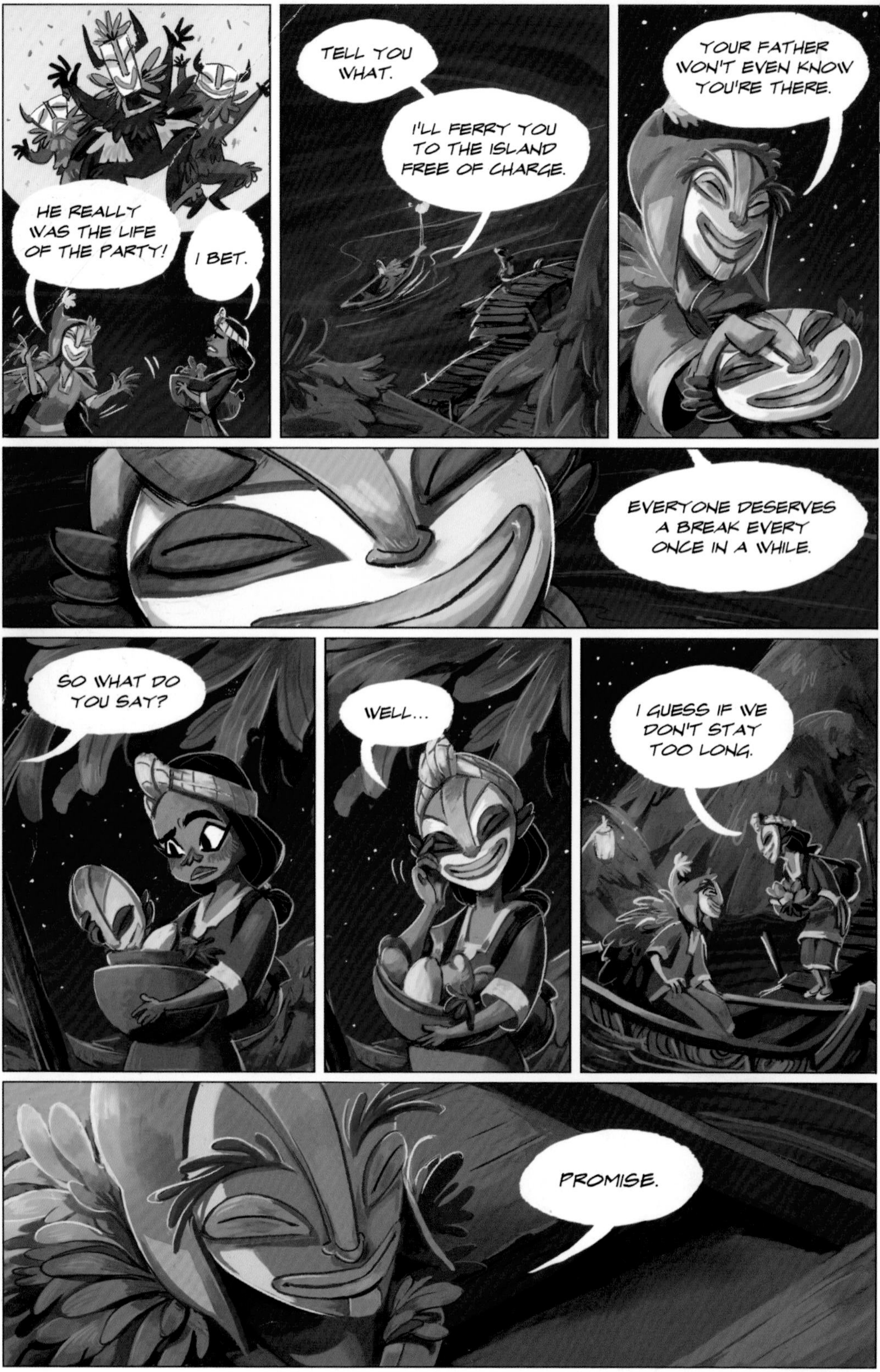
HE REALLY WAS THE LIFE OF THE PARTY!
I BET.
TELL YOU WHAT.
I'LL FERRY YOU TO THE ISLAND FREE OF CHARGE.
YOUR FATHER WON'T EVEN KNOW YOU'RE THERE.
EVERYONE DESERVES A BREAK EVERY ONCE IN A WHILE.
SO WHAT DO YOU SAY?
WELL...
I GUESS IF WE DON'T STAY TOO LONG.
PROMISE.

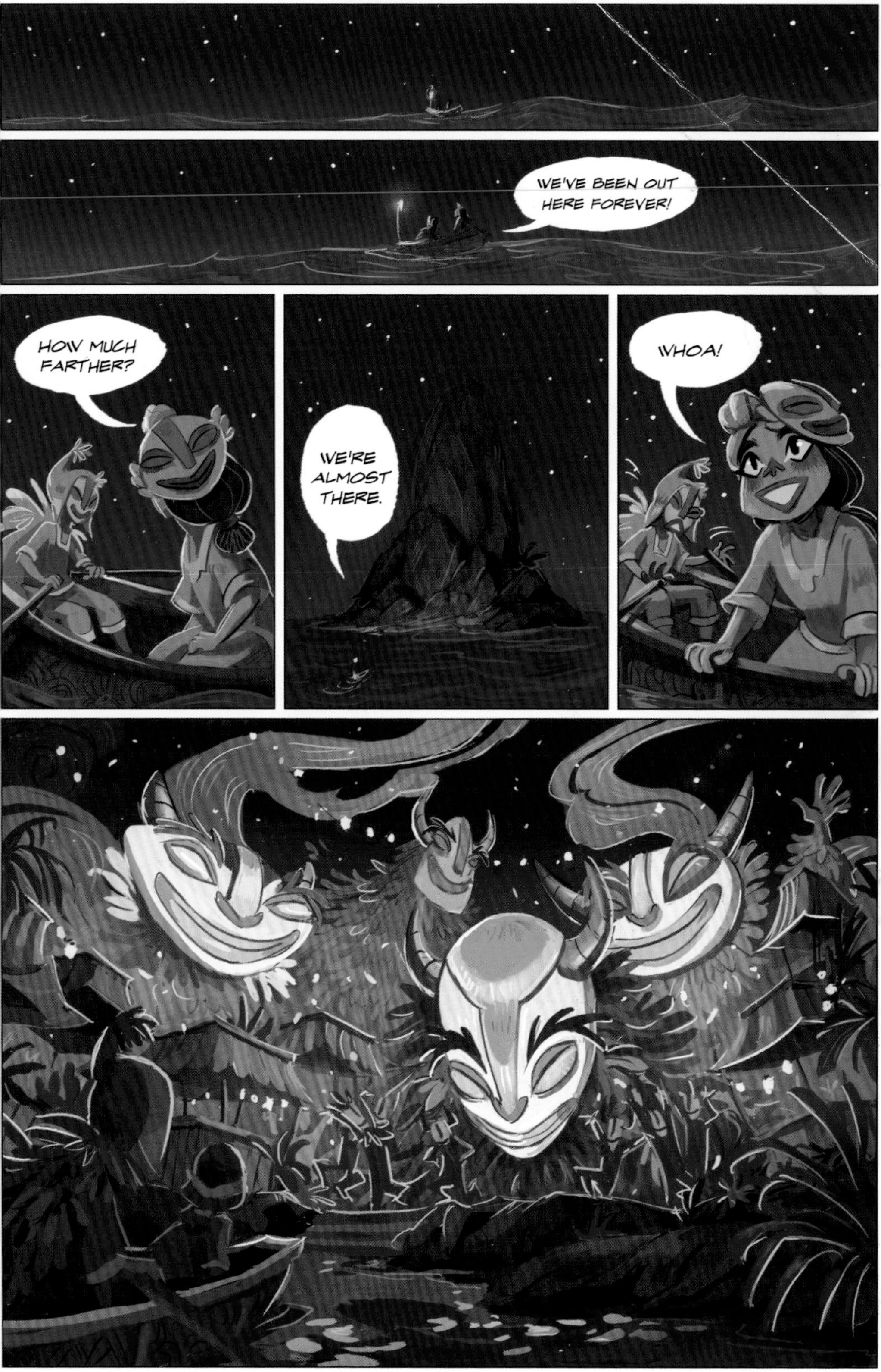
WE'VE BEEN OUT HERE FOREVER!
HOW MUCH FARTHER?
WE'RE ALMOST THERE.
WHOA!

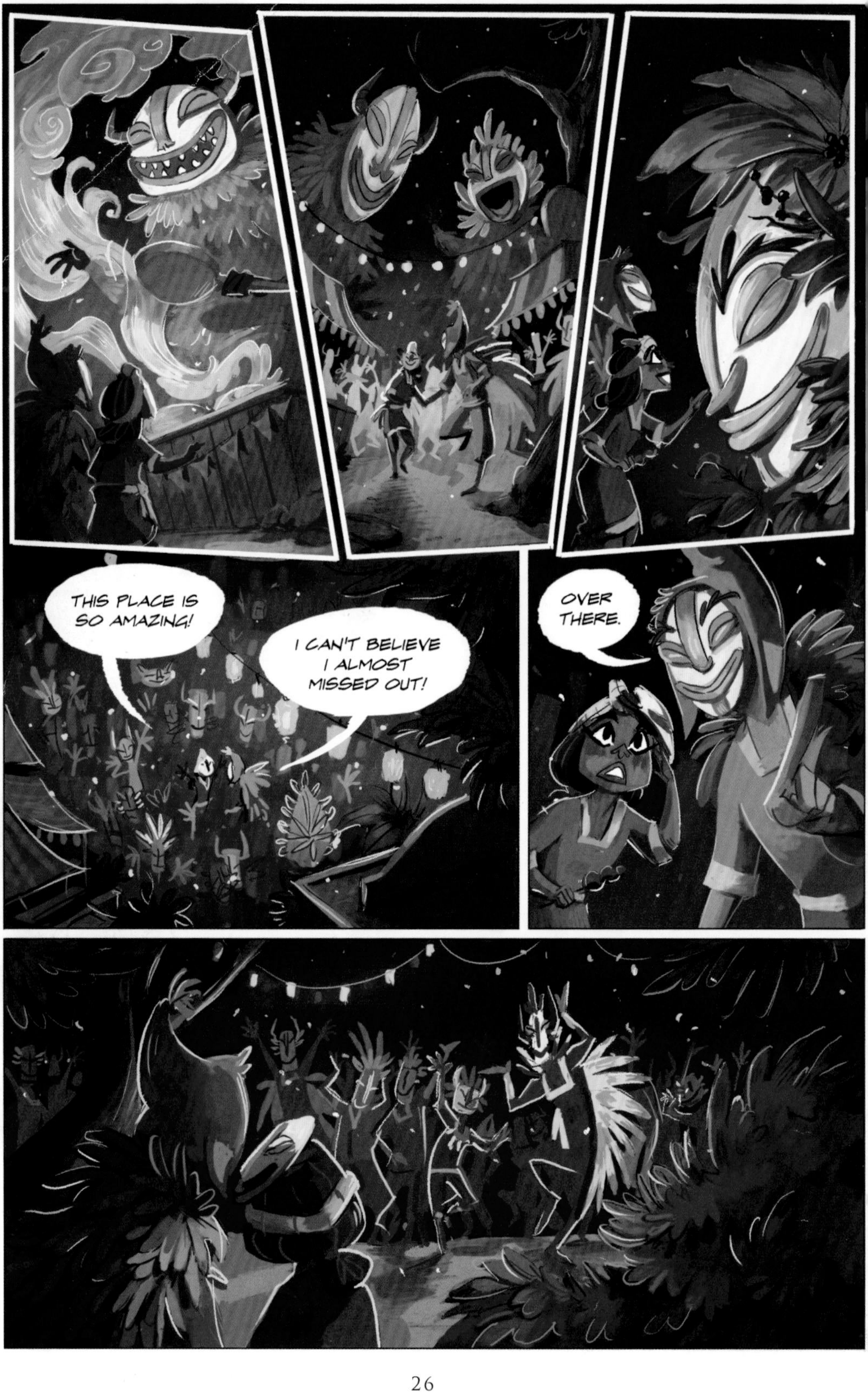
THIS PLACE IS SO AMAZING!
I CAN'T BELIEVE I ALMOST MISSED OUT!
OVER THERE.

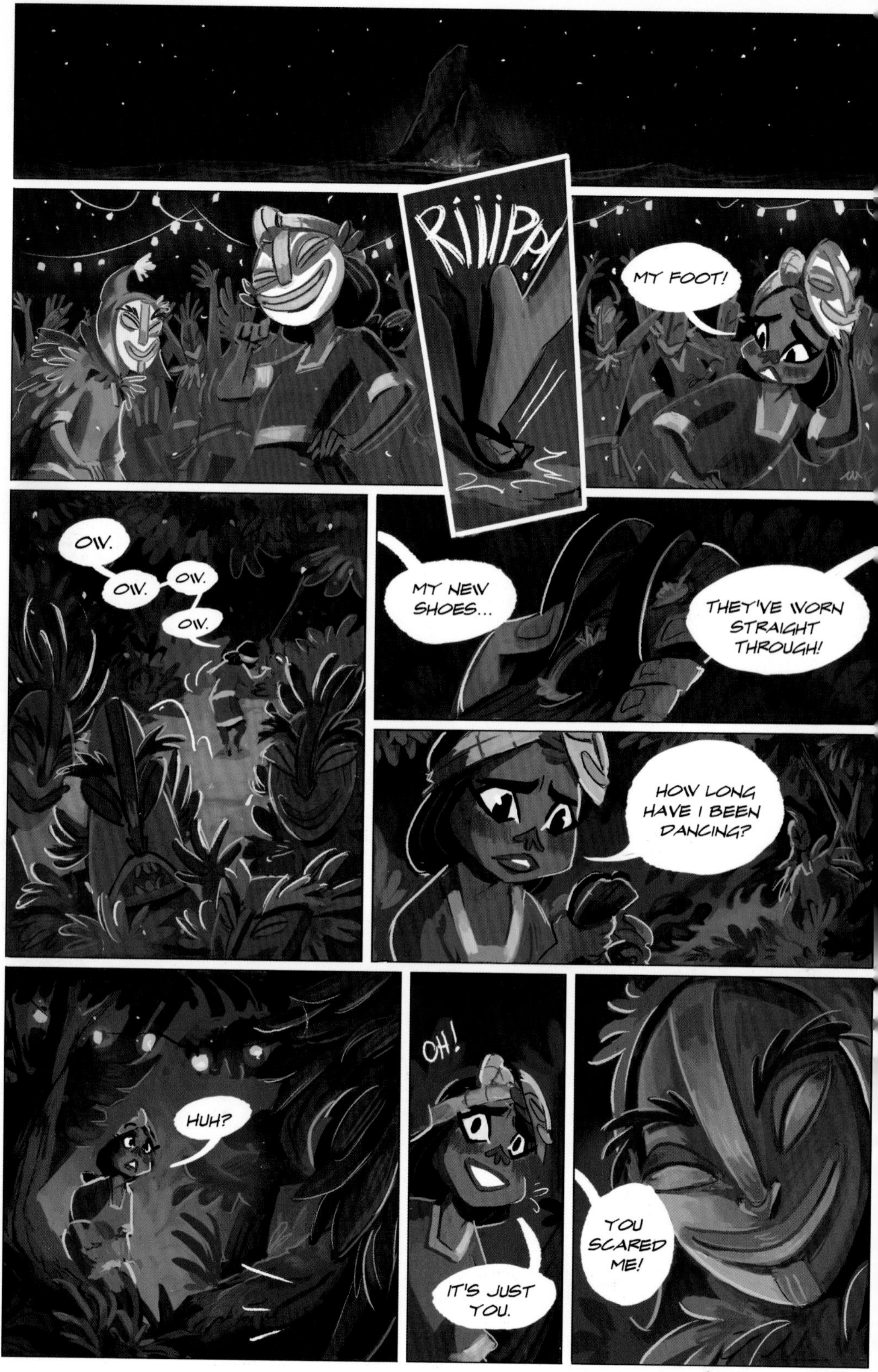
RIIIPP!
MY FOOT!
OW.
OW.
OW.
OW.
MY NEW SHOES...
THEY'VE WORN STRAIGHT THROUGH!
HOW LONG HAVE I BEEN DANCING?
HUH?
OH!
IT'S JUST YOU.
YOU SCARED ME!

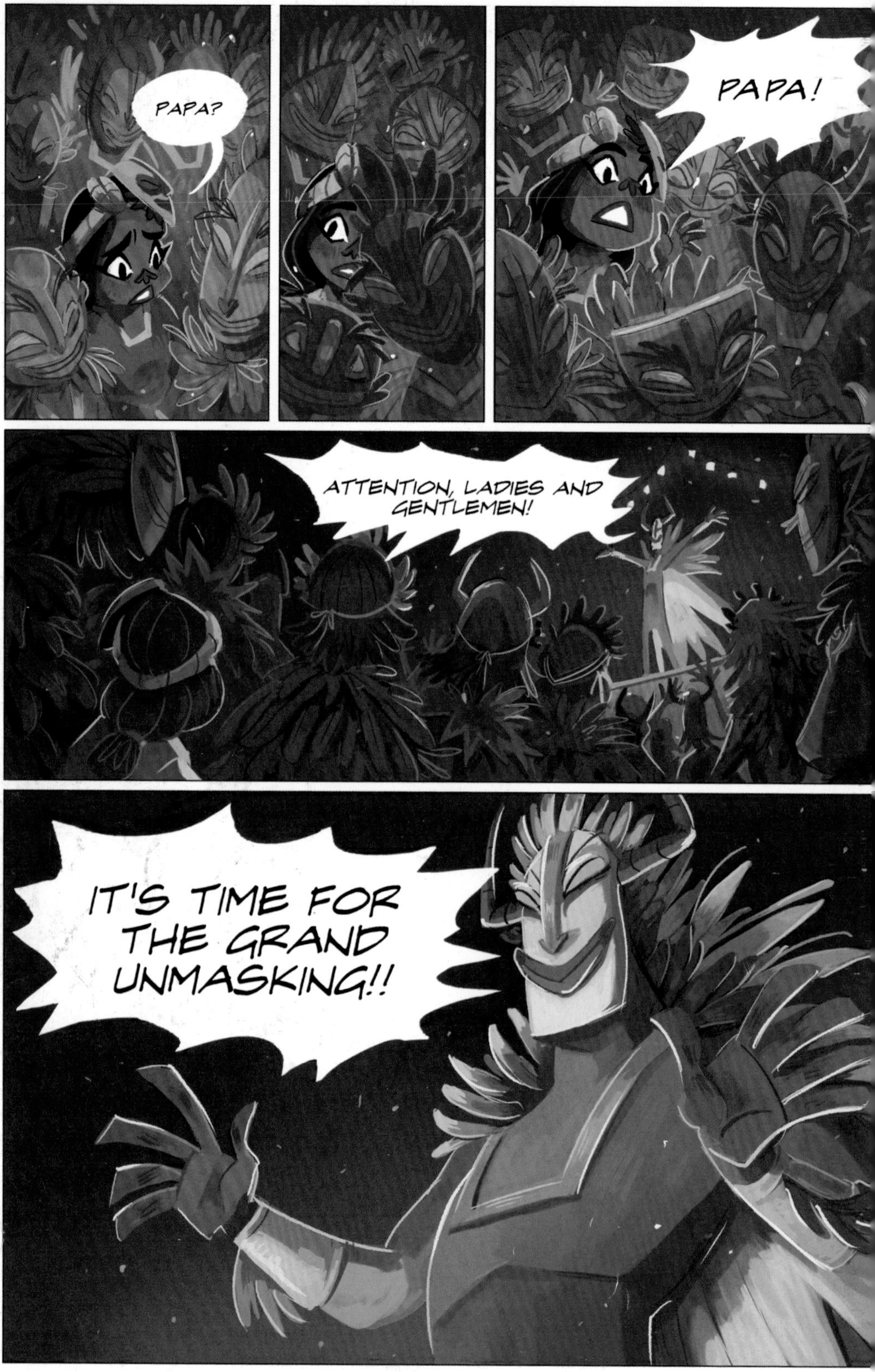
PAPA?
PAPA!
ATTENTION, LADIES AND GENTLEMEN!
IT'S TIME FOR THE GRAND UNMASKING!!

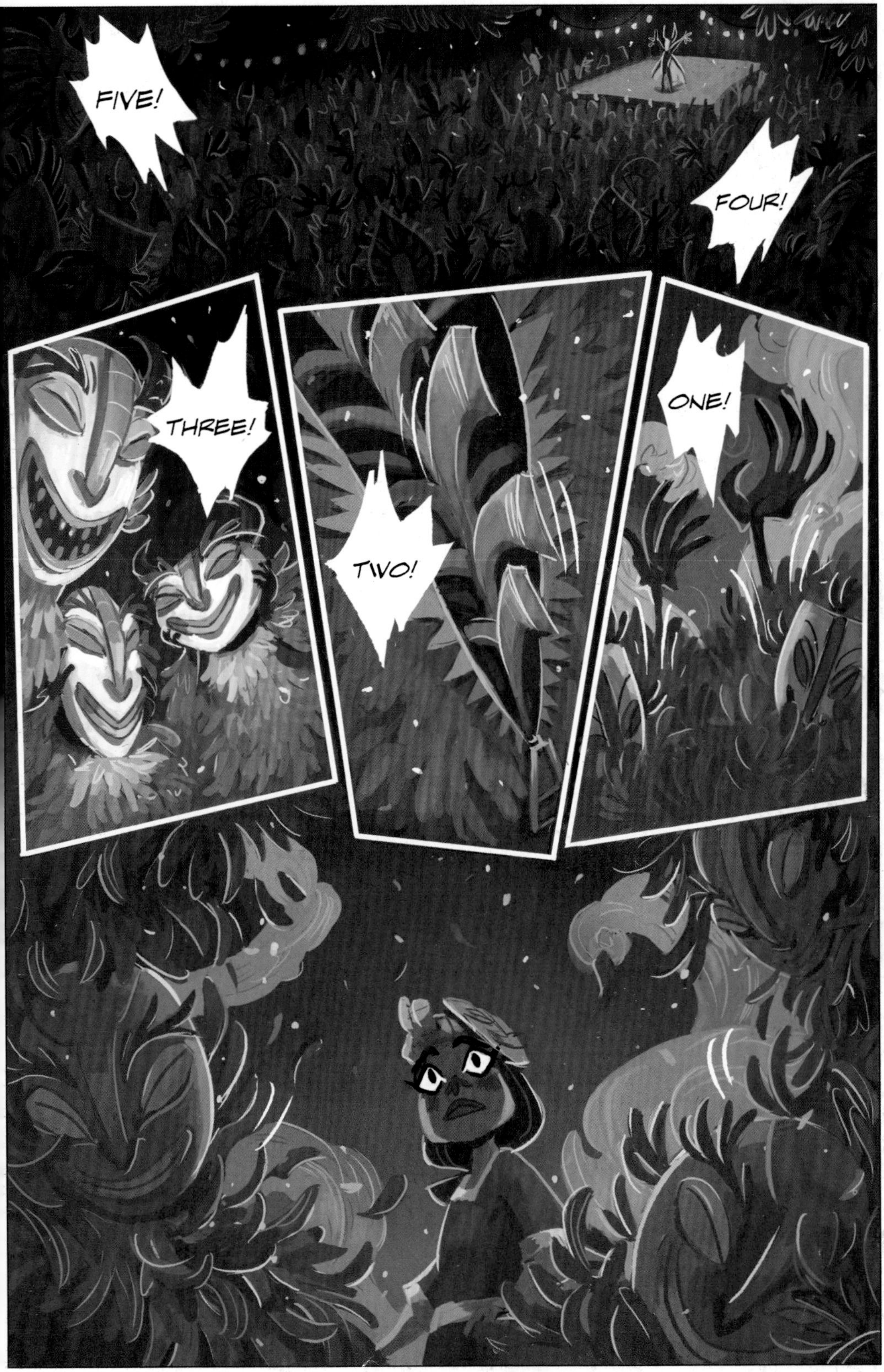
FIVE!
FOUR!
THREE!
TWO!
ONE!

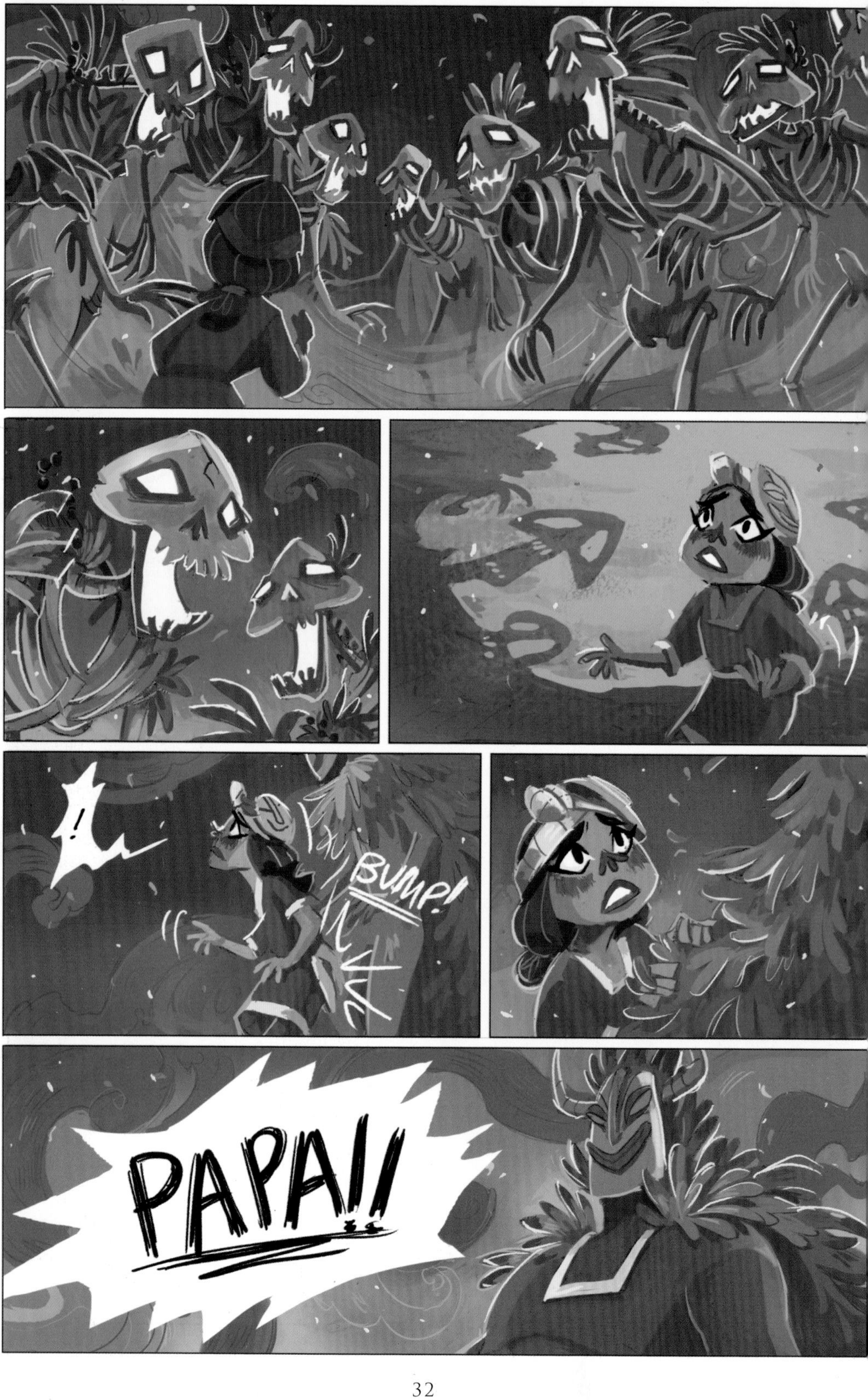
!
BUMP!
PAPA!!

PAPA! WE HAVE TO GET OUT OF HERE! THEY... THEY'RE ALL—!!

HAHA HAHA HA

I'M NOT YOUR FATHER, LITTLE GIRL.

TO TELL YOU THE TRUTH...

I CAN'T REMEMBER WHO I AM ANYMORE.

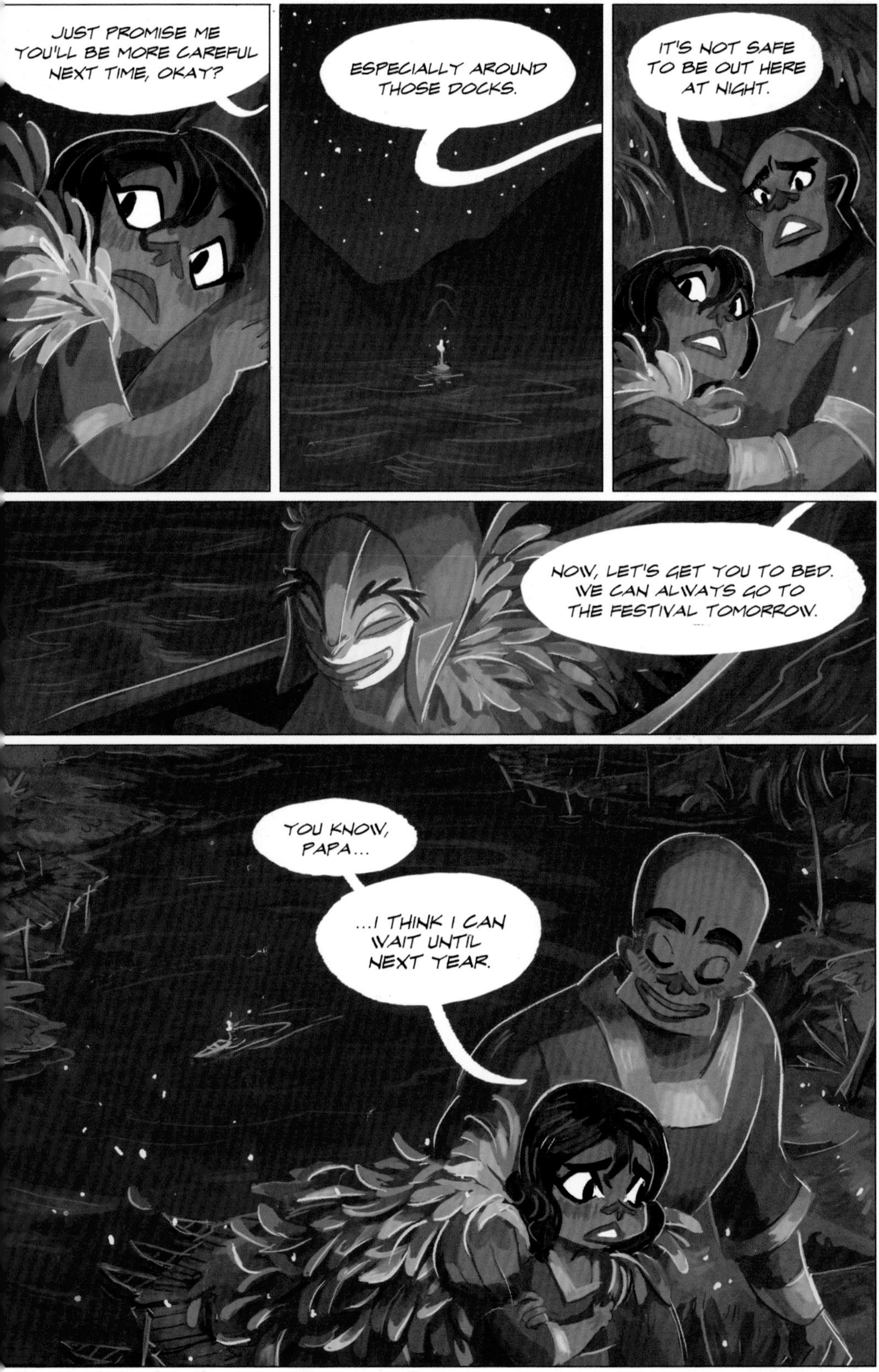
JUST PROMISE ME YOU'LL BE MORE CAREFUL NEXT TIME, OKAY?
ESPECIALLY AROUND THOSE DOCKS.
IT'S NOT SAFE TO BE OUT HERE AT NIGHT.
NOW, LET'S GET YOU TO BED. WE CAN ALWAYS GO TO THE FESTIVAL TOMORROW.
YOU KNOW, PAPA...
...I THINK I CAN WAIT UNTIL NEXT YEAR.

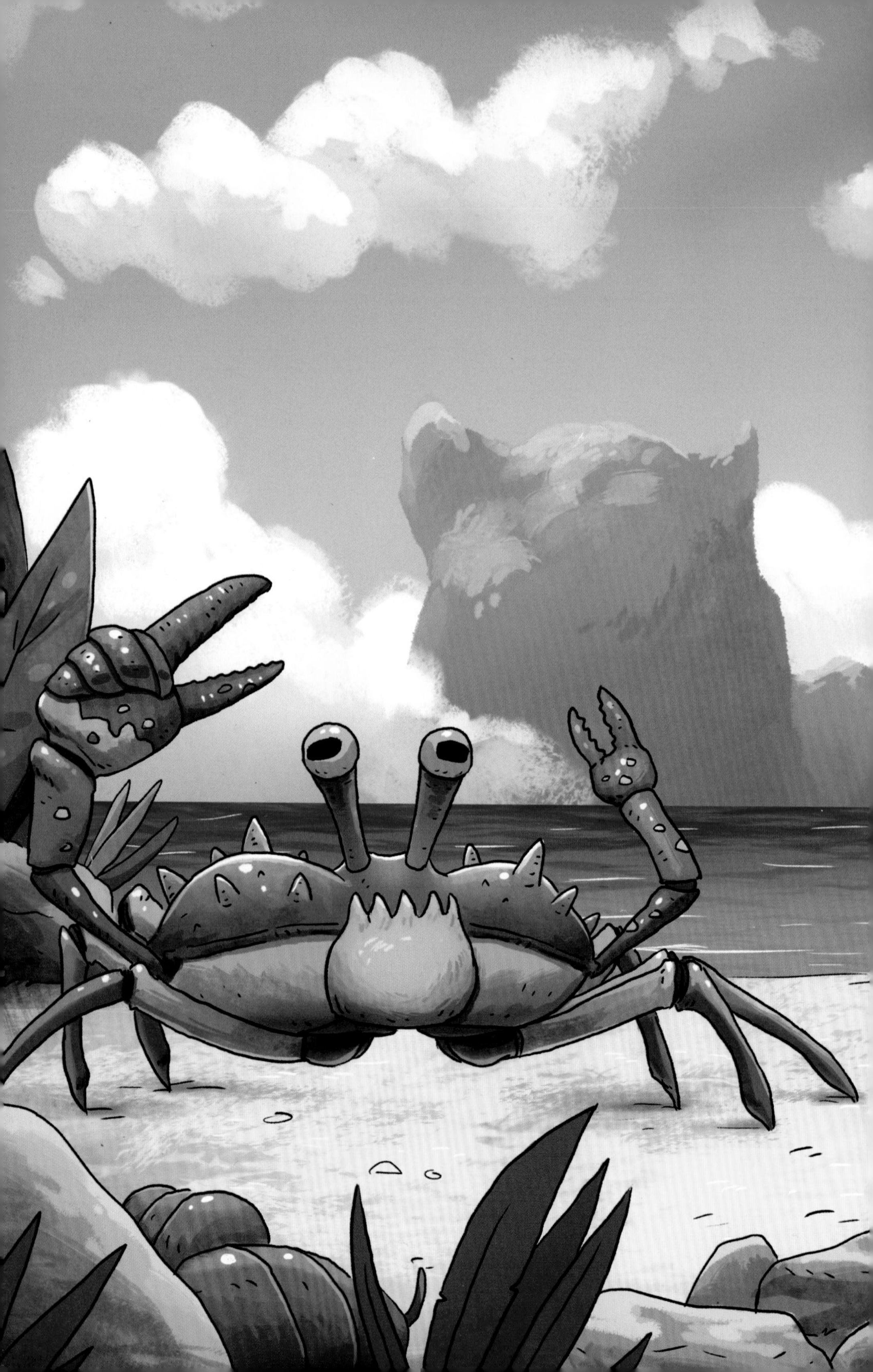

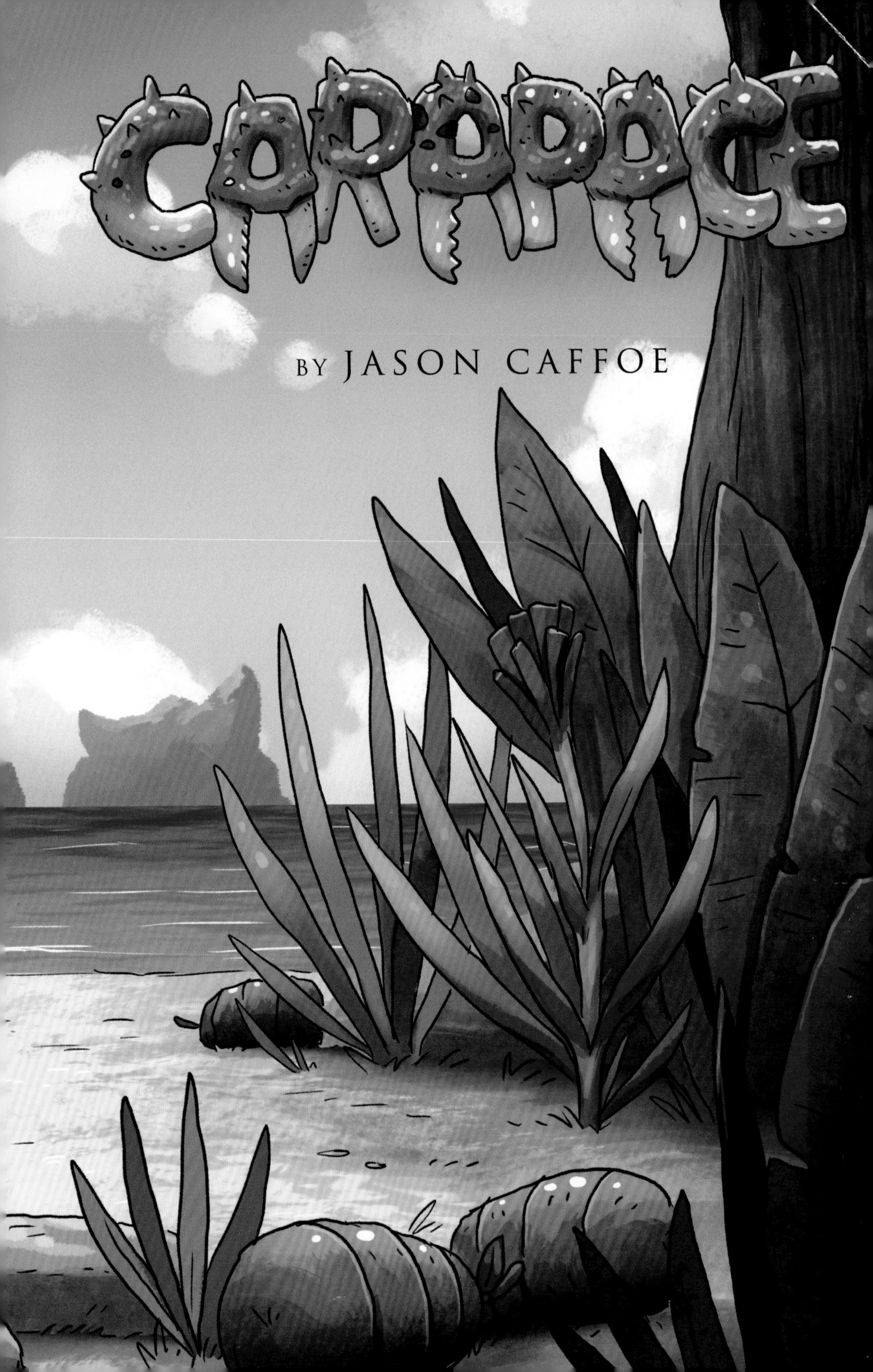
CARAPACE
BY JASON CAFFOE

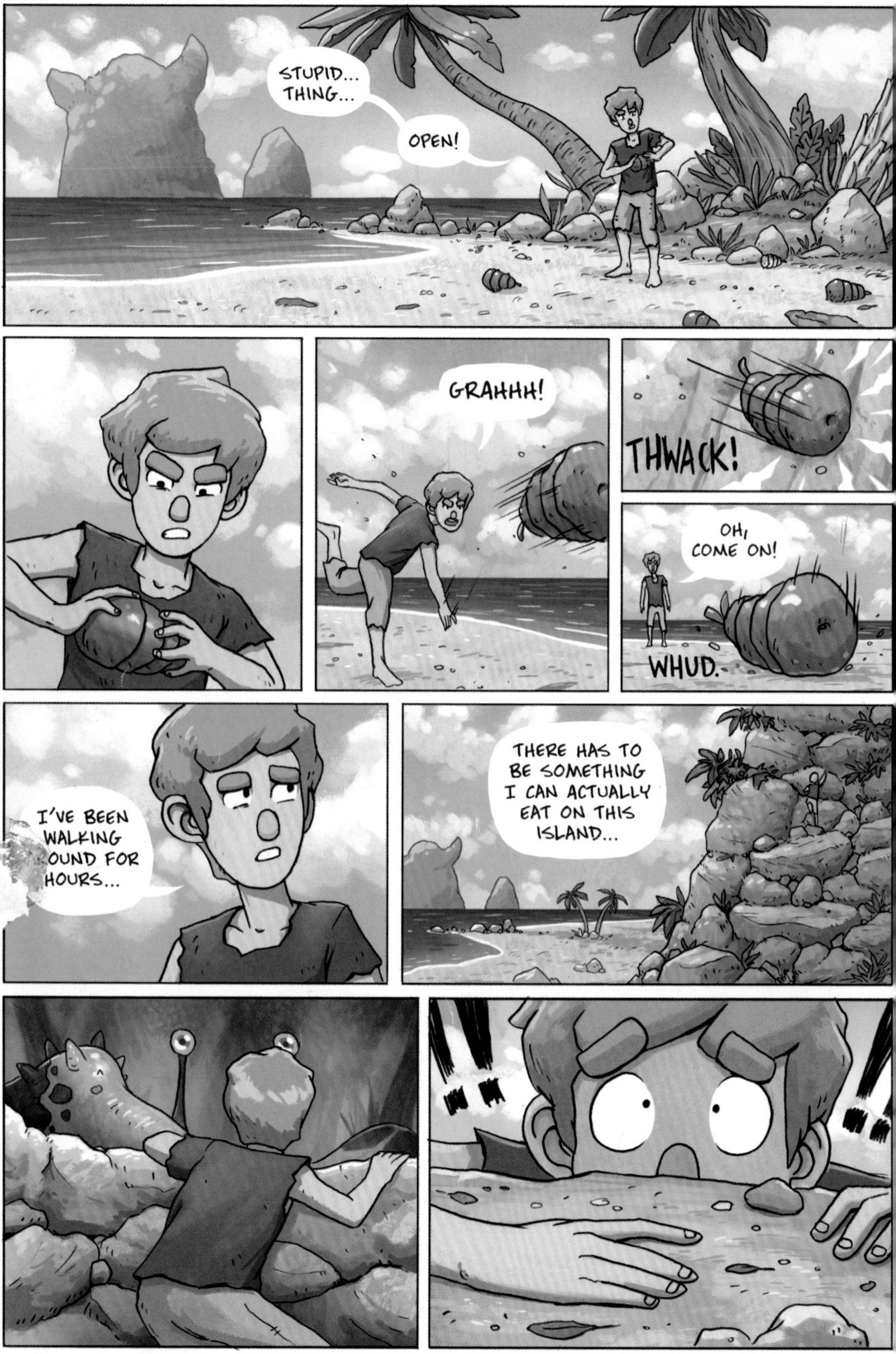
STUPID... THING...
OPEN!
GRAHHH!
THWACK!
OH, COME ON!
WHUD.
I'VE BEEN WALKING
OUND FOR HOURS...
THERE HAS TO BE SOMETHING I CAN ACTUALLY EAT ON THIS ISLAND...

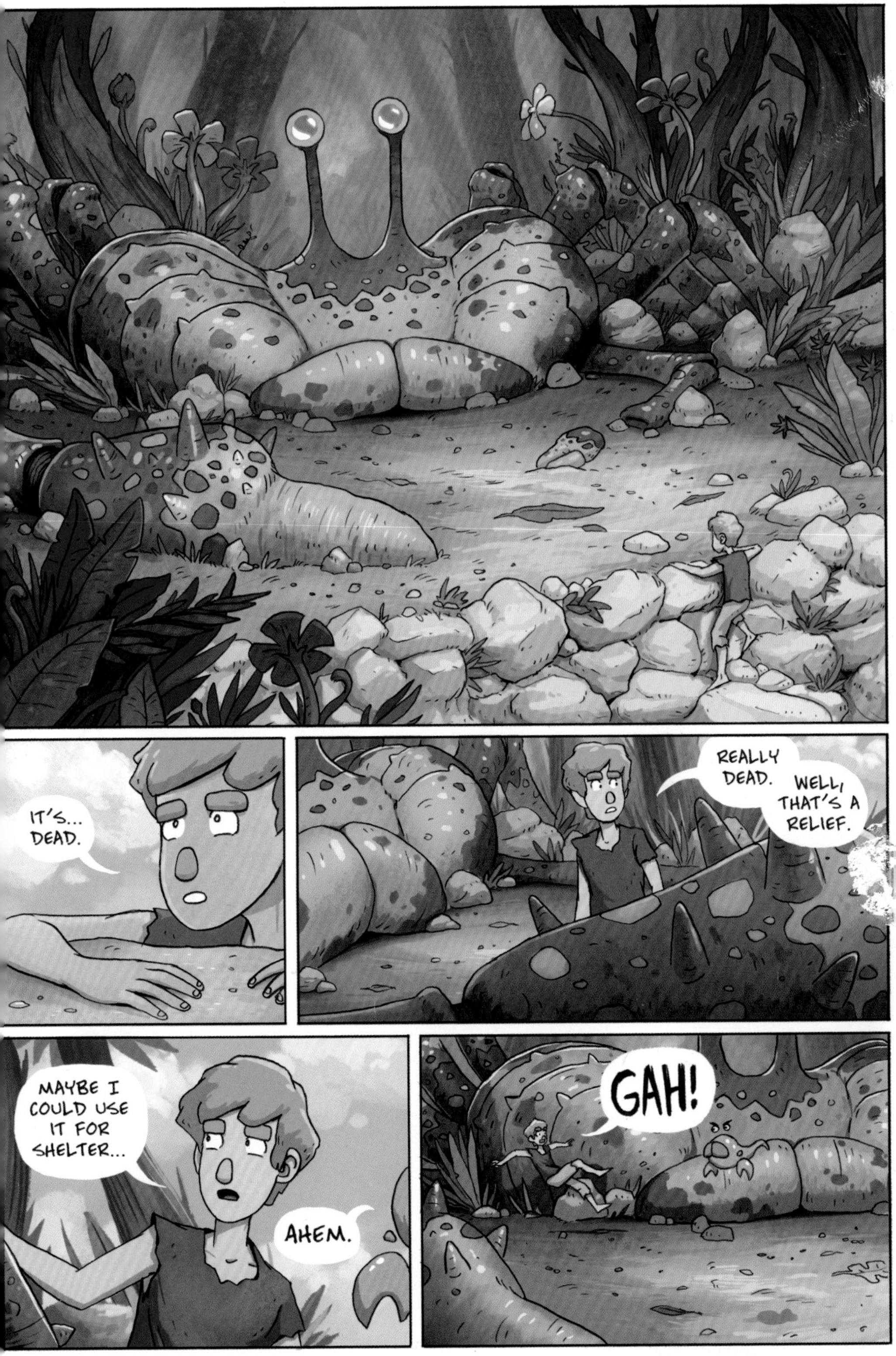

IT'S... DEAD.
REALLY DEAD.
WELL, THAT'S A RELIEF.
MAYBE I COULD USE IT FOR SHELTER...
AHEM.
GAH!

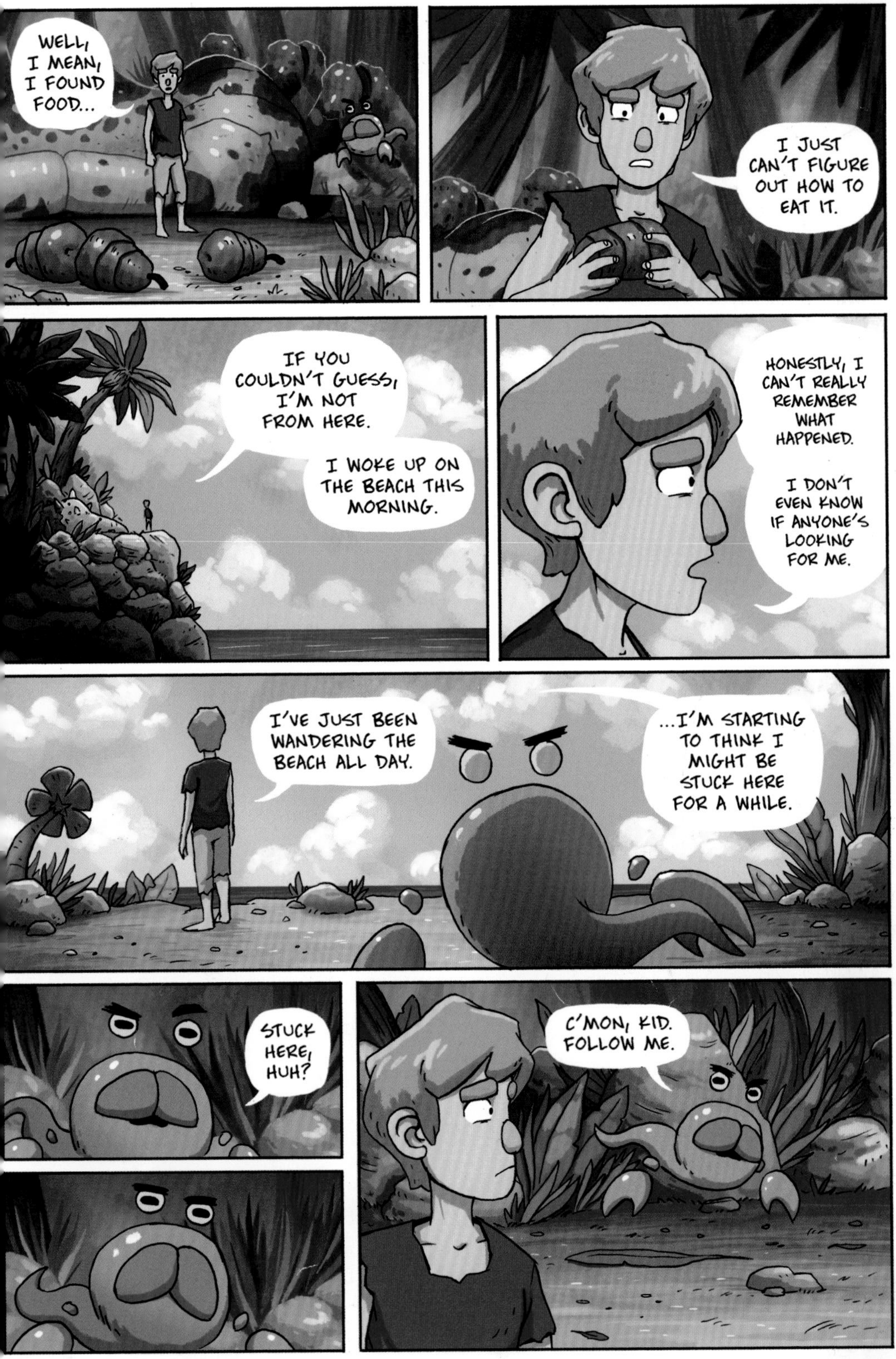
WELL, I MEAN, I FOUND FOOD...
I JUST CAN'T FIGURE OUT HOW TO EAT IT.
IF YOU COULDN'T GUESS, I'M NOT FROM HERE.
I WOKE UP ON THE BEACH THIS MORNING.
HONESTLY, I CAN'T REALLY REMEMBER WHAT HAPPENED.
I DON'T EVEN KNOW IF ANYONE'S LOOKING FOR ME.
I'VE JUST BEEN WANDERING THE BEACH ALL DAY.
...I'M STARTING TO THINK I MIGHT BE STUCK HERE FOR A WHILE.
STUCK HERE, HUH?
C'MON, KID. FOLLOW ME.

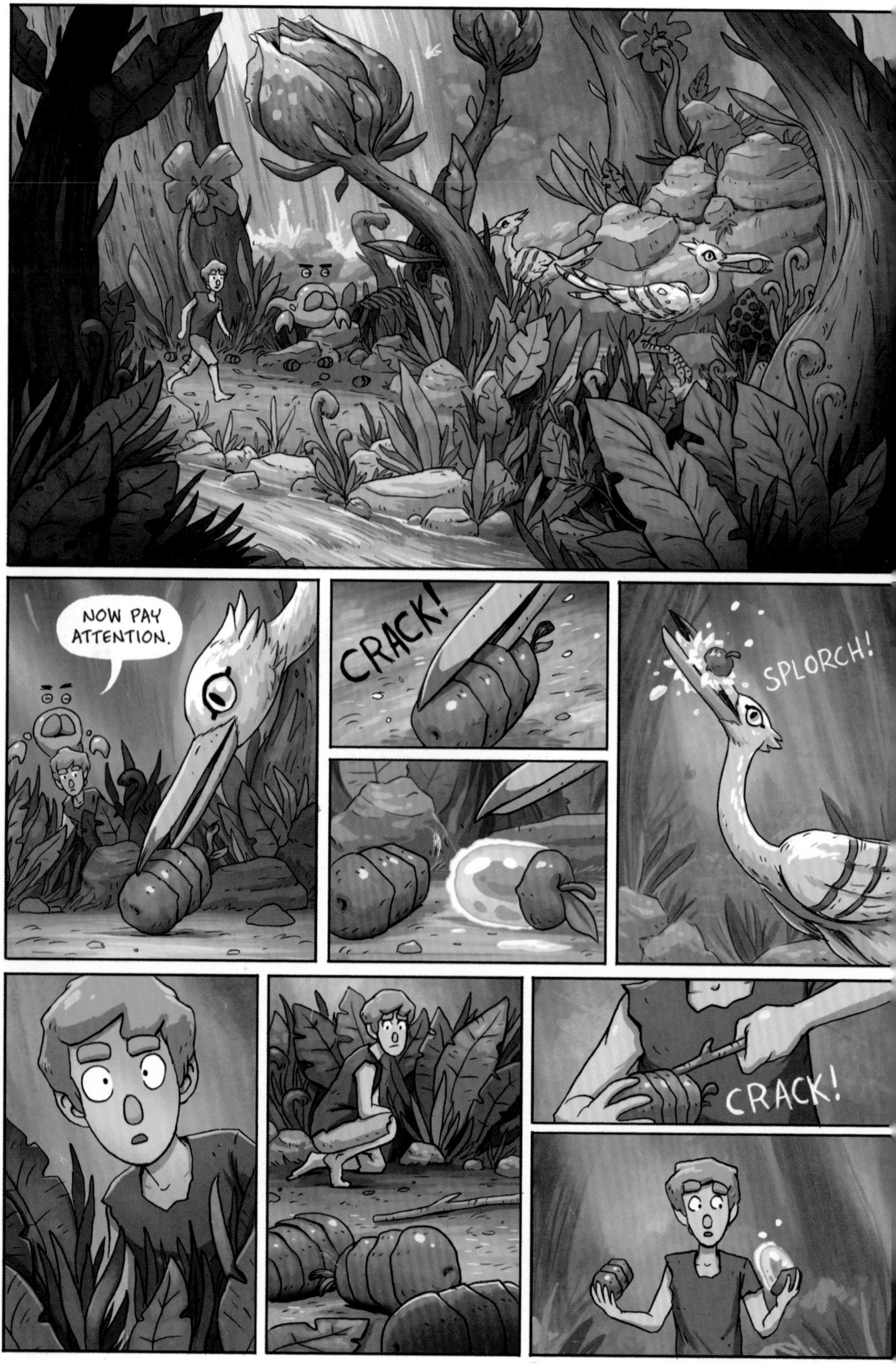
NOW PAY ATTENTION.
CRACK!
SPLORCH!
CRACK!

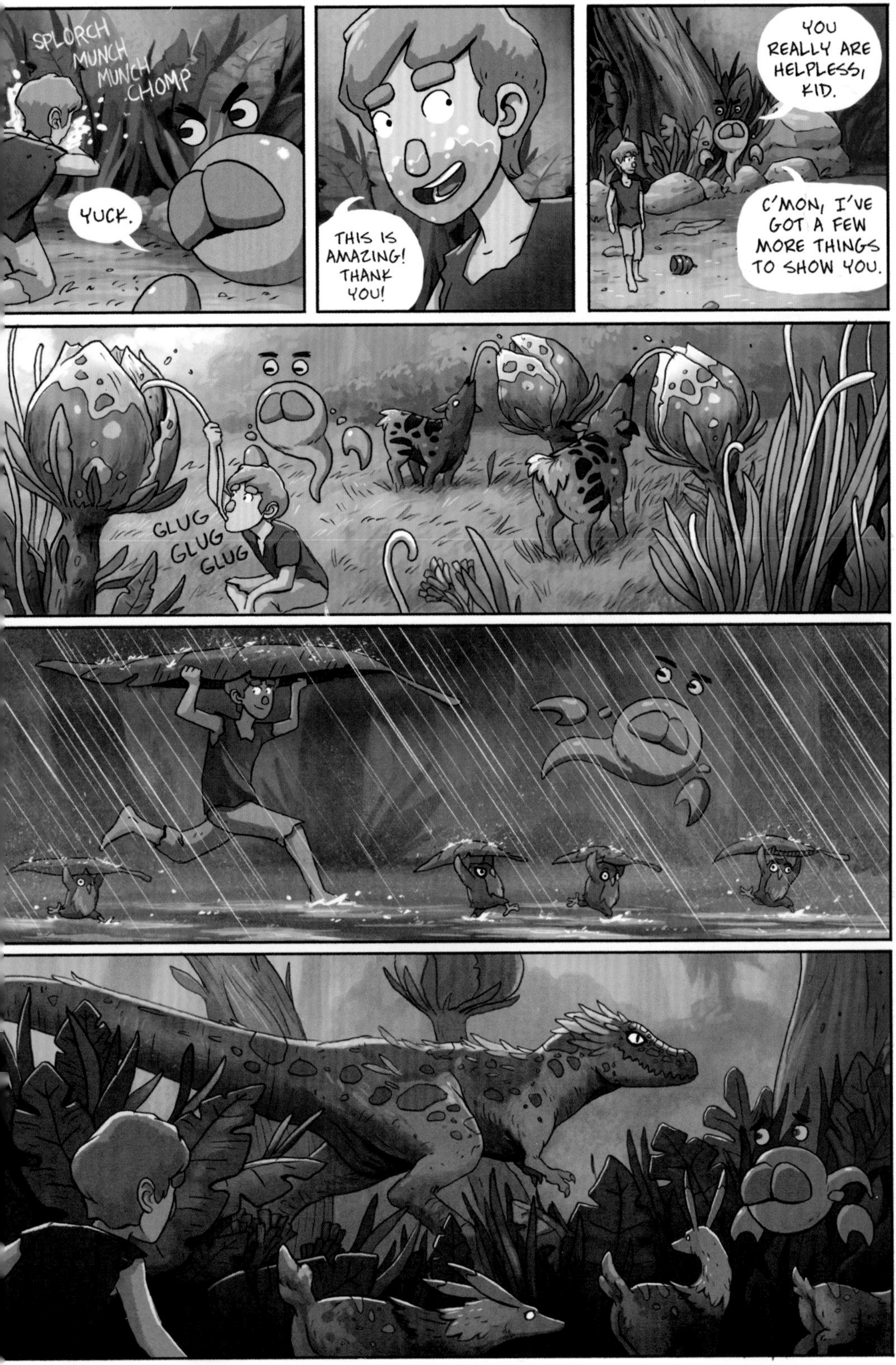
SPLORCH
MUNCH
MUNCH
CHOMP
YUCK.
THIS IS AMAZING! THANK YOU!
YOU REALLY ARE HELPLESS, KID.
C'MON, I'VE GOT A FEW MORE THINGS TO SHOW YOU.
GLUG
GLUG
GLUG

THIS ISLAND IS AMAZING! EVEN THIS LITTLE GUY IS HARD AT WORK.

SNIP!

MAN, I BET I COULD DO A LOT WITH CLAWS LIKE THOSE.

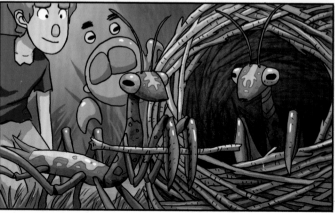

Y'KNOW, KID...I MIGHT BE ABLE TO HELP YOU OUT WITH THAT.

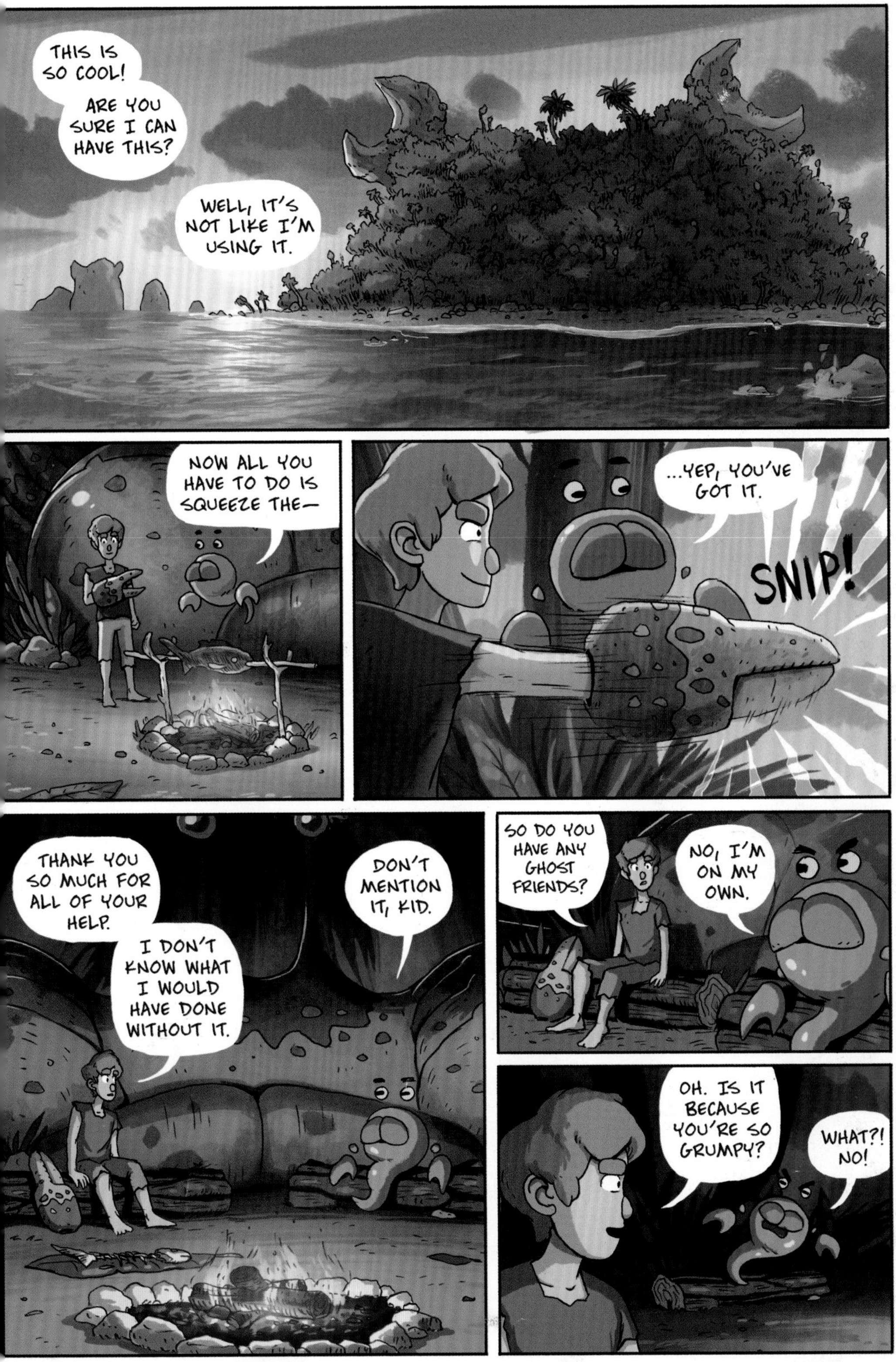
THIS IS SO COOL!
ARE YOU SURE I CAN HAVE THIS?
WELL, IT'S NOT LIKE I'M USING IT.
NOW ALL YOU HAVE TO DO IS SQUEEZE THE—
...YEP, YOU'VE GOT IT.
SNIP!
THANK YOU SO MUCH FOR ALL OF YOUR HELP.
I DON'T KNOW WHAT I WOULD HAVE DONE WITHOUT IT.
DON'T MENTION IT, KID.
SO DO YOU HAVE ANY GHOST FRIENDS?
NO, I'M ON MY OWN.
OH. IS IT BECAUSE YOU'RE SO GRUMPY?
WHAT?! NO!

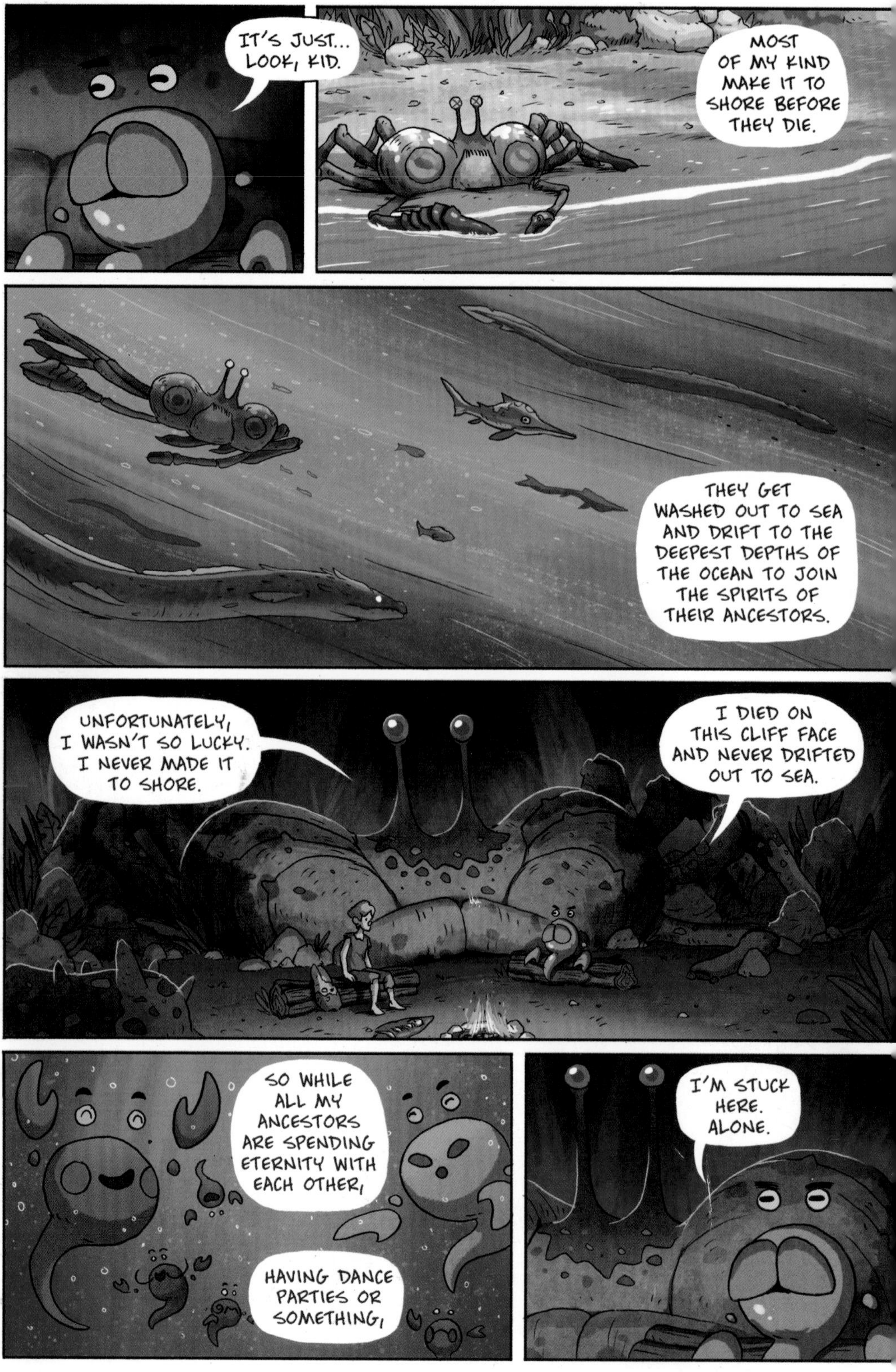
IT'S JUST... LOOK, KID.
MOST OF MY KIND MAKE IT TO SHORE BEFORE THEY DIE.
THEY GET WASHED OUT TO SEA AND DRIFT TO THE DEEPEST DEPTHS OF THE OCEAN TO JOIN THE SPIRITS OF THEIR ANCESTORS.
UNFORTUNATELY, I WASN'T SO LUCKY. I NEVER MADE IT TO SHORE.
I DIED ON THIS CLIFF FACE AND NEVER DRIFTED OUT TO SEA.
SO WHILE ALL MY ANCESTORS ARE SPENDING ETERNITY WITH EACH OTHER,
HAVING DANCE PARTIES OR SOMETHING,
I'M STUCK HERE. ALONE.

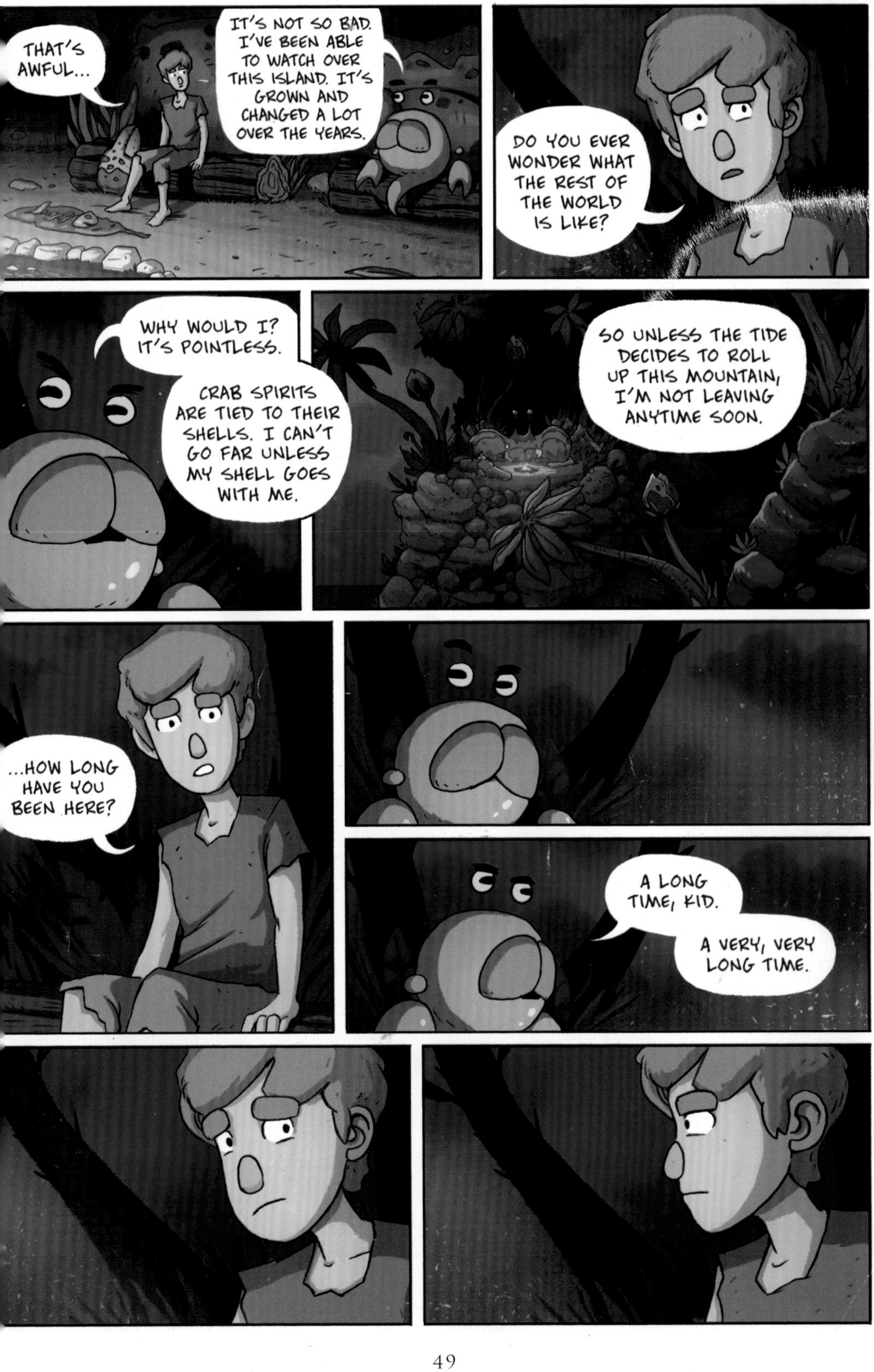
THAT'S AWFUL...
IT'S NOT SO BAD. I'VE BEEN ABLE TO WATCH OVER THIS ISLAND. IT'S GROWN AND CHANGED A LOT OVER THE YEARS.
DO YOU EVER WONDER WHAT THE REST OF THE WORLD IS LIKE?
WHY WOULD I? IT'S POINTLESS.
CRAB SPIRITS ARE TIED TO THEIR SHELLS. I CAN'T GO FAR UNLESS MY SHELL GOES WITH ME.
SO UNLESS THE TIDE DECIDES TO ROLL UP THIS MOUNTAIN, I'M NOT LEAVING ANYTIME SOON.
...HOW LONG HAVE YOU BEEN HERE?
A LONG TIME, KID.
A VERY, VERY LONG TIME.

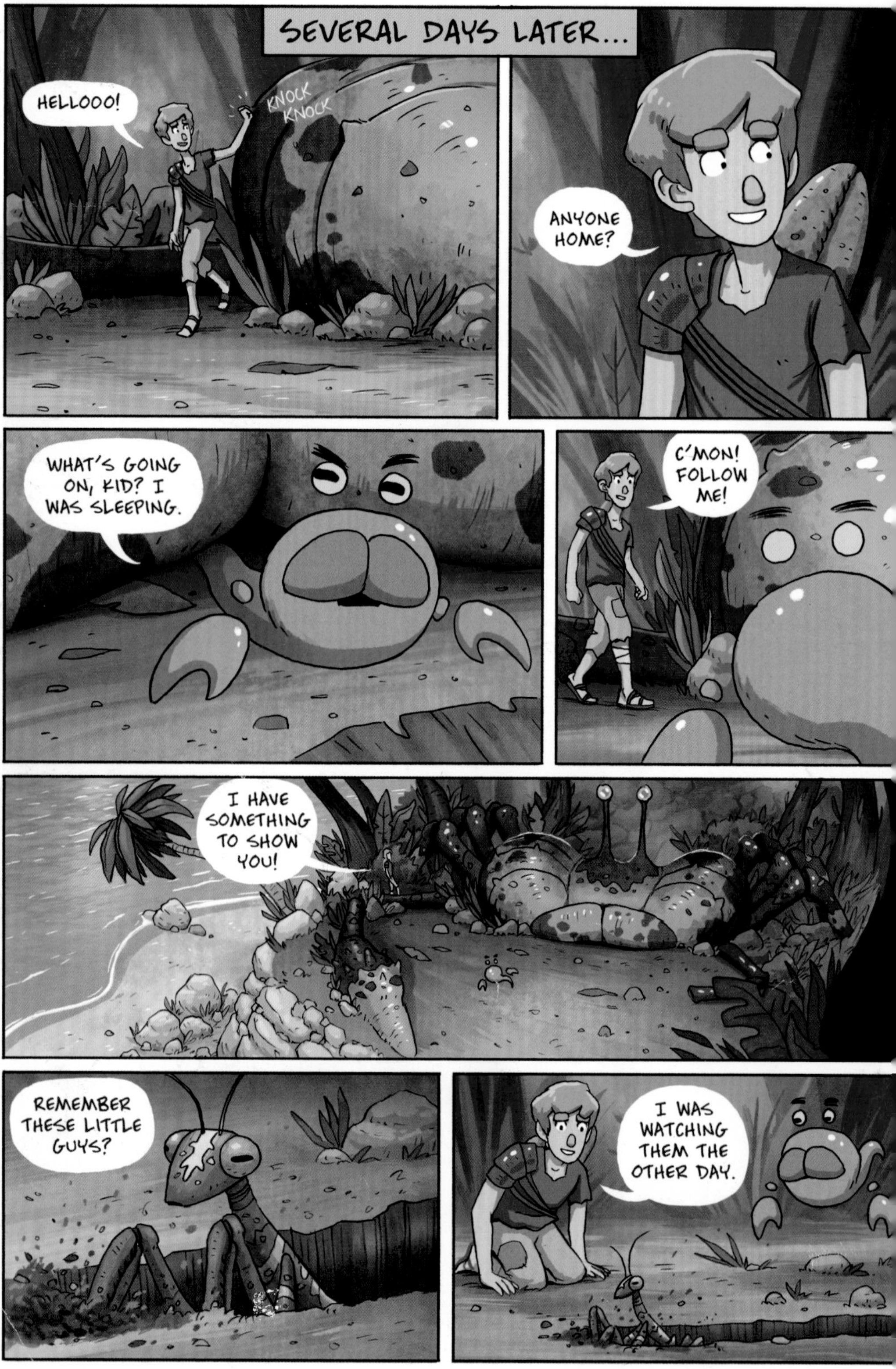
SEVERAL DAYS LATER...
HELLOOO!
KNOCK KNOCK
ANYONE HOME?
WHAT'S GOING ON, KID? I WAS SLEEPING.
C'MON! FOLLOW ME!
I HAVE SOMETHING TO SHOW YOU!
REMEMBER THESE LITTLE GUYS?
I WAS WATCHING THEM THE OTHER DAY.

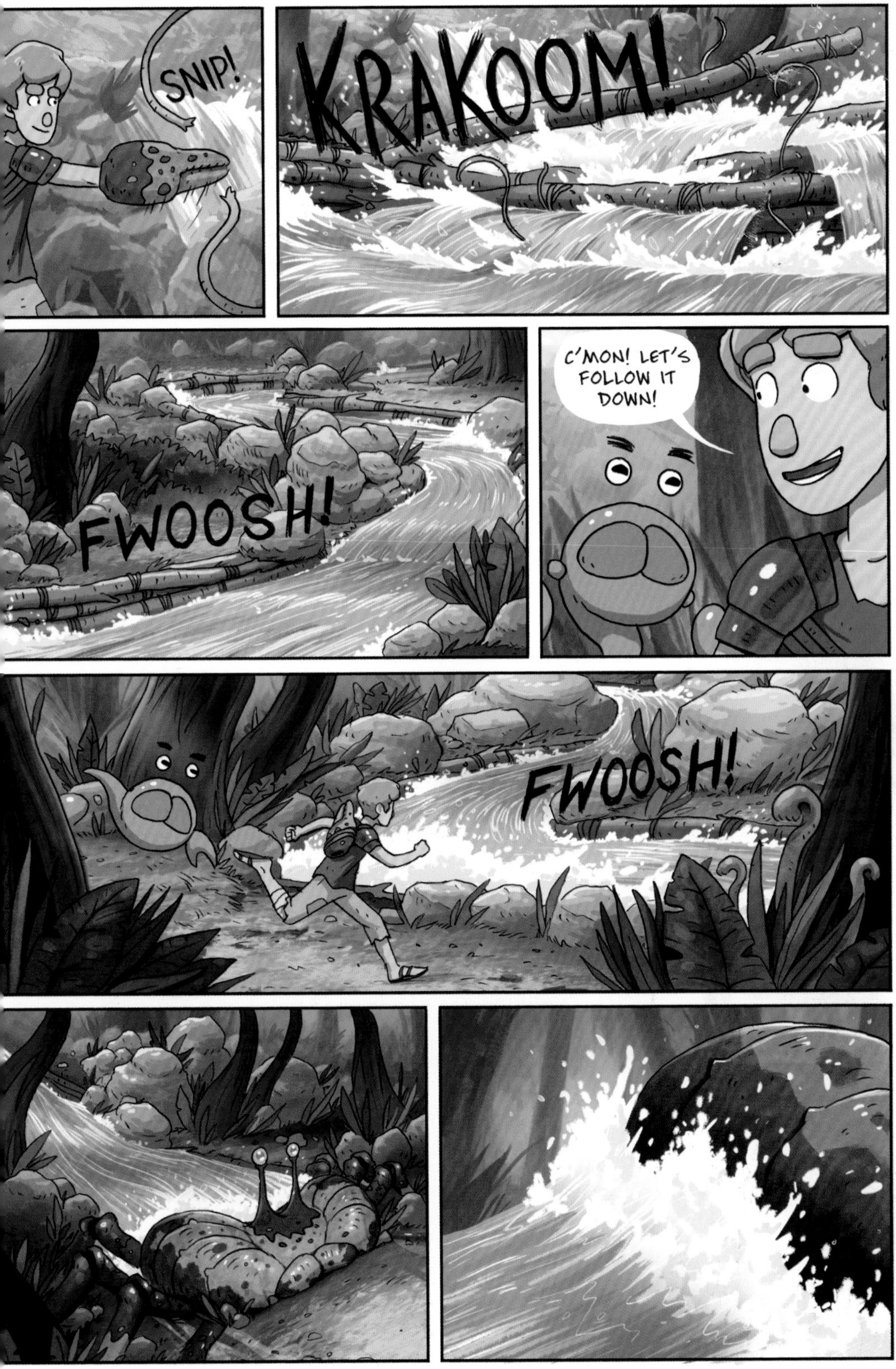
SNIP!
KRAKOOM!
FWOOSH!
C'MON! LET'S FOLLOW IT DOWN!
FWOOSH!

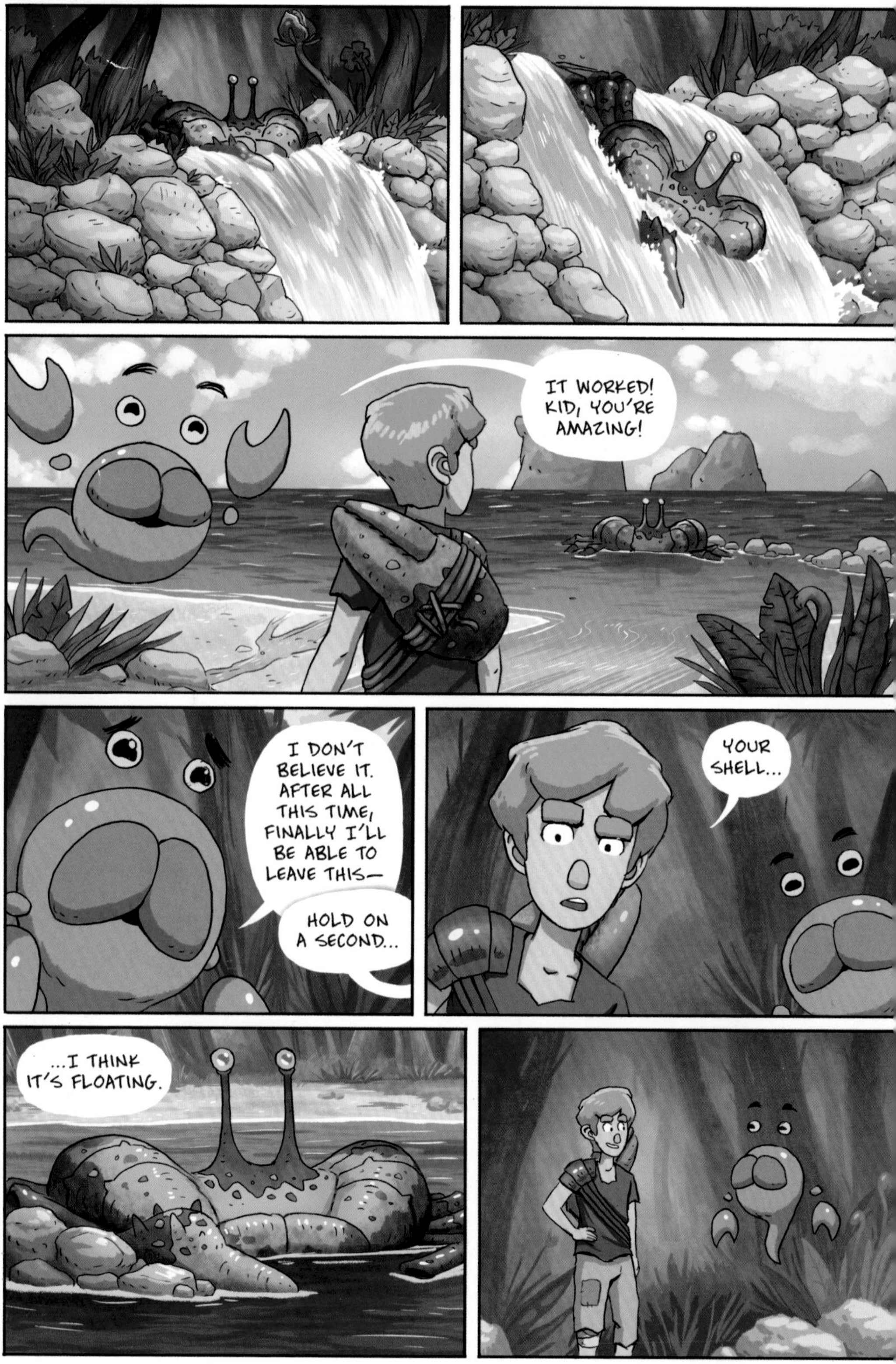
IT WORKED! KID, YOU'RE AMAZING!
I DON'T BELIEVE IT. AFTER ALL THIS TIME, FINALLY I'LL BE ABLE TO LEAVE THIS—
HOLD ON A SECOND...
YOUR SHELL...
...I THINK IT'S FLOATING.

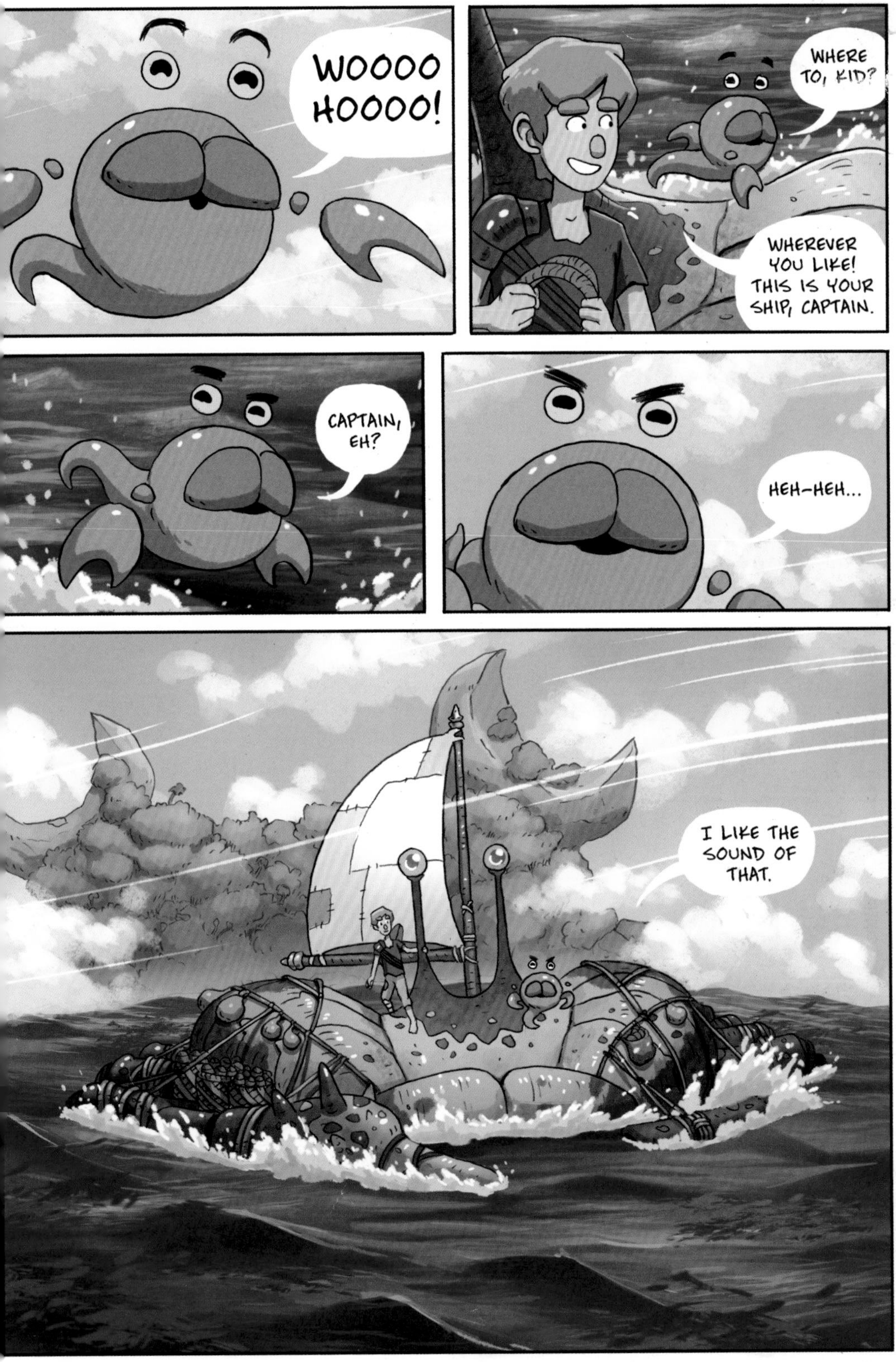
WOOOO HOOOO!
WHERE TO, KID?
WHEREVER YOU LIKE! THIS IS YOUR SHIP, CAPTAIN.
CAPTAIN, EH?
HEH-HEH...
I LIKE THE SOUND OF THAT.

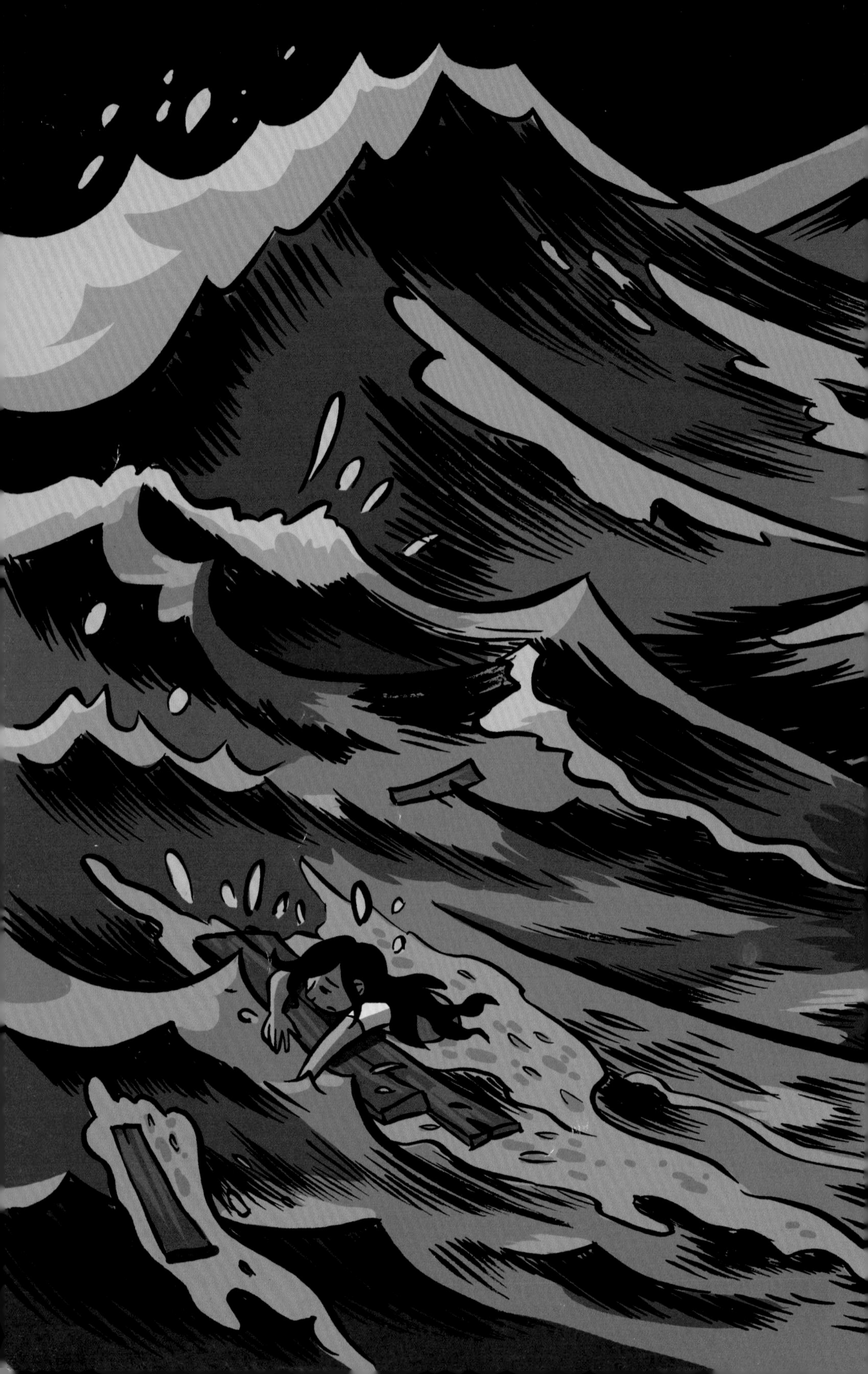

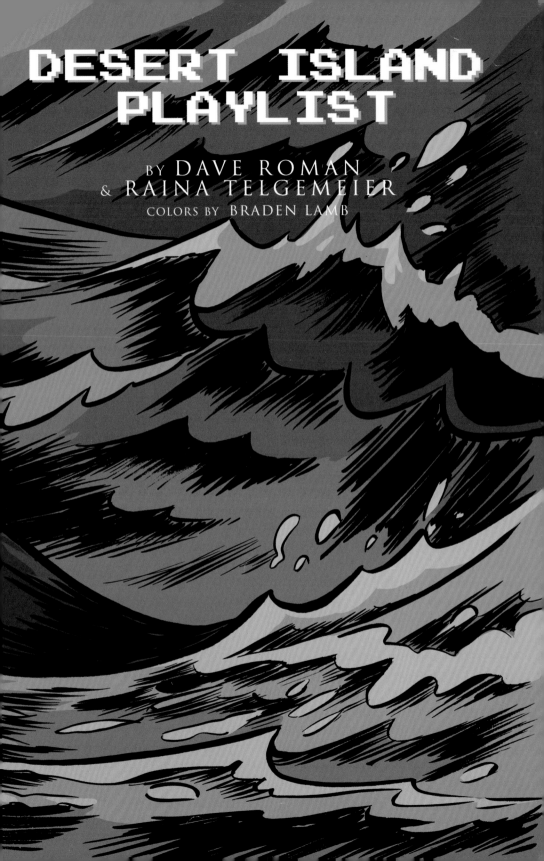

DESERT ISLAND PLAYLIST

BY DAVE ROMAN
& RAINA TELGEMEIER
COLORS BY BRADEN LAMB

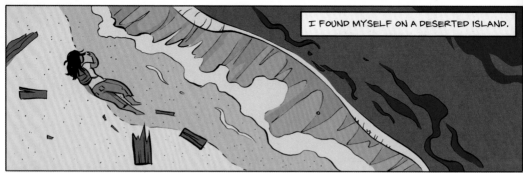

I FOUND MYSELF ON A DESERTED ISLAND.

WITH ONLY A BACKPACK...

Brush
Brush

A FEW KEEPSAKES...

ZZZZZZZip

58

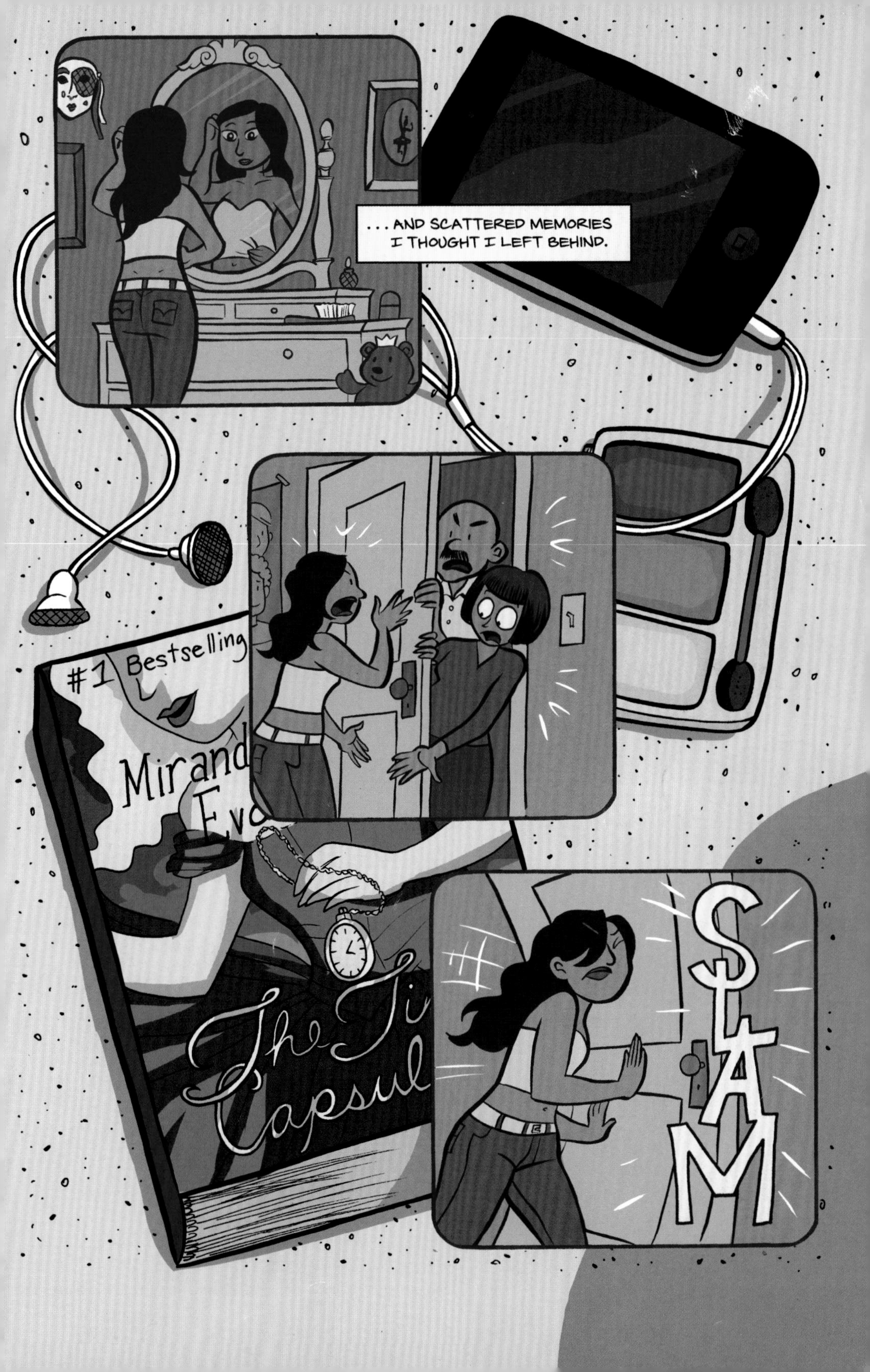

. . . AND SCATTERED MEMORIES I THOUGHT I LEFT BEHIND.
#1 Bestselling
Mirand
Ev
The Ti
Capsul
SLAM

YOU MUST HAVE GOTTEN MESSED UP IN THE STORM.

SAME OLD SONGS STUCK ON REPEAT.

HEH.

BUT IF I COULD HAVE CHOSEN ANY THREE SONGS TO HAVE ON A DESERT ISLAND . . .

IT **WOULD** BE THESE SONGS.

I SEARCHED THE COAST, BUT THERE DIDN'T SEEM TO BE ANY OTHER SIGNS OF LIFE.

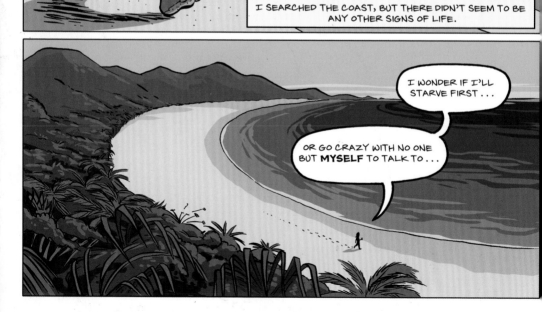

I WONDER IF I'LL STARVE FIRST . . .

OR GO CRAZY WITH NO ONE BUT **MYSELF** TO TALK TO . . .

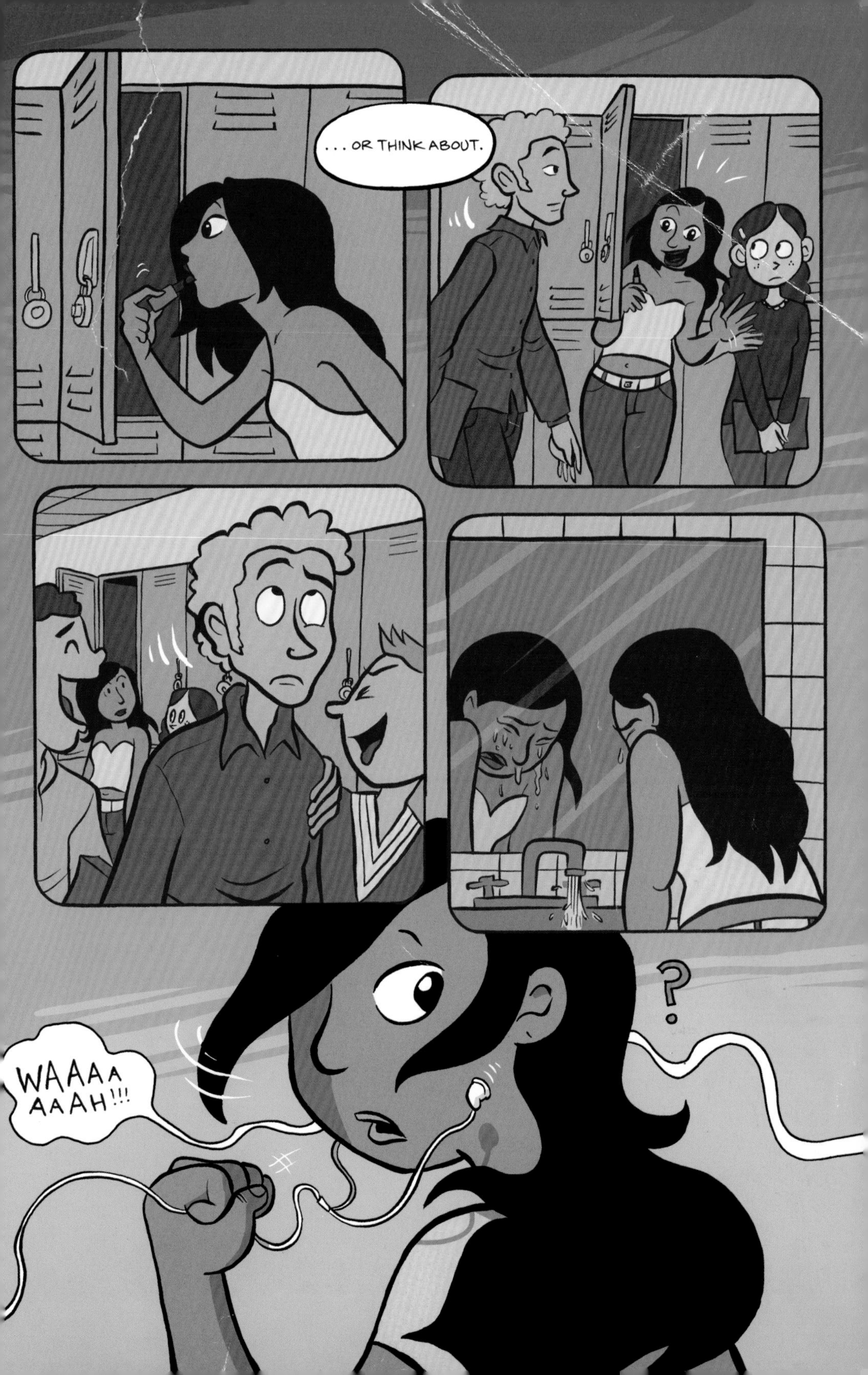
. . . OR THINK ABOUT.
?
WAAAA AAAH!!!

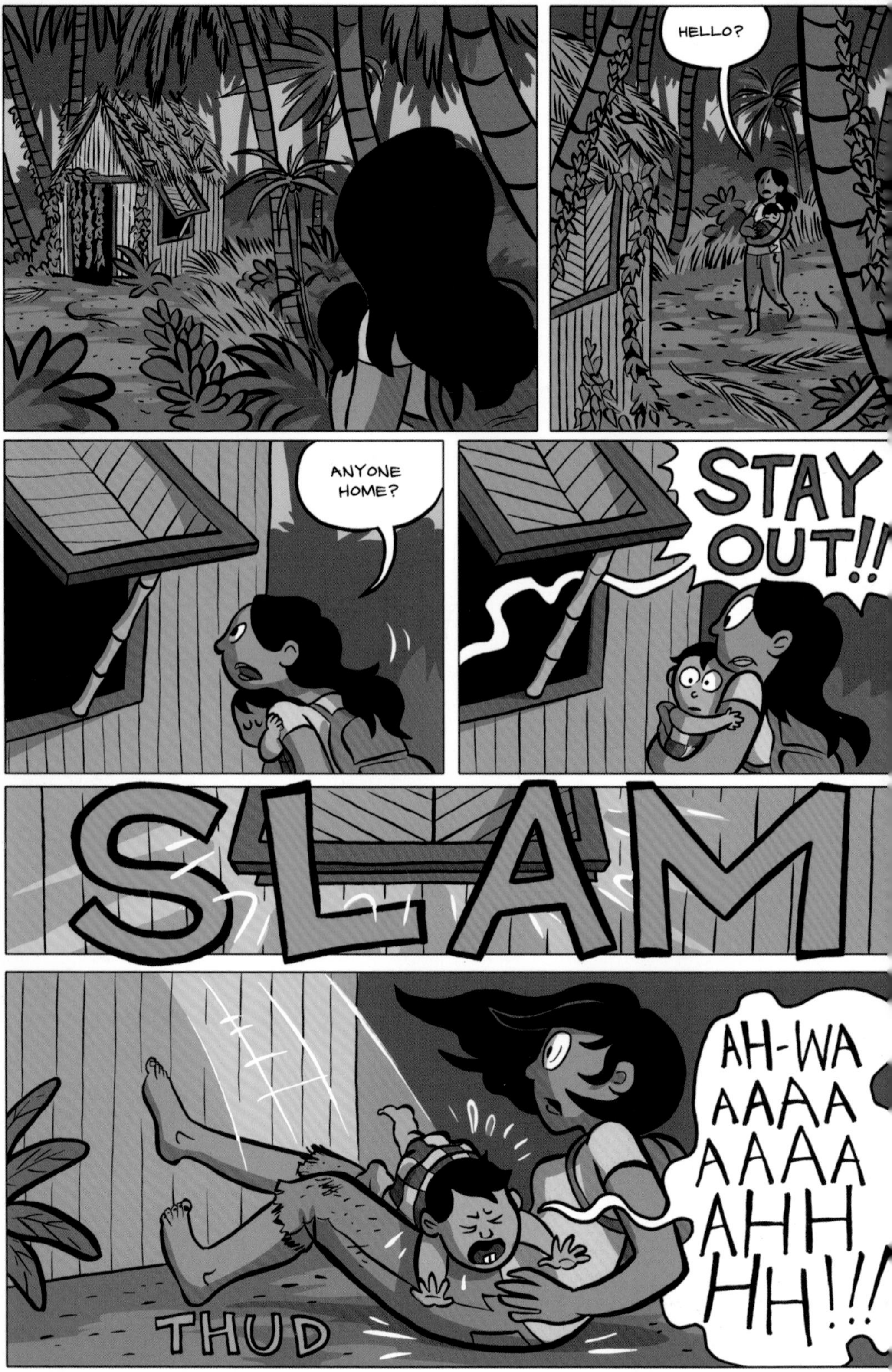
HELLO?
ANYONE HOME?
STAY OUT!!
SLAM
AH-WA AAAA AAAA AHH HH!!!
THUD

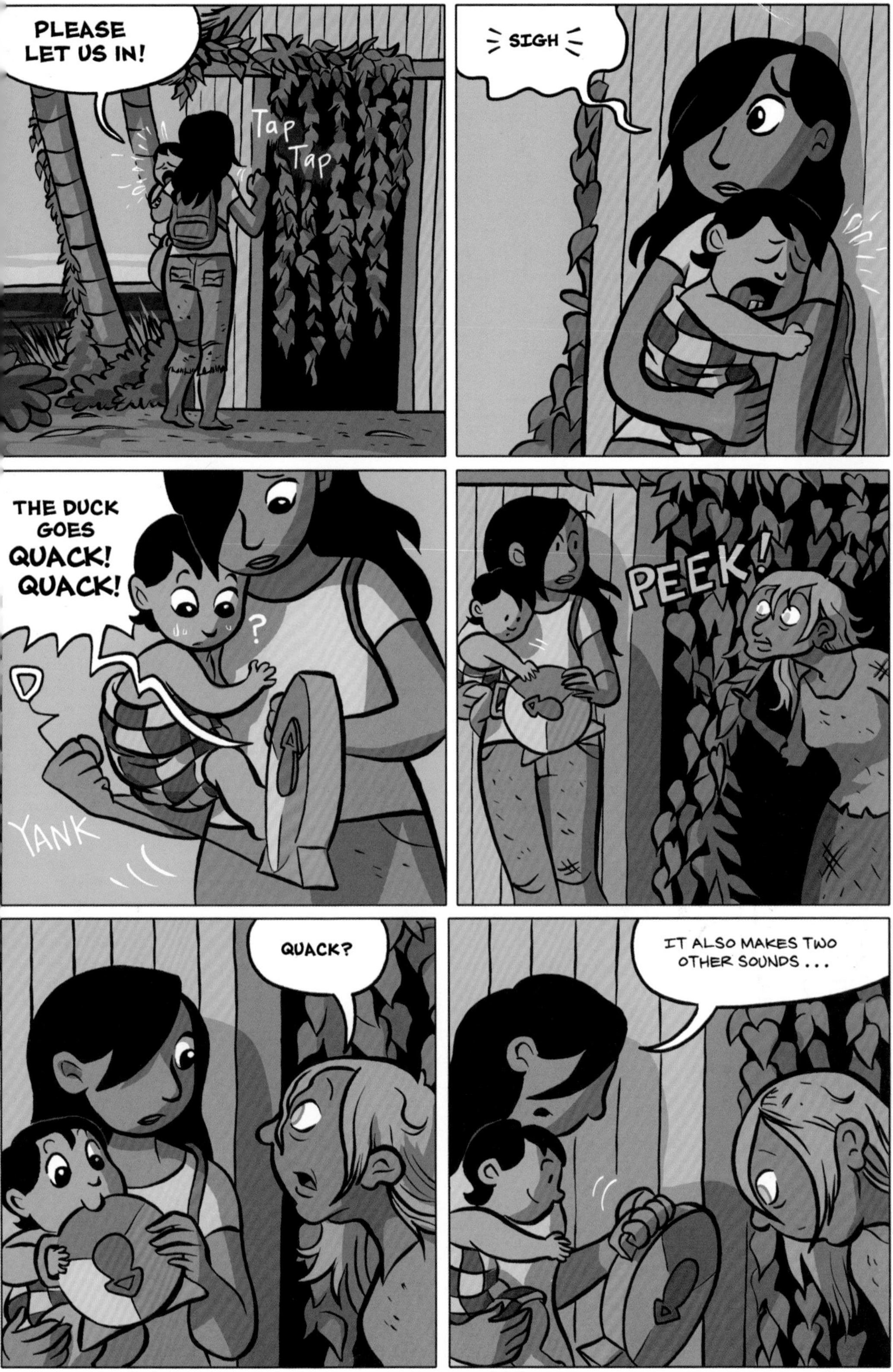
PLEASE LET US IN!
Tap Tap
SIGH
THE DUCK GOES QUACK! QUACK!
?
YANK
PEEK!
QUACK?
IT ALSO MAKES TWO OTHER SOUNDS . . .

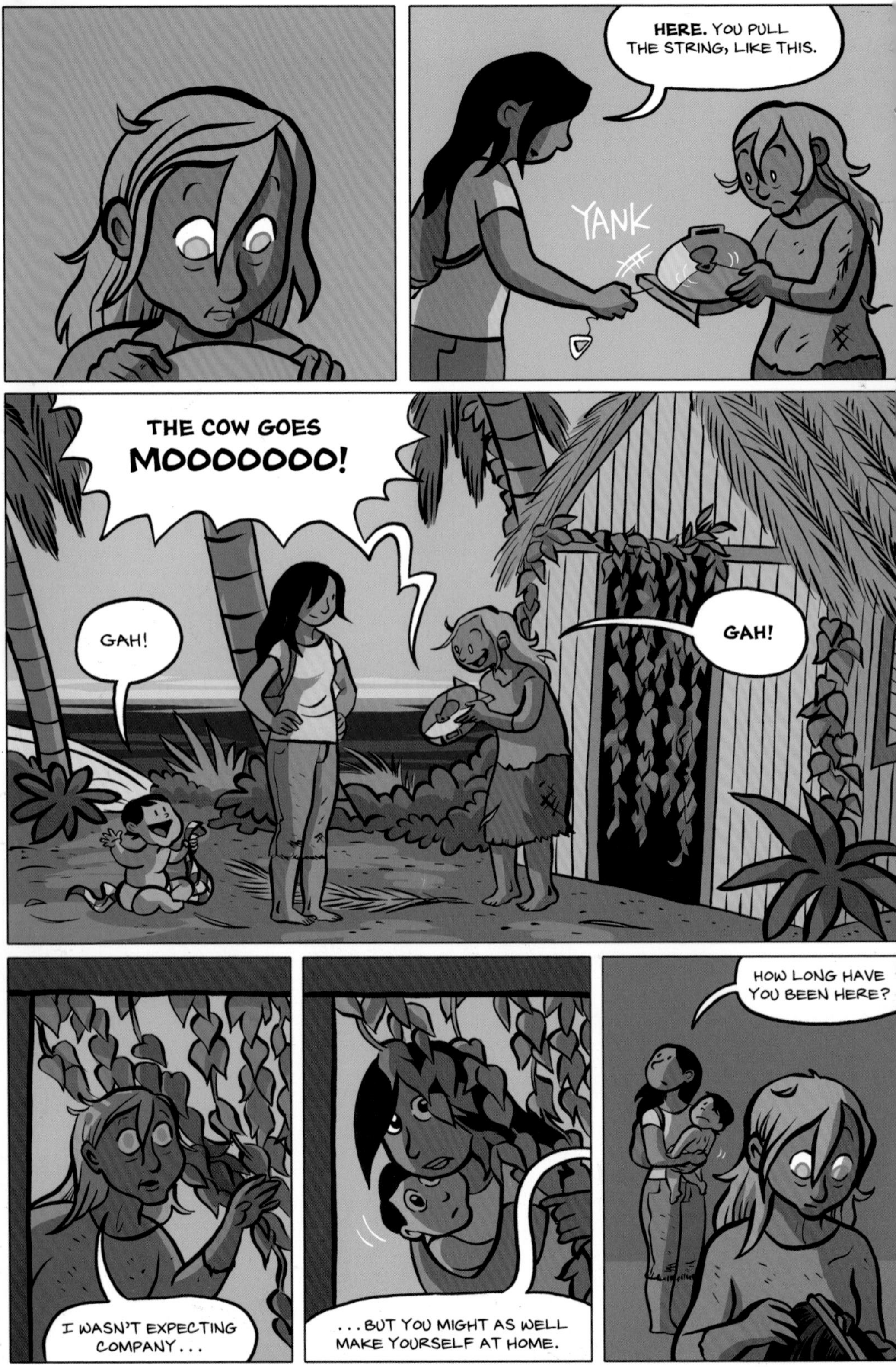

HERE. YOU PULL THE STRING, LIKE THIS.
YANK
THE COW GOES MOOOOOOO!
GAH!
GAH!
HOW LONG HAVE YOU BEEN HERE?
I WASN'T EXPECTING COMPANY...
...BUT YOU MIGHT AS WELL MAKE YOURSELF AT HOME.

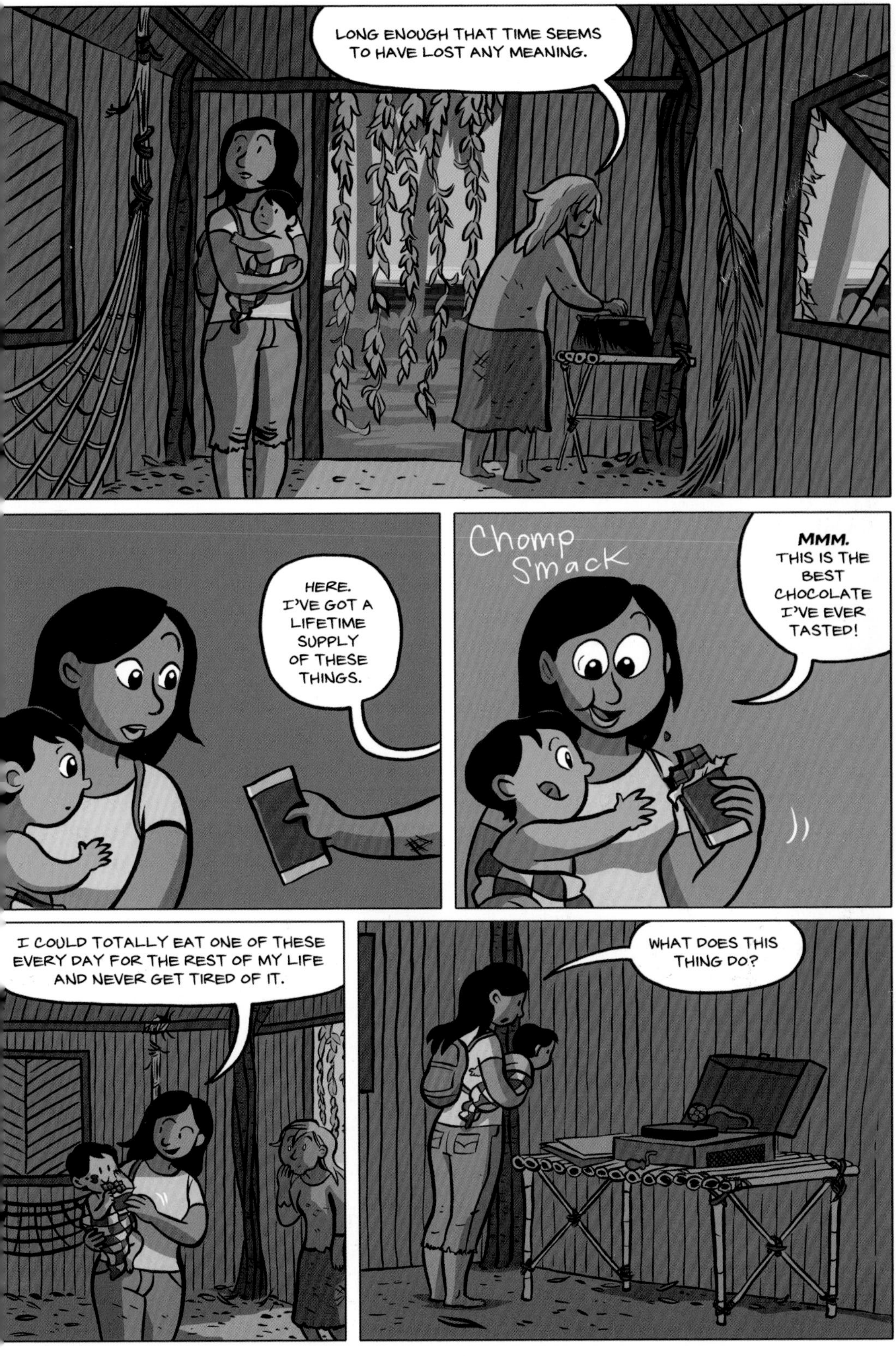
LONG ENOUGH THAT TIME SEEMS TO HAVE LOST ANY MEANING.
HERE. I'VE GOT A LIFETIME SUPPLY OF THESE THINGS.
Chomp Smack
MMM. THIS IS THE BEST CHOCOLATE I'VE EVER TASTED!
I COULD TOTALLY EAT ONE OF THESE EVERY DAY FOR THE REST OF MY LIFE AND NEVER GET TIRED OF IT.
WHAT DOES THIS THING DO?

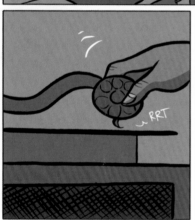

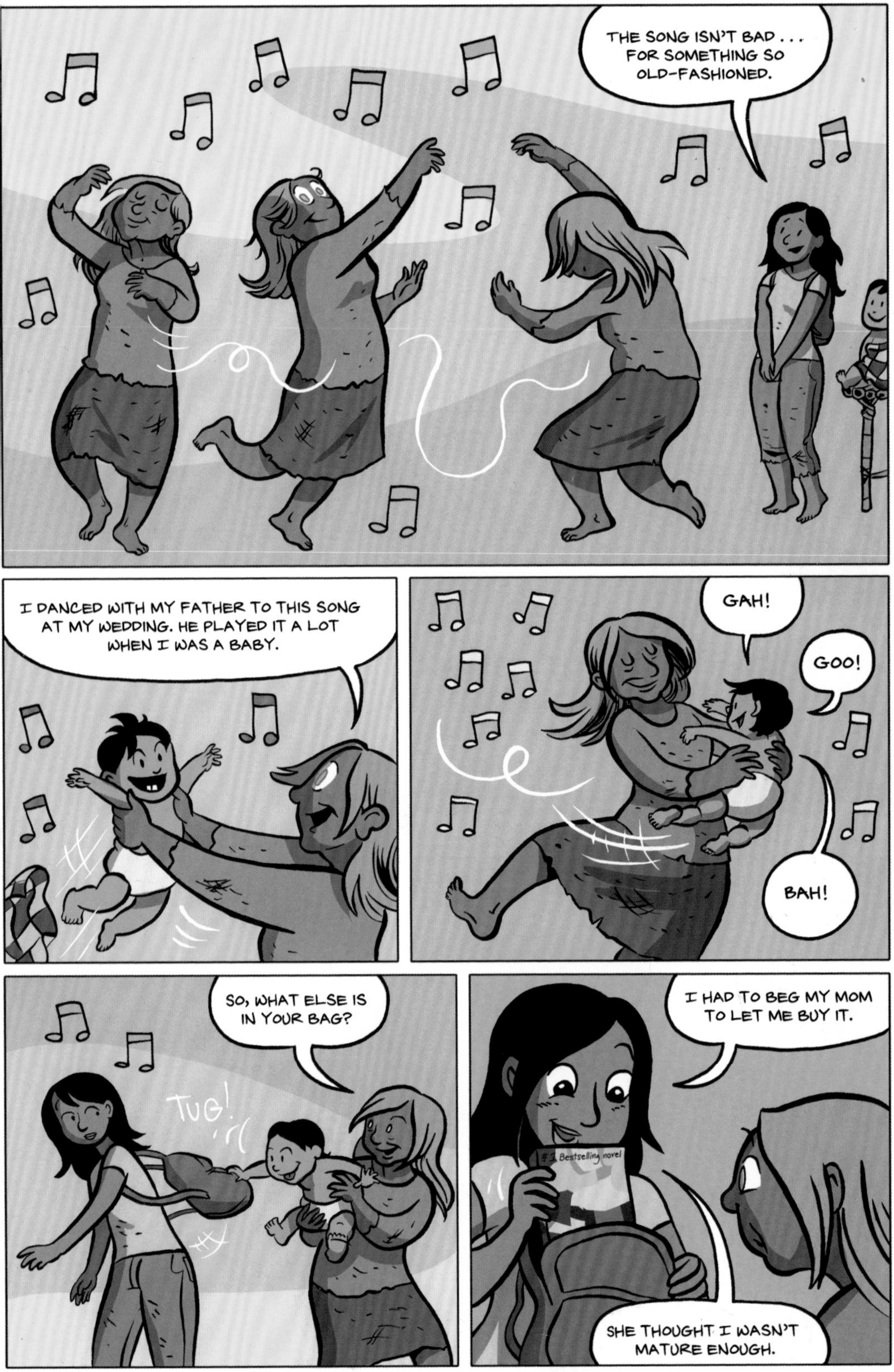
THE SONG ISN'T BAD . . . FOR SOMETHING SO OLD-FASHIONED.
I DANCED WITH MY FATHER TO THIS SONG AT MY WEDDING. HE PLAYED IT A LOT WHEN I WAS A BABY.
GAH!
GOO!
BAH!
SO, WHAT ELSE IS IN YOUR BAG?
TUG!
I HAD TO BEG MY MOM TO LET ME BUY IT.
#1 Bestselling novel
SHE THOUGHT I WASN'T MATURE ENOUGH.

AH, YES!

I'VE READ **THE TIME CAPSULE** OVER AND OVER!

FlipFlip Flip

#1 Bestselling Novel

CAN'T TELL YOU HOW MANY TIMES I GOT MY HEART BROKEN AND WISHED I COULD BE LIKE ONE OF THE CHARACTERS IN THIS BOOK.

BUT THIS JUST CAME OUT A FEW WEEKS AGO . . . IF YOU'VE BEEN TRAPPED ON AN ISLAND, HOW COULD YOU HAVE READ IT **ALREADY**?

DON'T BELIEVE ME, EH? CHECK OVER THERE. NEAR MY BED.

AMAZING!!

EVEN THE SAME EDITION!

PERHAPS A BIT **WORN** FROM SO MANY READINGS.

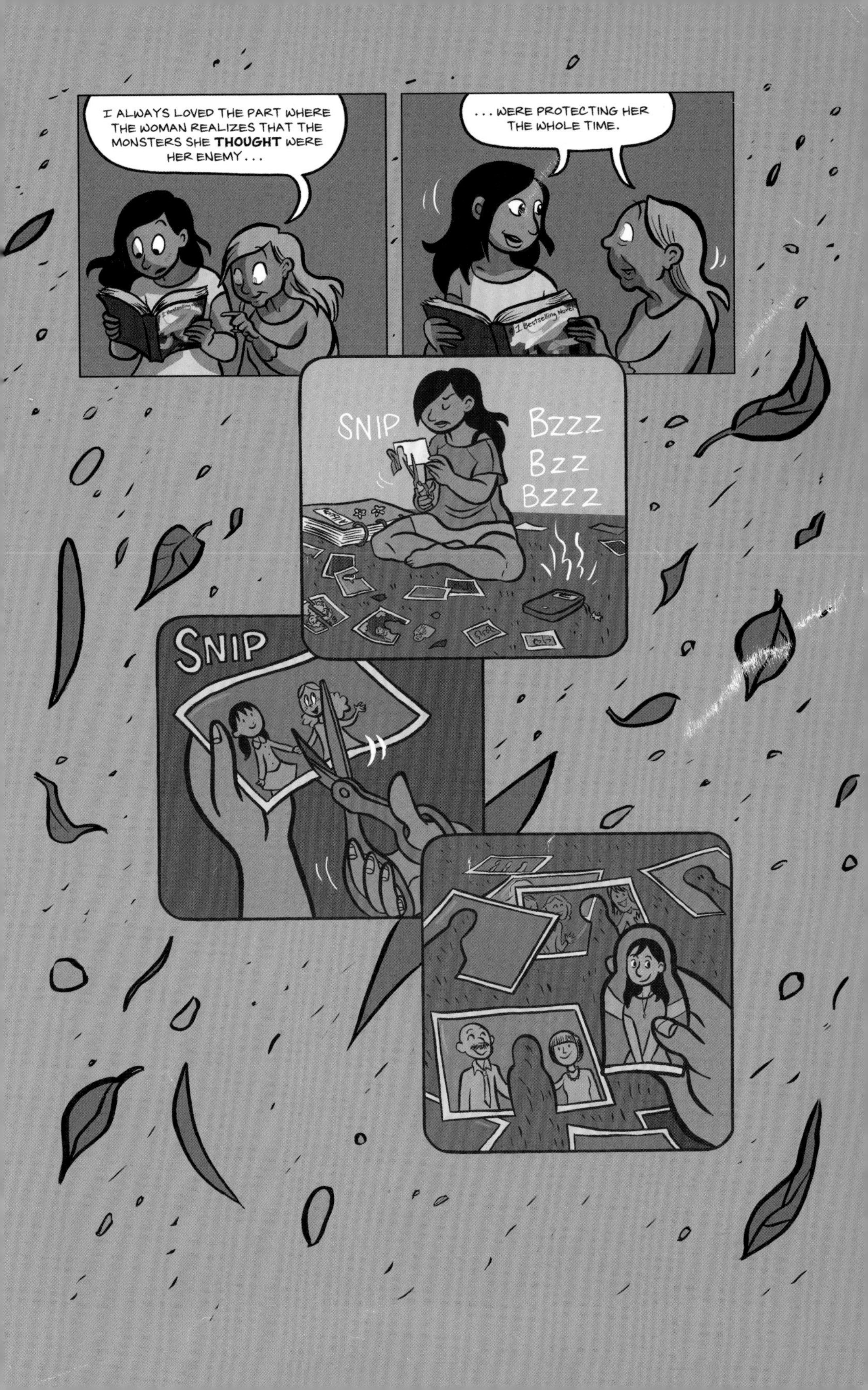

I ALWAYS LOVED THE PART WHERE THE WOMAN REALIZES THAT THE MONSTERS SHE **THOUGHT** WERE HER ENEMY . . .
. . . WERE PROTECTING HER THE WHOLE TIME.
#1 Bestselling Novel
SNIP
Bzzz
Bzz
Bzzz
SNIP

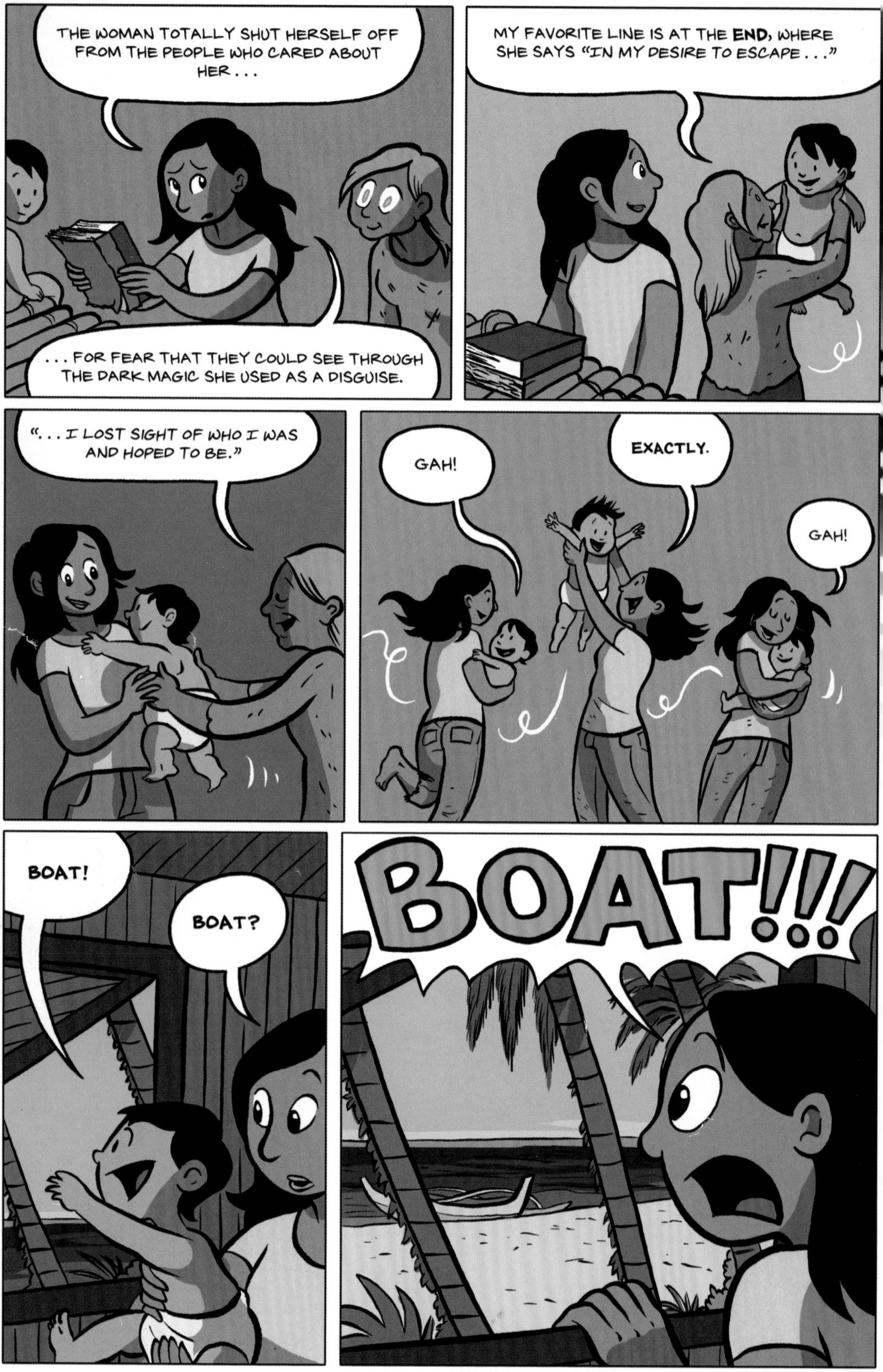
THE WOMAN TOTALLY SHUT HERSELF OFF FROM THE PEOPLE WHO CARED ABOUT HER . . .
. . . FOR FEAR THAT THEY COULD SEE THROUGH THE DARK MAGIC SHE USED AS A DISGUISE.
MY FAVORITE LINE IS AT THE **END**, WHERE SHE SAYS "IN MY DESIRE TO ESCAPE . . ."
". . . I LOST SIGHT OF WHO I WAS AND HOPED TO BE."
GAH!
EXACTLY.
GAH!
BOAT!
BOAT?
BOAT!!!

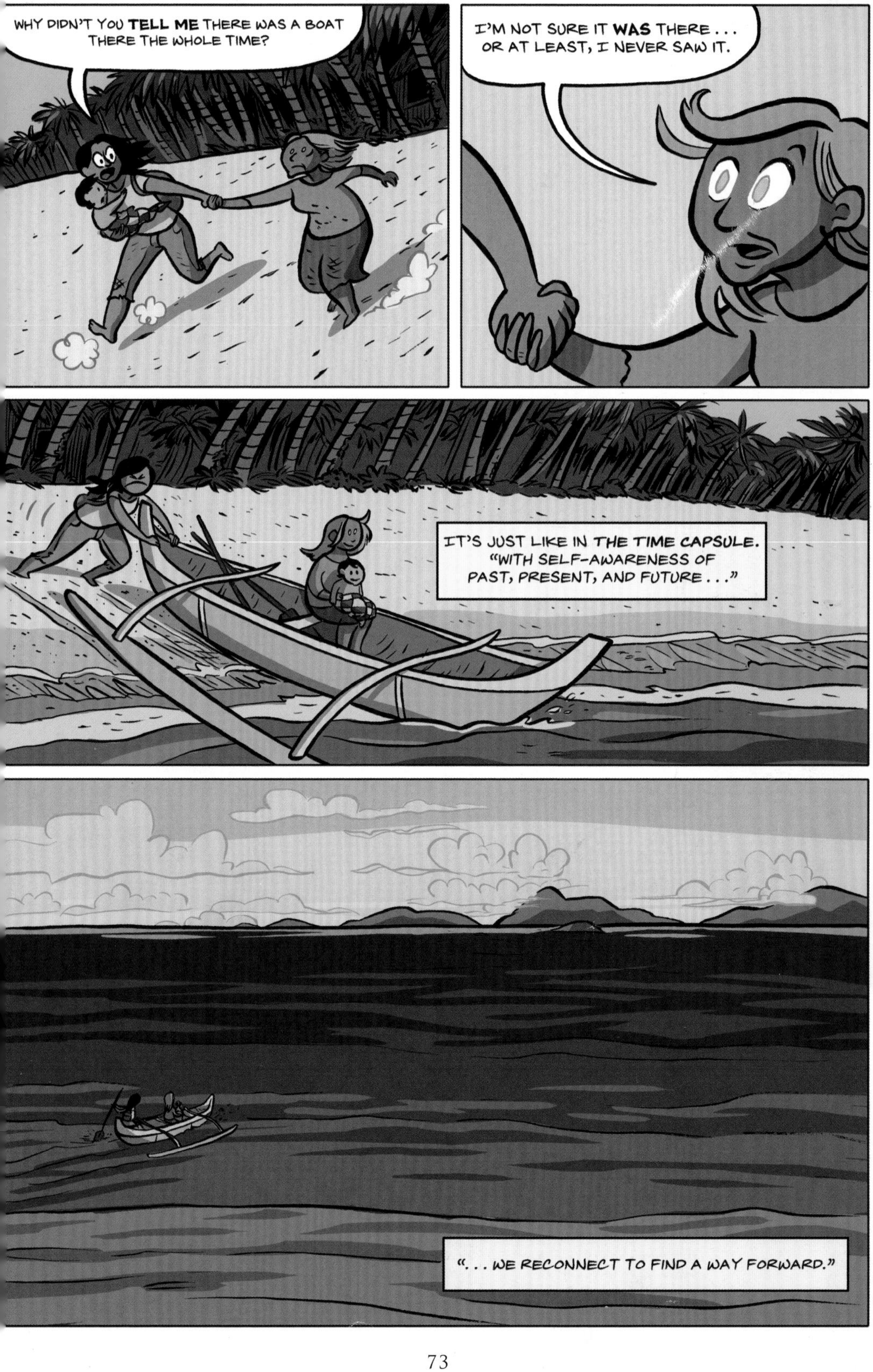
WHY DIDN'T YOU **TELL ME** THERE WAS A BOAT THERE THE WHOLE TIME?
I'M NOT SURE IT **WAS** THERE . . . OR AT LEAST, I NEVER SAW IT.
IT'S JUST LIKE IN **THE TIME CAPSULE.** "WITH SELF-AWARENESS OF PAST, PRESENT, AND FUTURE . . ."
". . . WE RECONNECT TO FIND A WAY FORWARD."

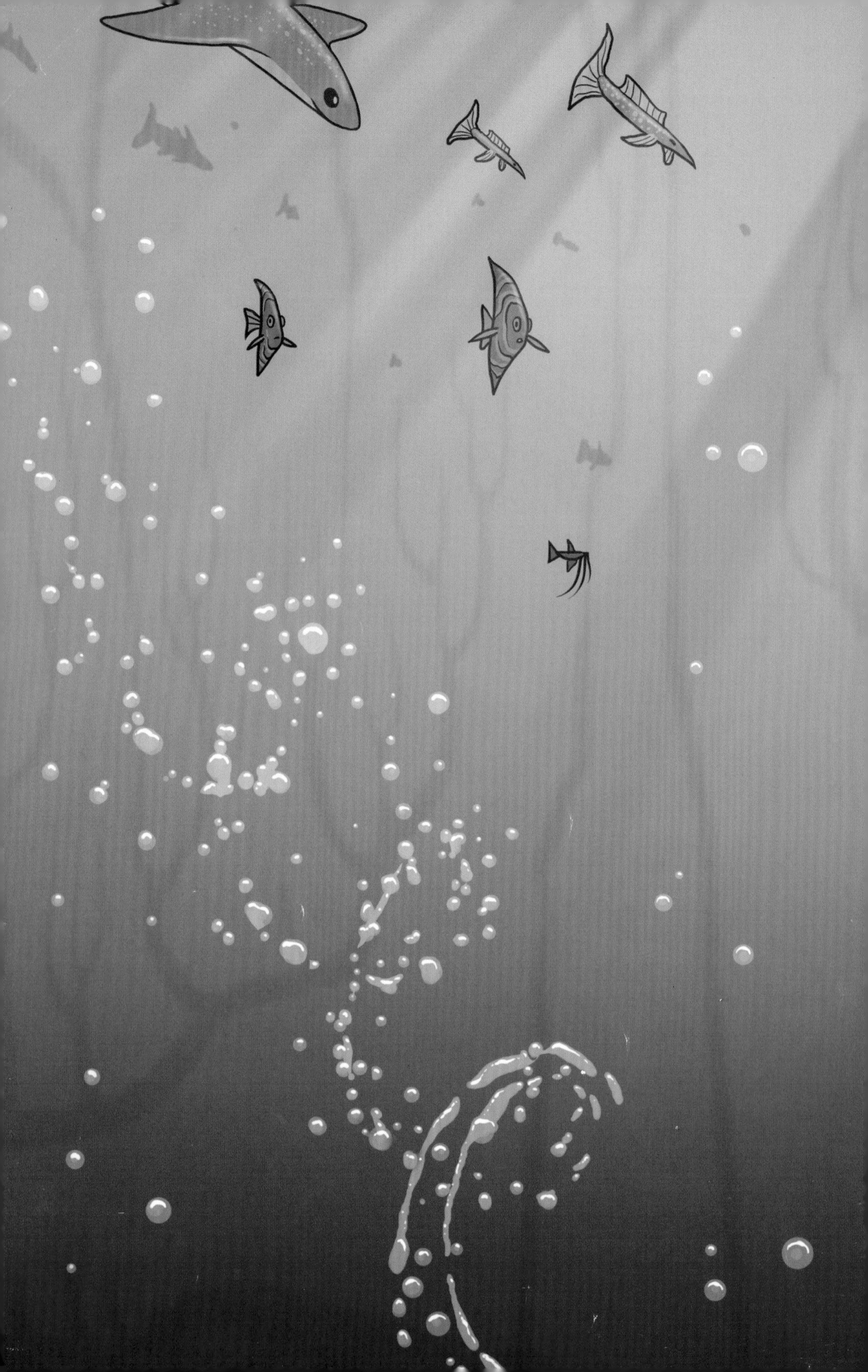

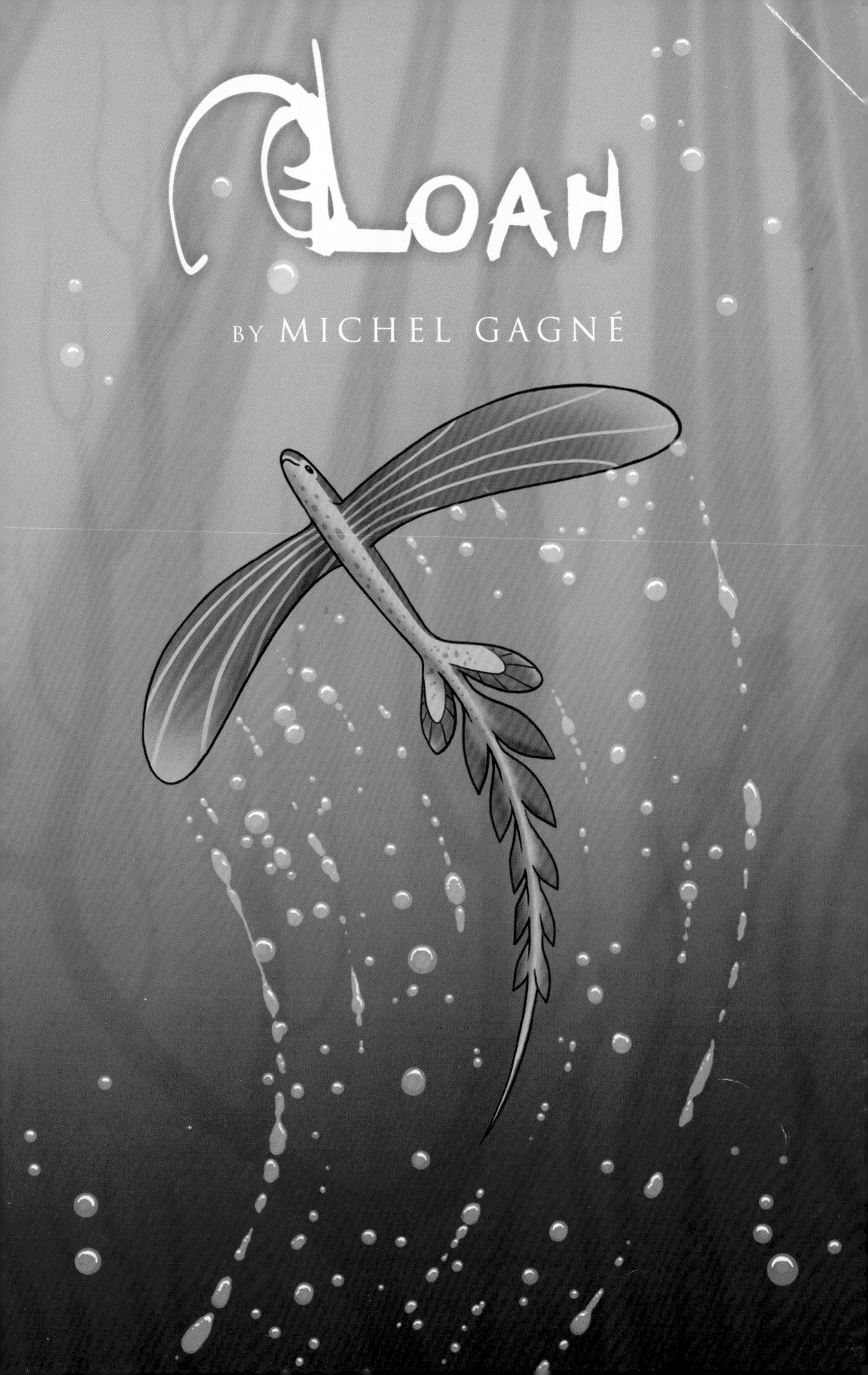
CLOAH
BY MICHEL GAGNÉ

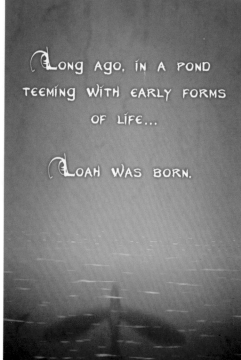

Long ago, in a pond teeming with early forms of life...

Loah was born.

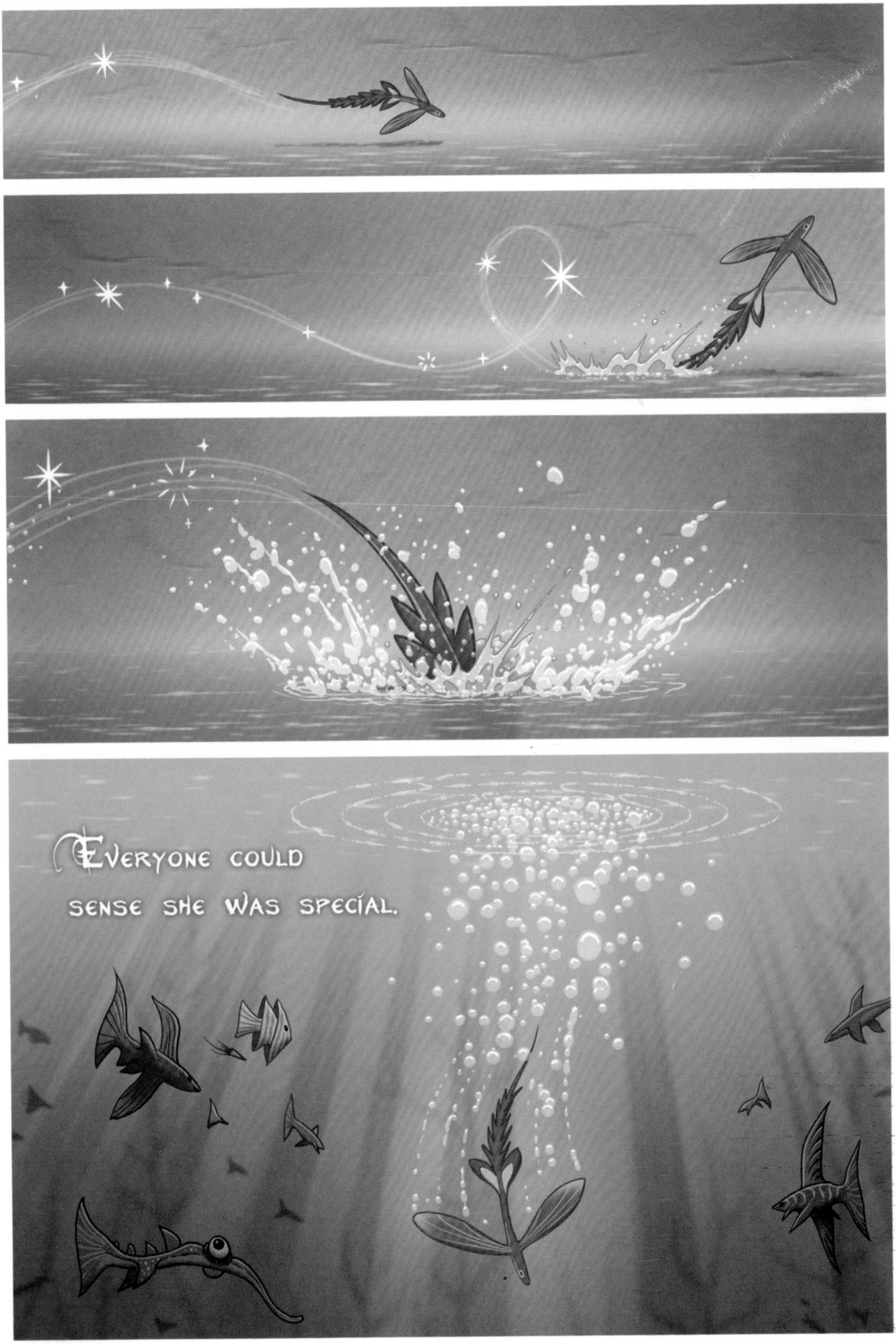
Everyone could
sense she was special.

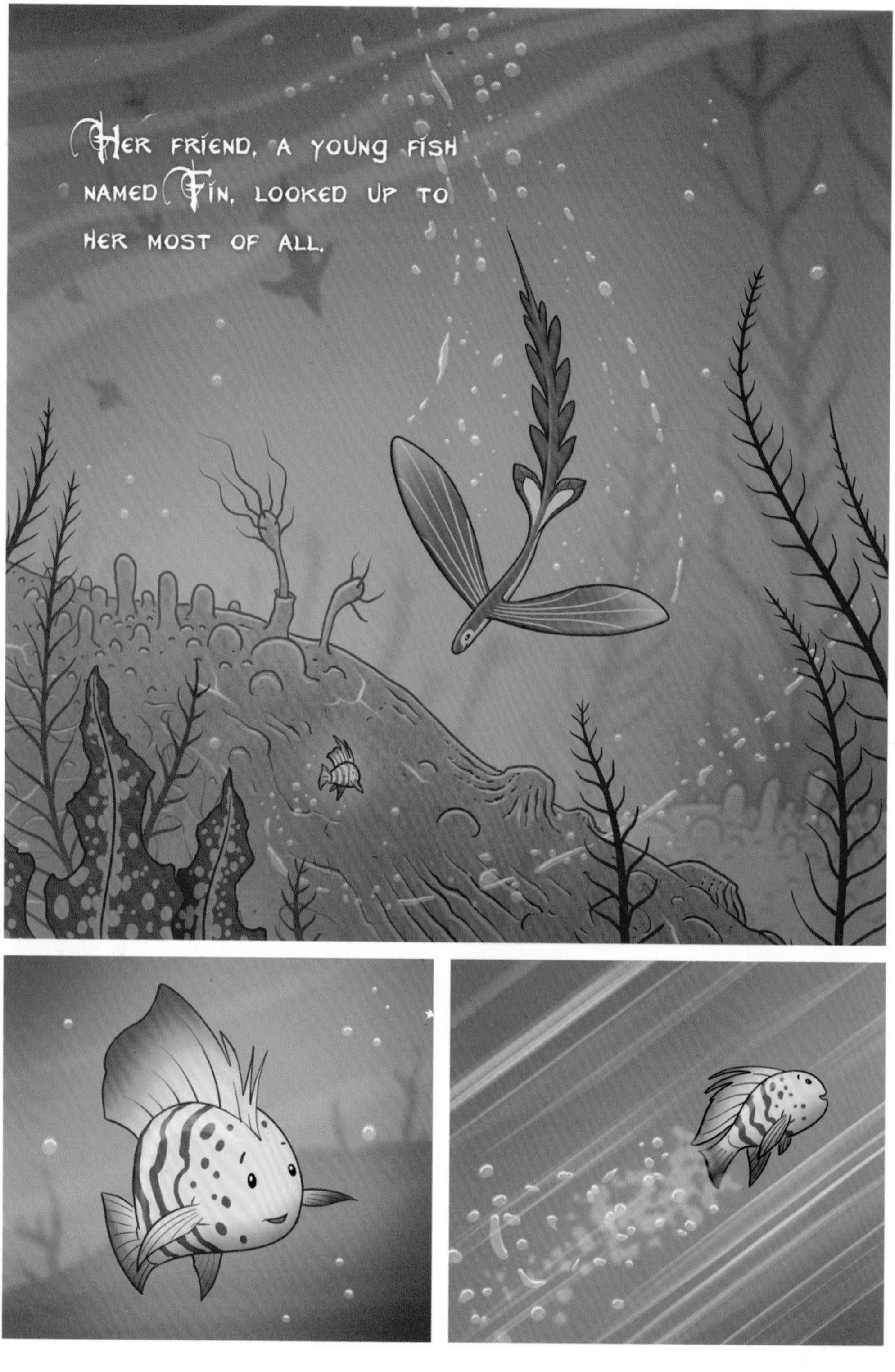
HER FRIEND, A YOUNG FISH NAMED FIN, LOOKED UP TO HER MOST OF ALL.

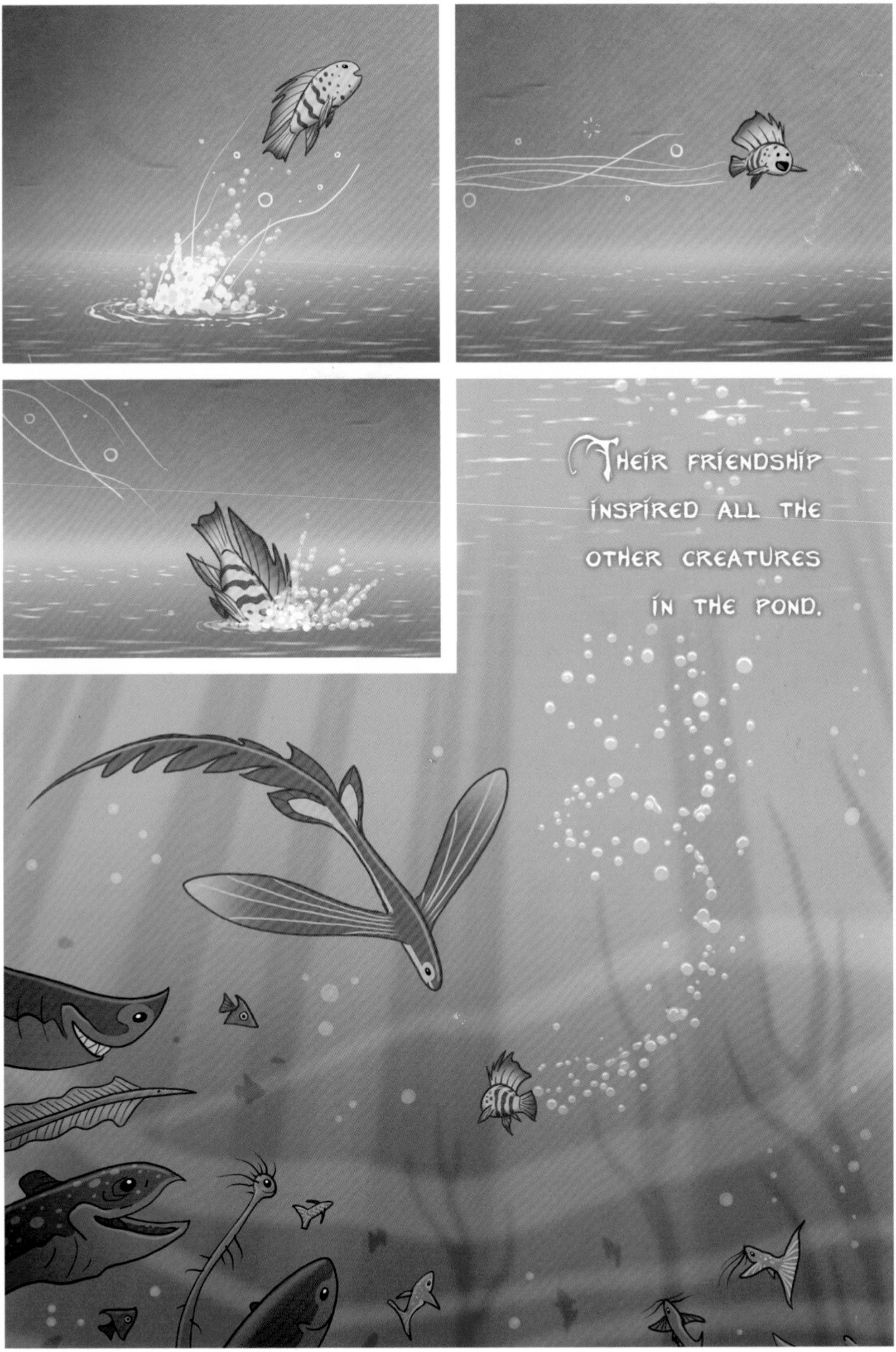
Their friendship inspired all the other creatures in the pond.

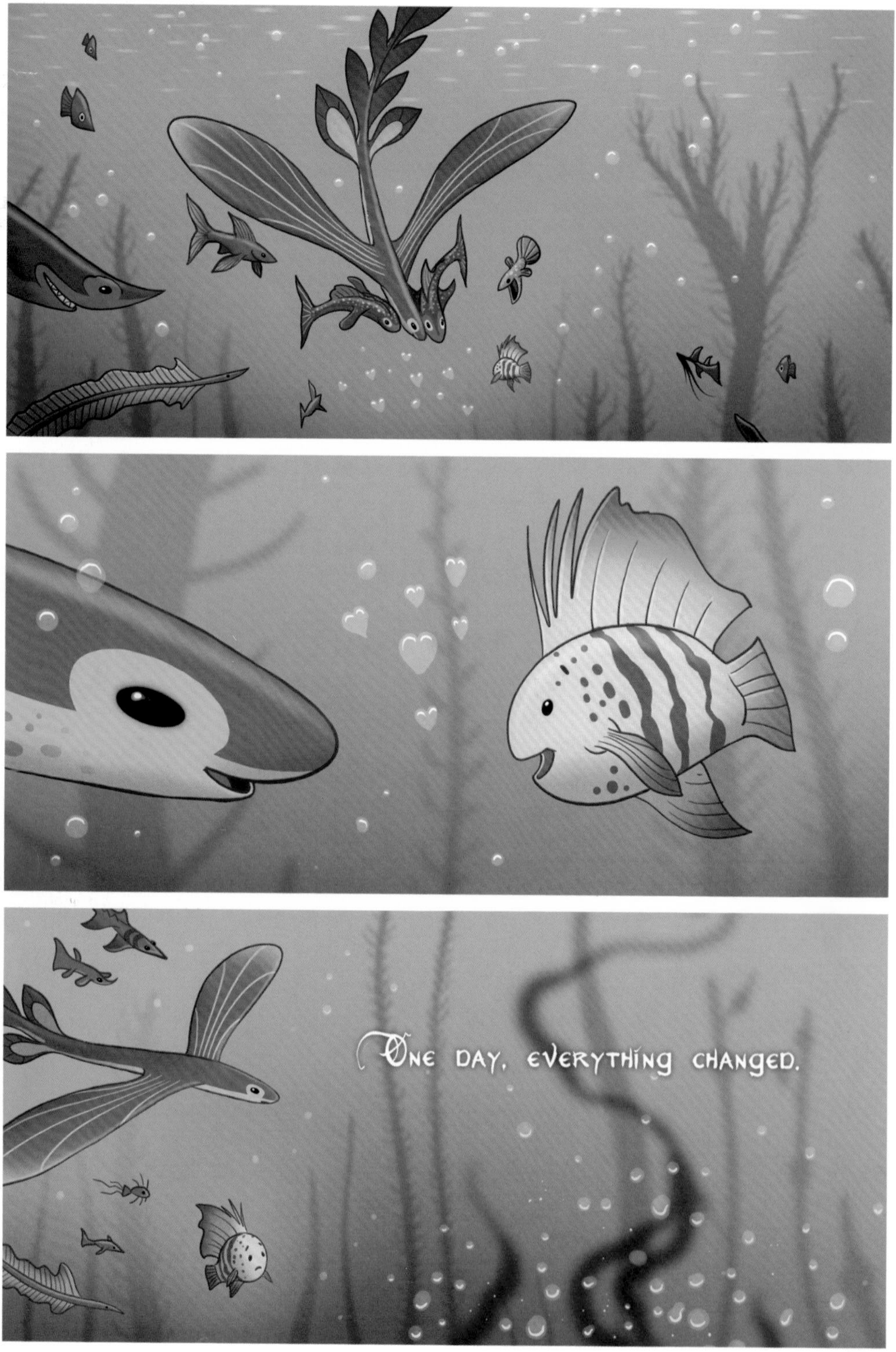
One day, everything changed.

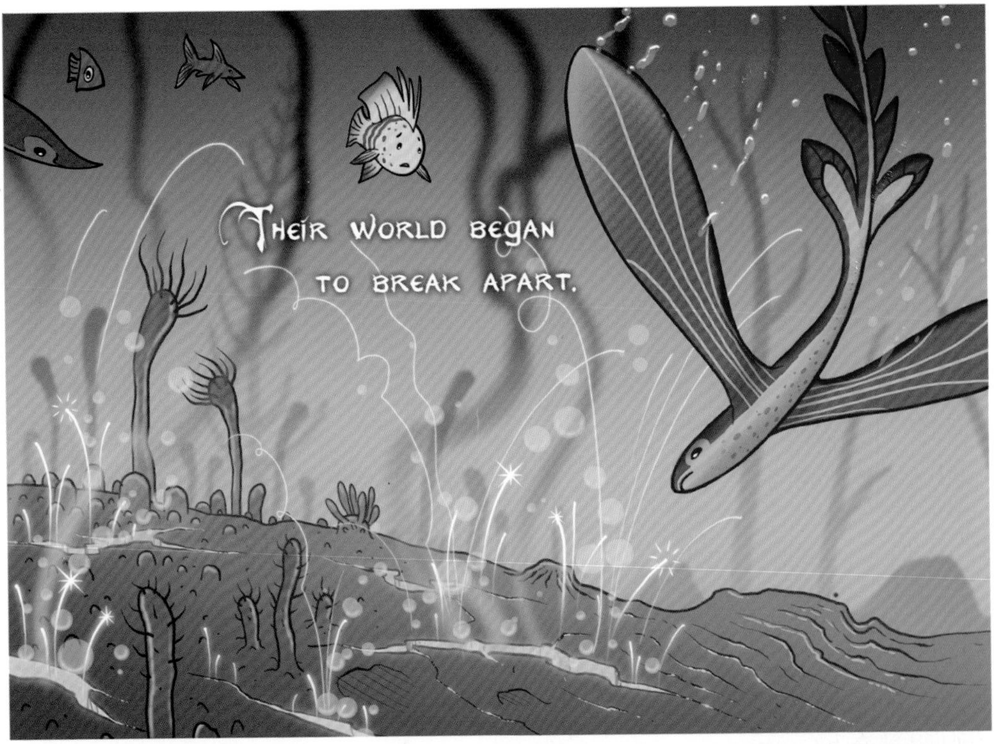
THEIR WORLD BEGAN
TO BREAK APART.

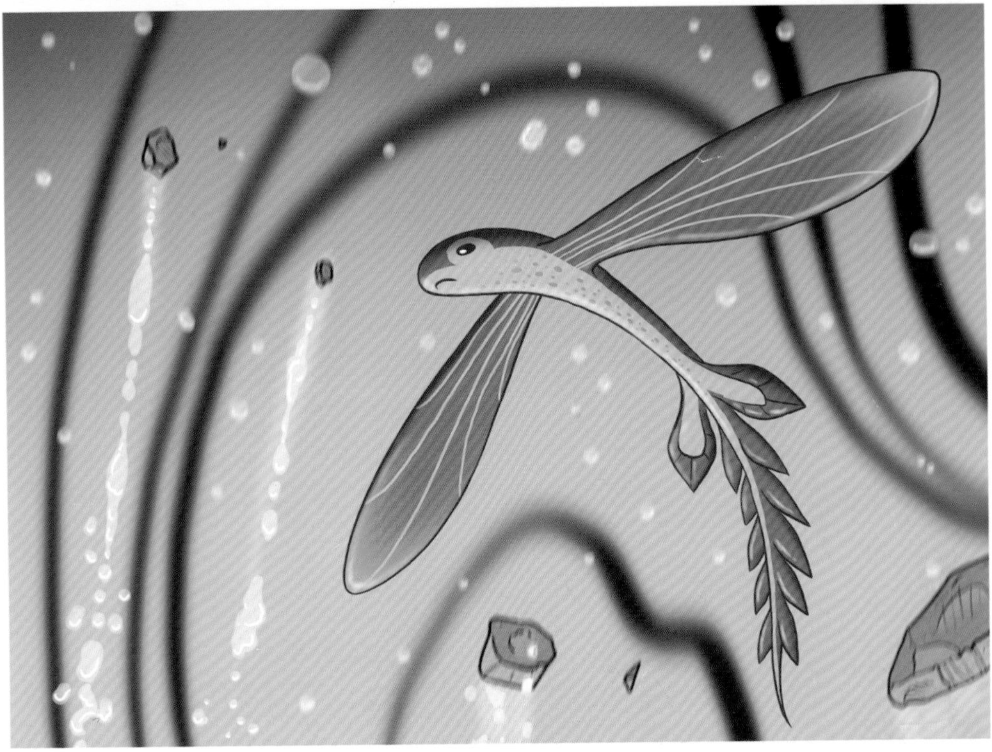

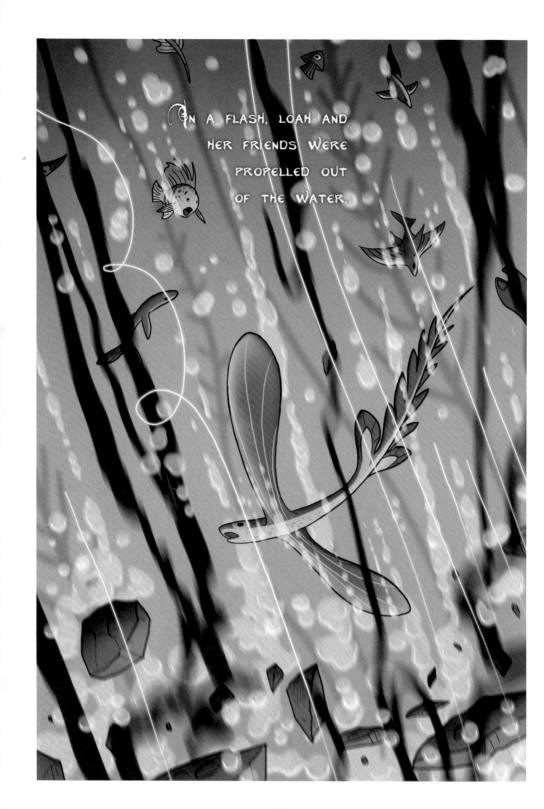

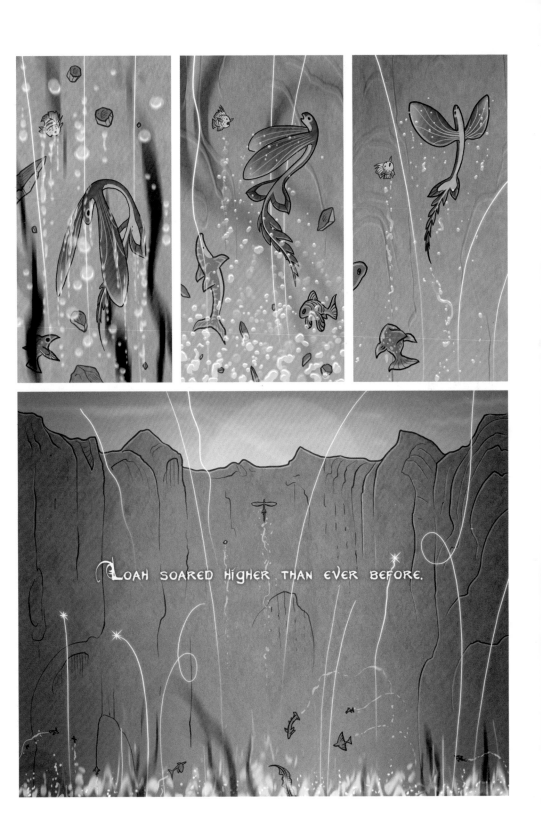

LOAH SOARED HIGHER THAN EVER BEFORE.

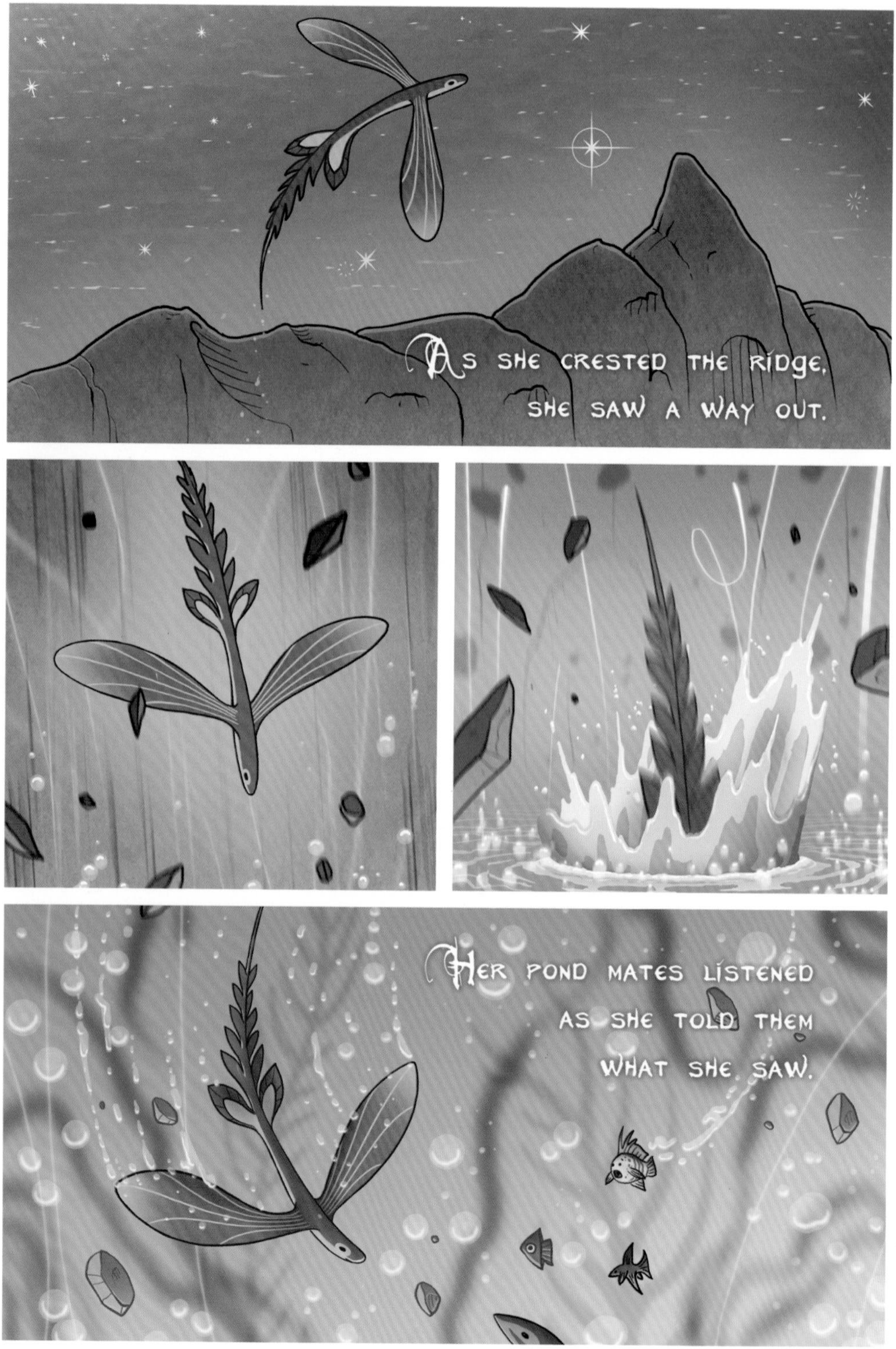
As she crested the ridge,
she saw a way out.
Her pond mates listened
as she told them
what she saw.

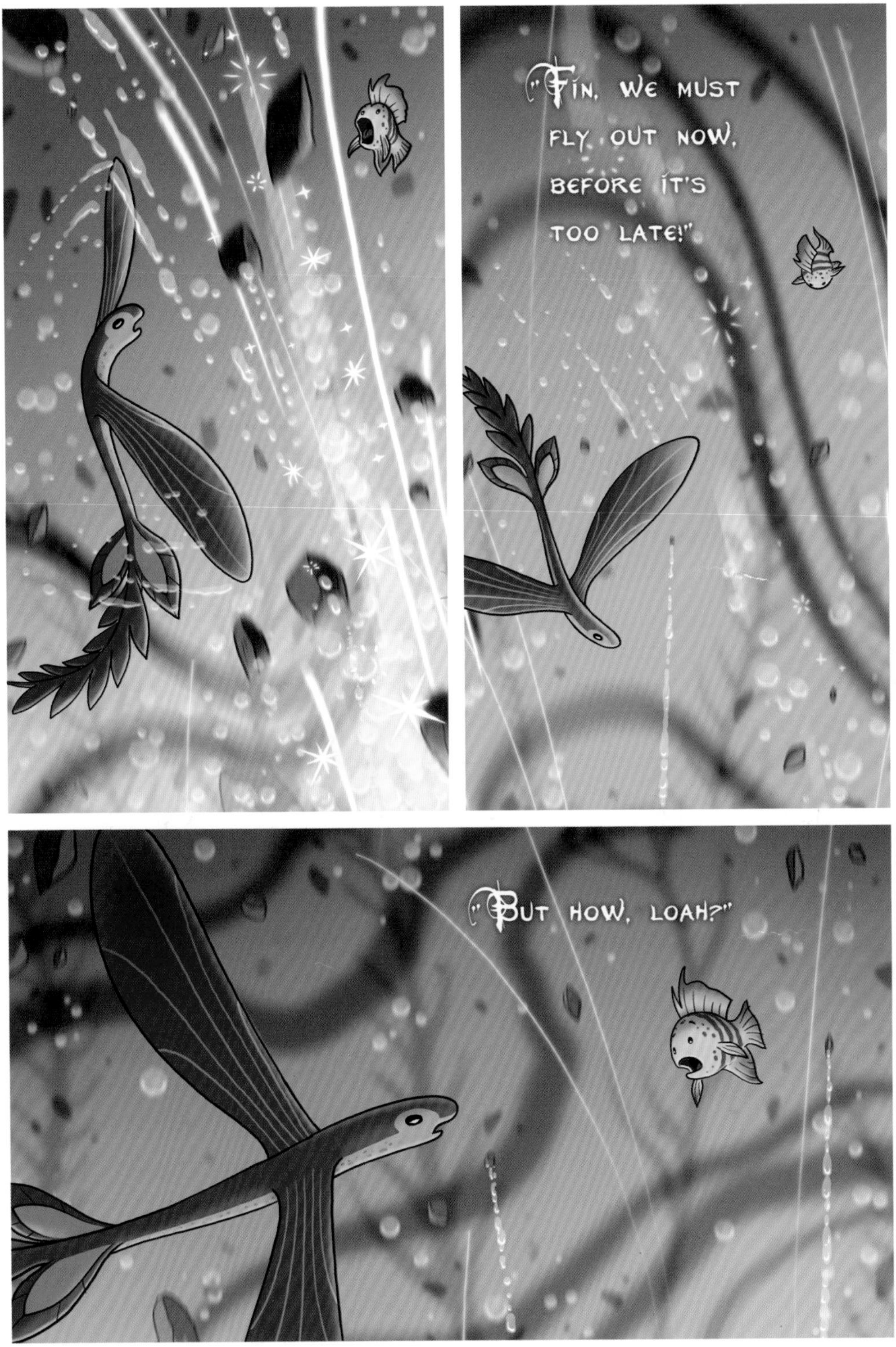
"Fin, we must fly out now, before it's too late!"
"But how, Loah?"

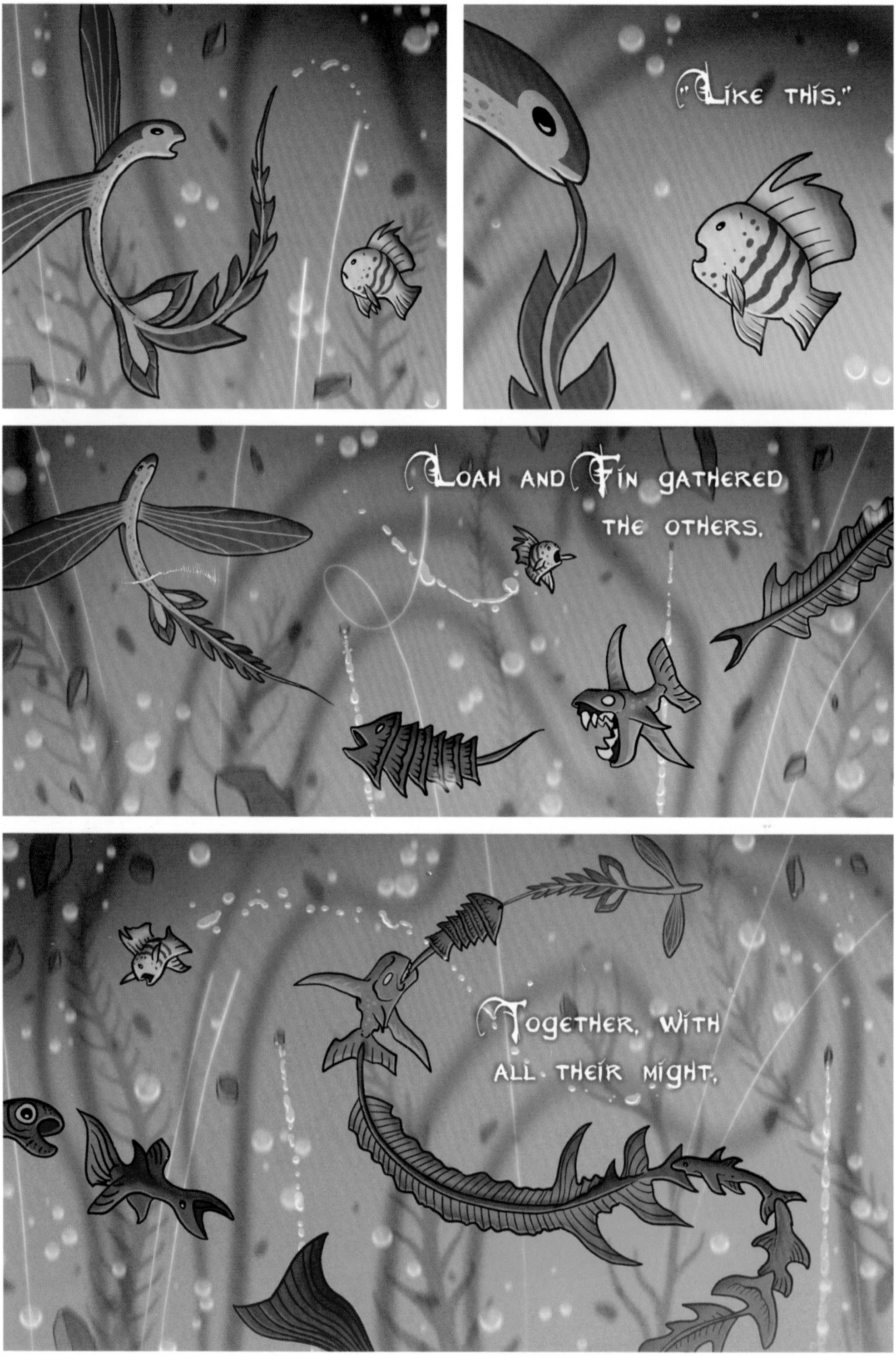
"Like this."
Loah and Fin gathered the others.
Together, with all their might,

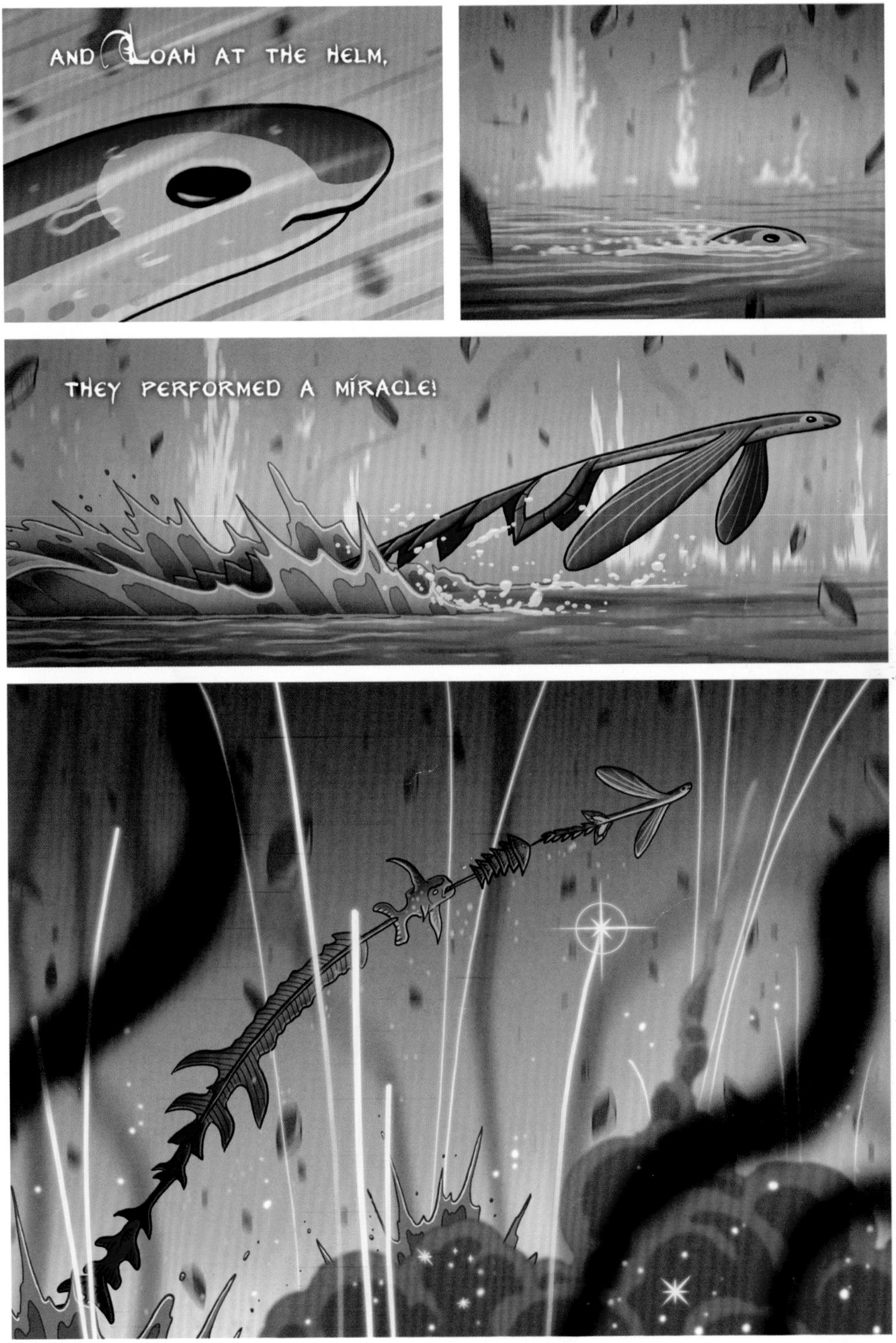
AND NOAH AT THE HELM,
THEY PERFORMED A MIRACLE!

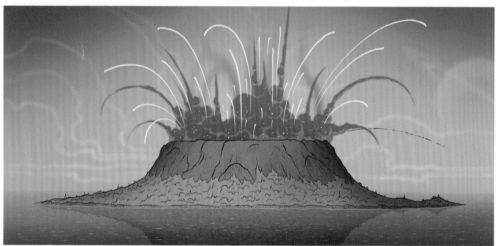

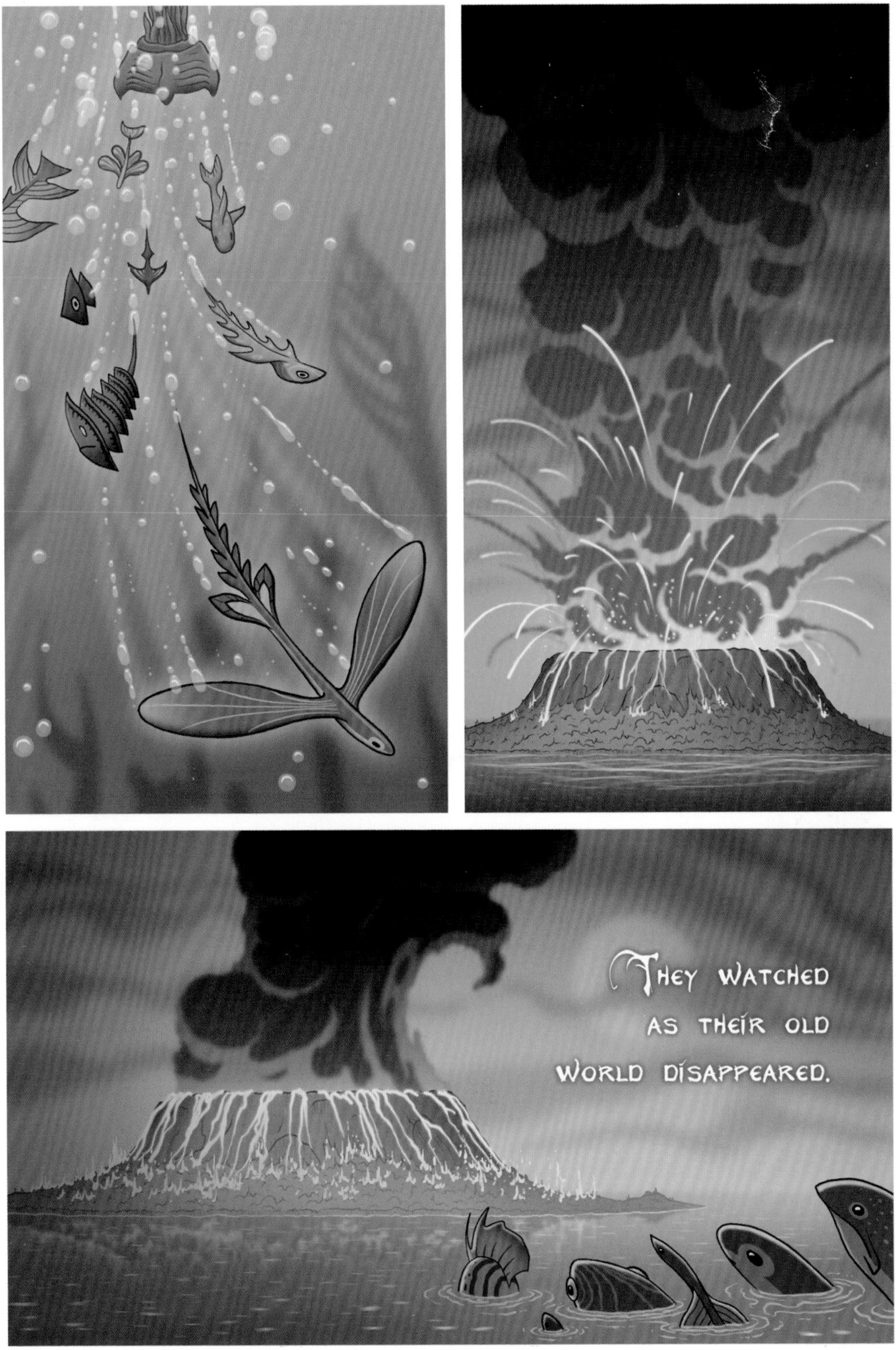
THEY WATCHED AS THEIR OLD WORLD DISAPPEARED.

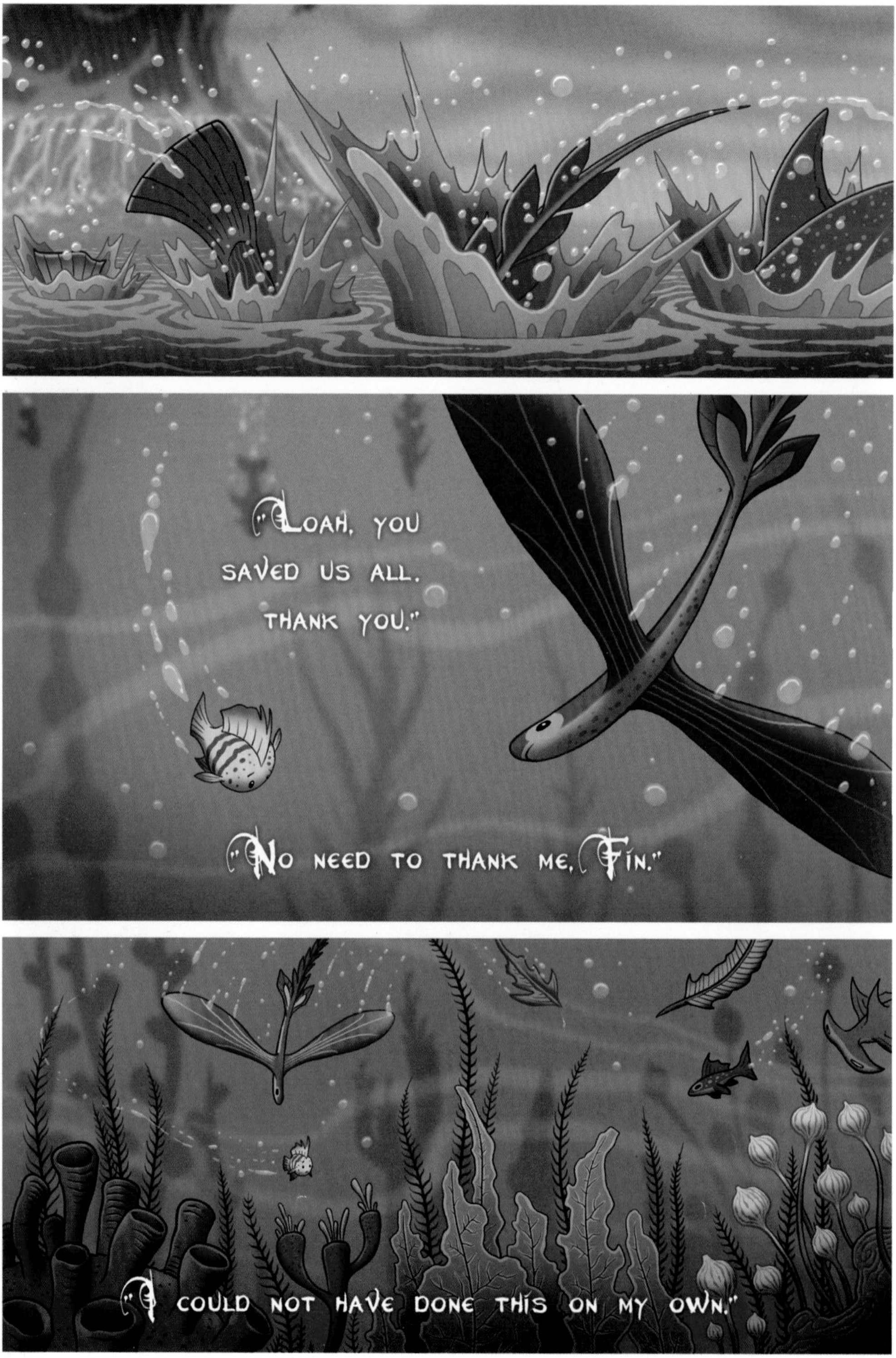
"Loah, you saved us all. thank you."
"No need to thank me, Fin."
"I could not have done this on my own."

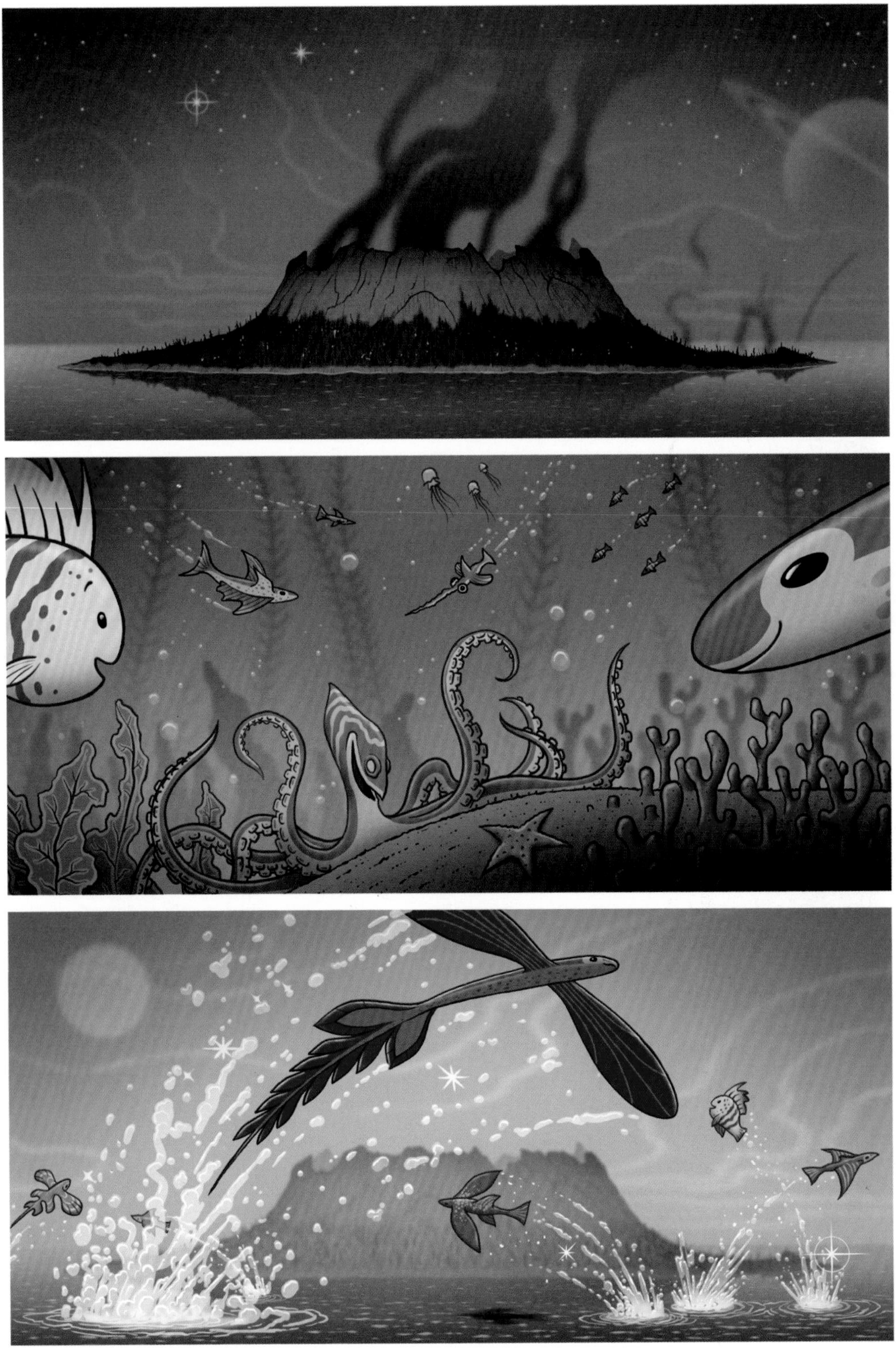

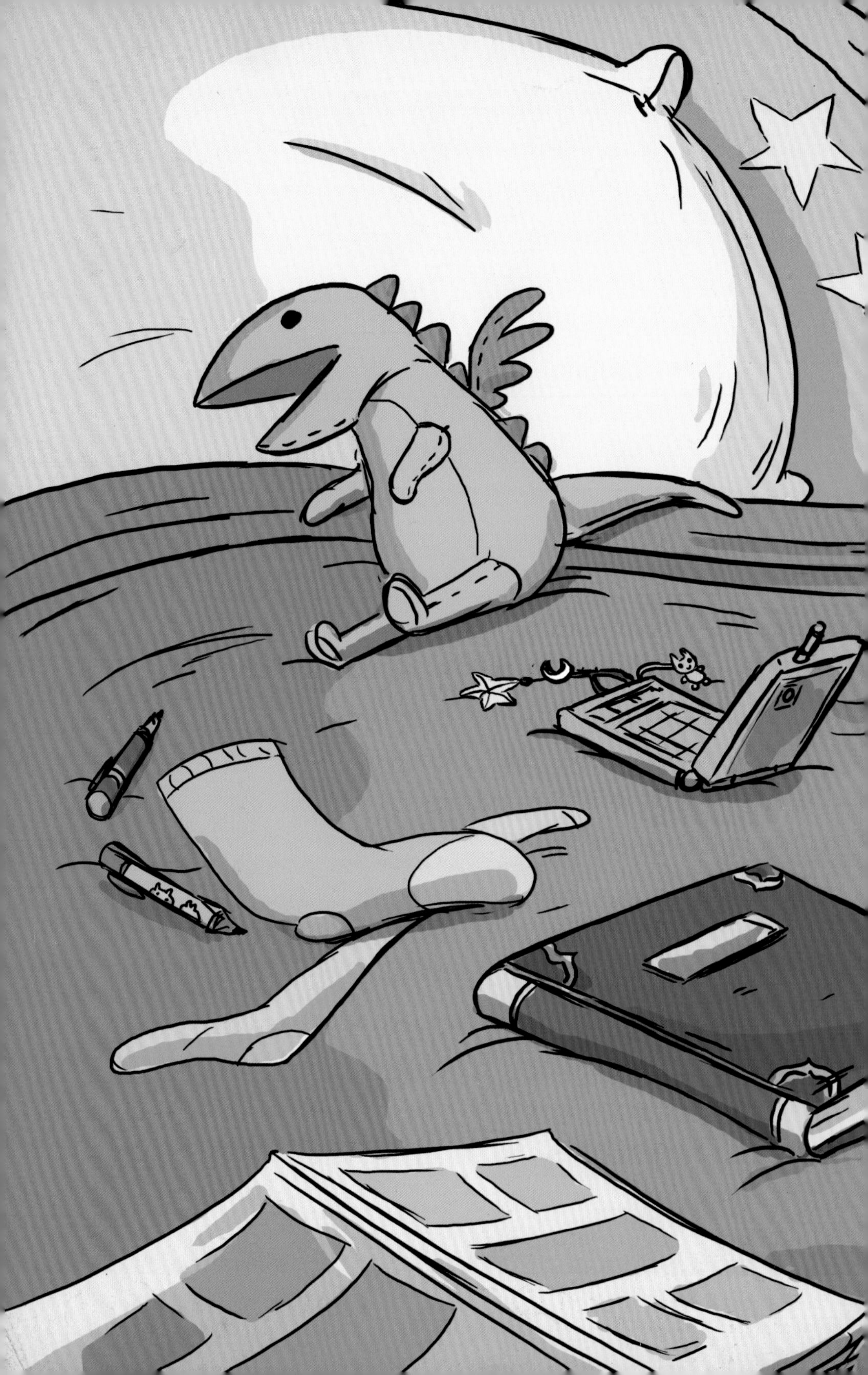

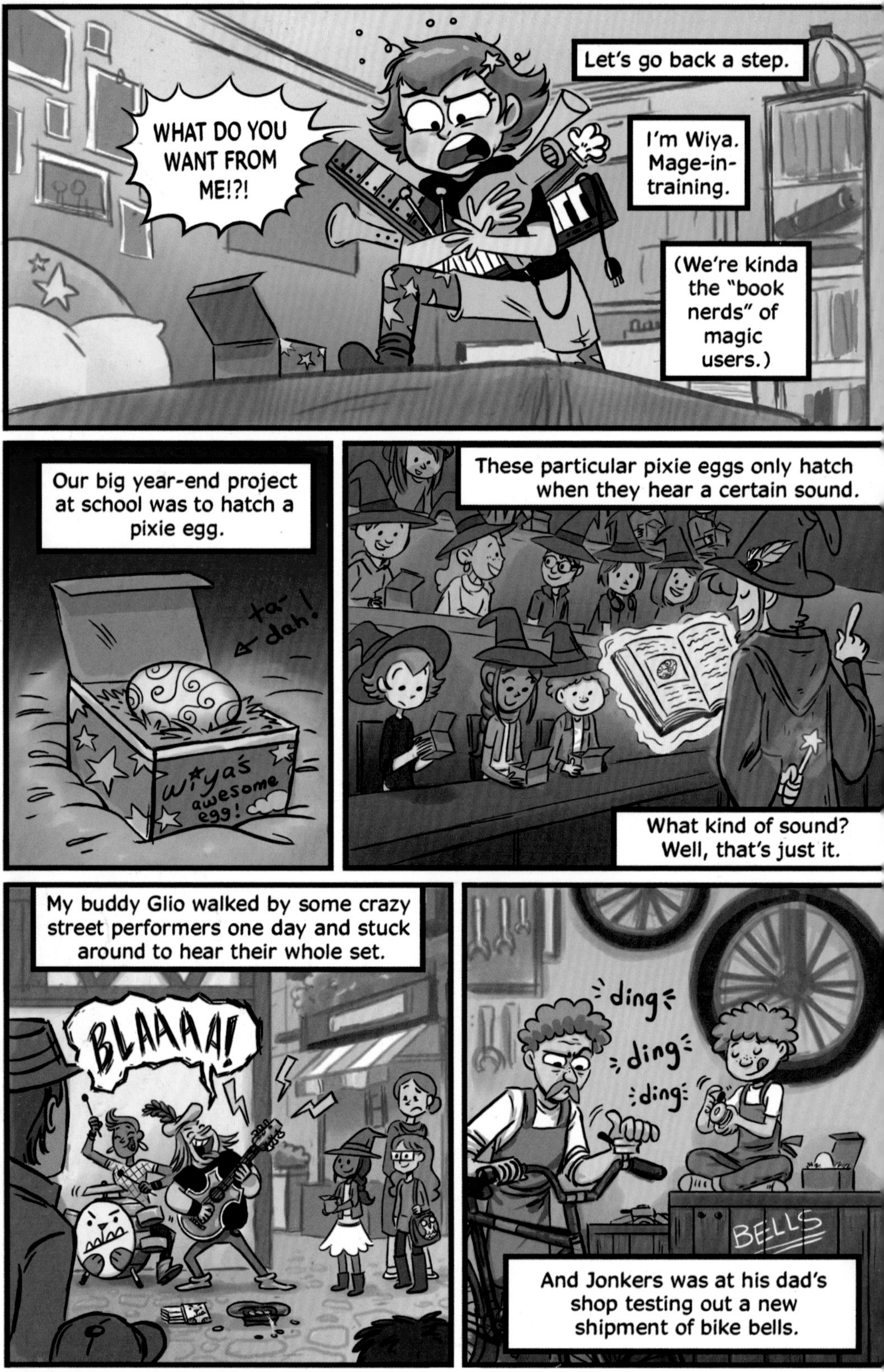
WHAT DO YOU WANT FROM ME!?!
Let's go back a step.
I'm Wiya. Mage-in-training.
(We're kinda the "book nerds" of magic users.)
Our big year-end project at school was to hatch a pixie egg.
ta-dah!
wiya's awesome egg!
These particular pixie eggs only hatch when they hear a certain sound.
What kind of sound? Well, that's just it.
My buddy Glio walked by some crazy street performers one day and stuck around to hear their whole set.
BLAAAA!
ding
ding
ding
BELLS
And Jonkers was at his dad's shop testing out a new shipment of bike bells.

Shortly after? BAM! Hatched pixies.

So I tried everything. Instruments and bells.

Ducks and crunchy crackers.

Vehicles of all kinds.

And nature in all its glory!

But I began to realize...

I'm gonna be the ONLY one in class who doesn't hatch a pixie.

That's nice, dear.

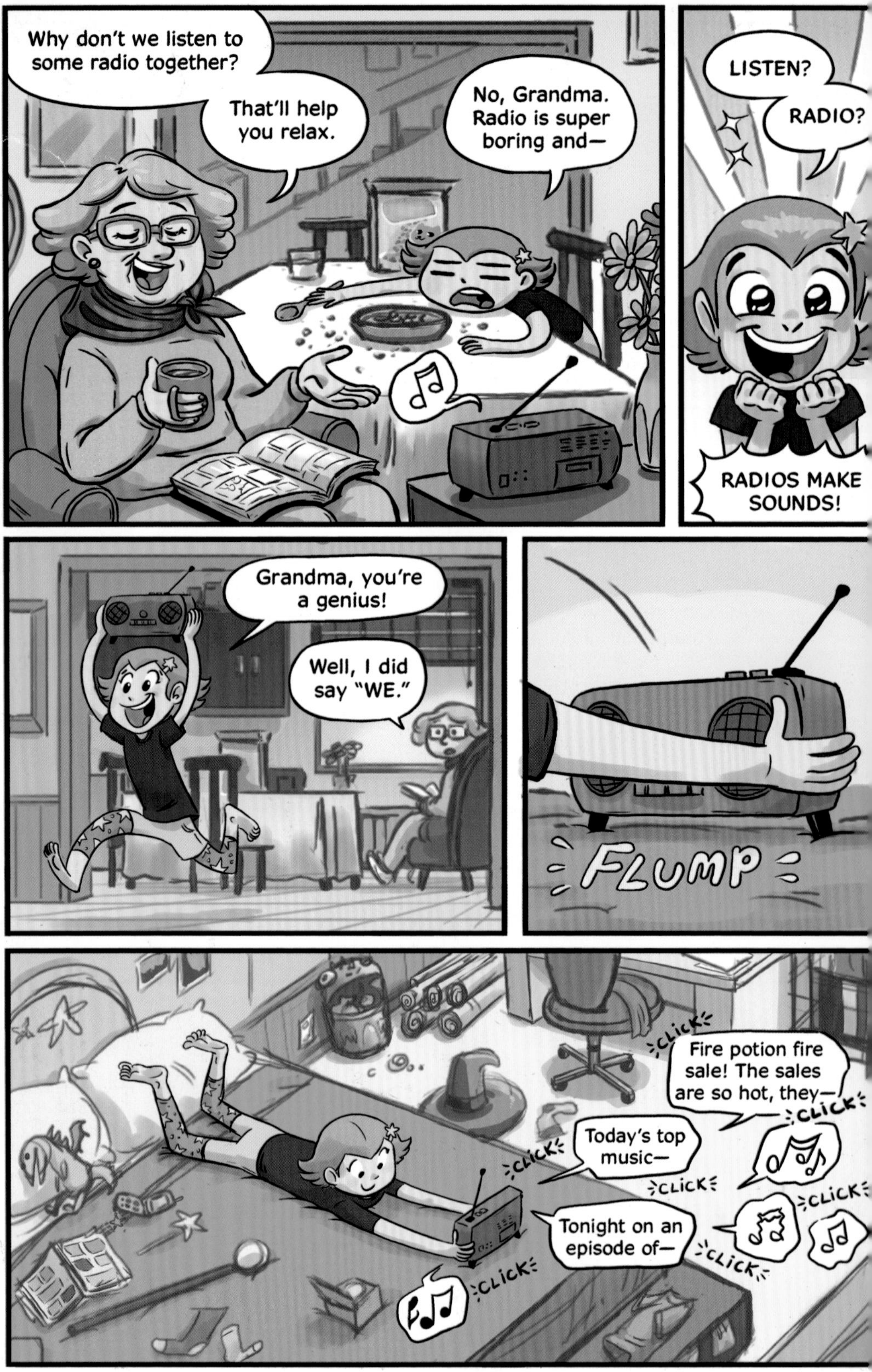
Why don't we listen to some radio together?
That'll help you relax.
No, Grandma. Radio is super boring and—
LISTEN?
RADIO?
RADIOS MAKE SOUNDS!
Grandma, you're a genius!
Well, I did say "WE."
FLUMP
CLICK
Fire potion fire sale! The sales are so hot, they—
CLICK
Today's top music—
CLICK
CLICK
CLICK
Tonight on an episode of—
CLICK
CLICK

—win a trip for you and three hundred of your best friends!

:CLICK:

🎵 baby, baby, baaaabies— 🎵

:CLICK:

—do you need a lawyer? I'm happy to be a lawyer—

blah blah blah stock market—

ZZZ

blah blah blah

:CLICK:

Day 126—

—here on Radio Adrift and our last day in town.

I just want to thank you all for the warm welcome.

But as it is in life, all good things must come to an end.

Wha?

That's it!

We're going to take a musical break now—

97

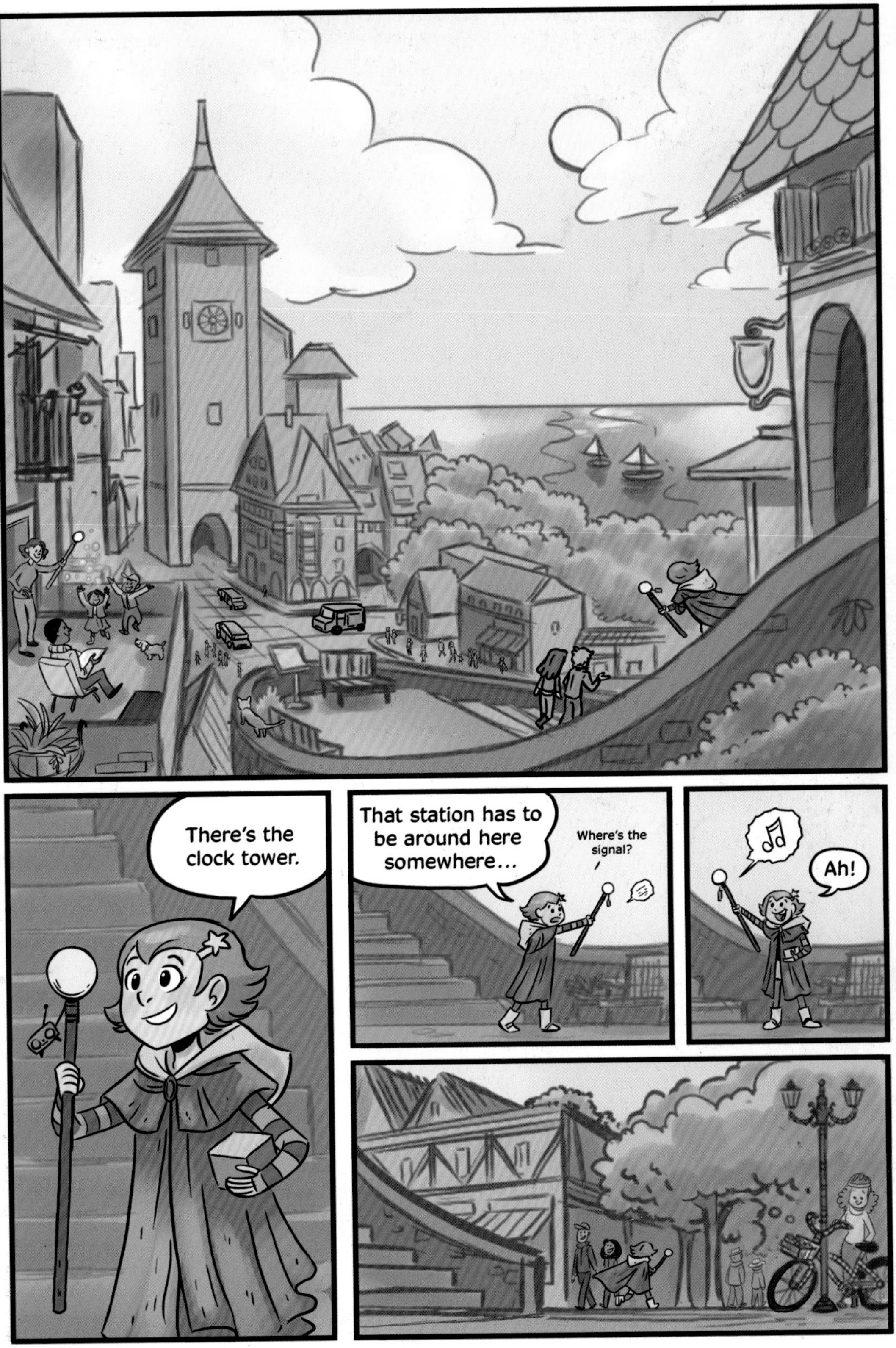
There's the clock tower.
That station has to be around here somewhere...
Where's the signal?
Ah!

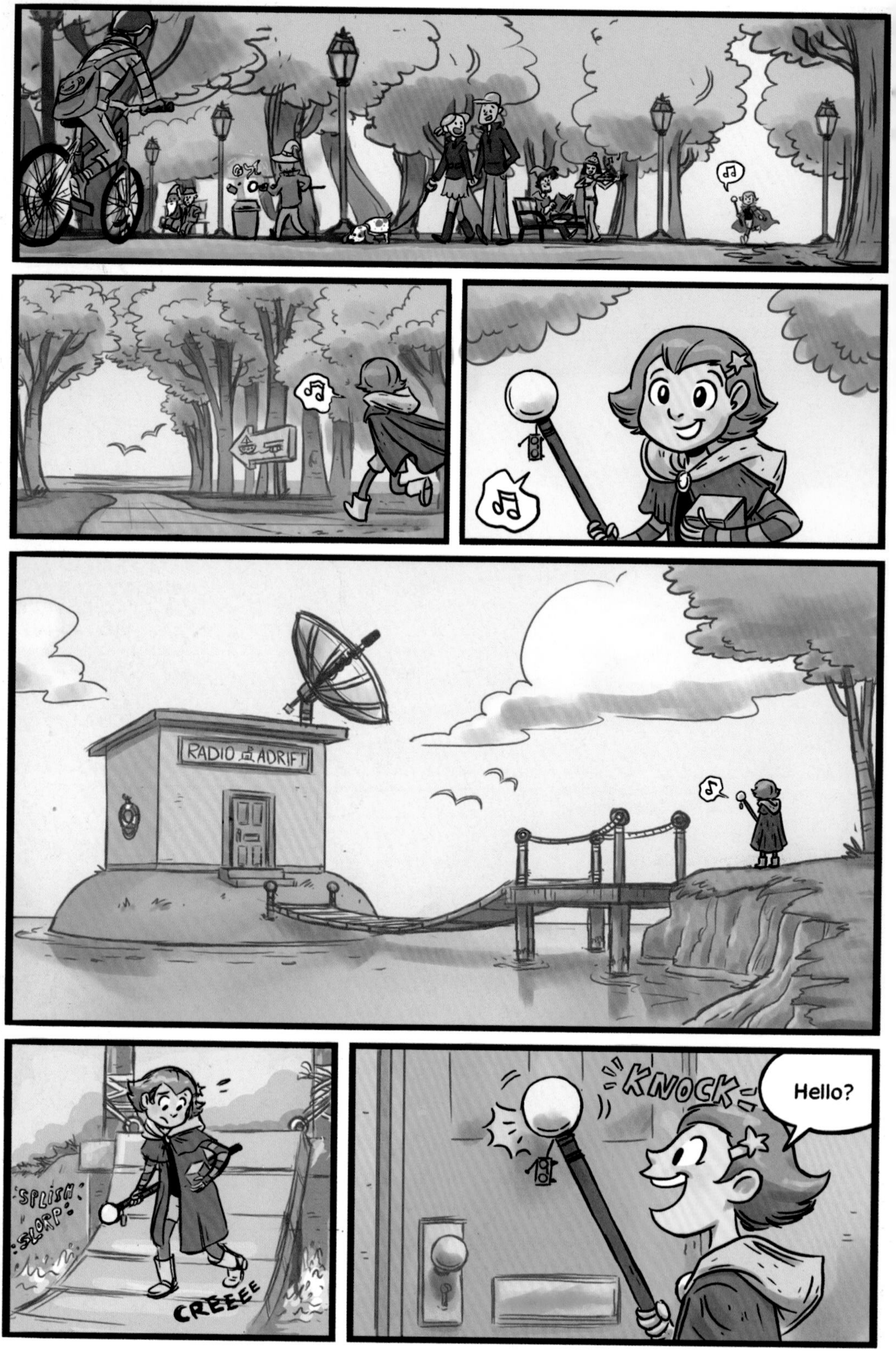
RADIO ADRIFT
SPLISH
SLORP
CREEEE
KNOCK
Hello?

Hello, I'm Bert. DJ, host, and engineer here at **Radio Adrift.**

My card.

Oh! Nice.

I'm Wiya, mage-in-training.

?

And this is an egg. Talk to it!

Uh, hi there, Egg.

Huh?

So you're a mage? That's excellent.

I heard this town had a **magic academy.** I was hoping to interview someone from there.

Prestigious place, right? Heard it's tough to get into.

Yeeeeeah, well, it's, y'know.

It's just something I do.

Not much to say.

tap tap

Why ain't you workin', Egg?

You're right! We should save it for the show.

Keep it natural.

Oh, sure.

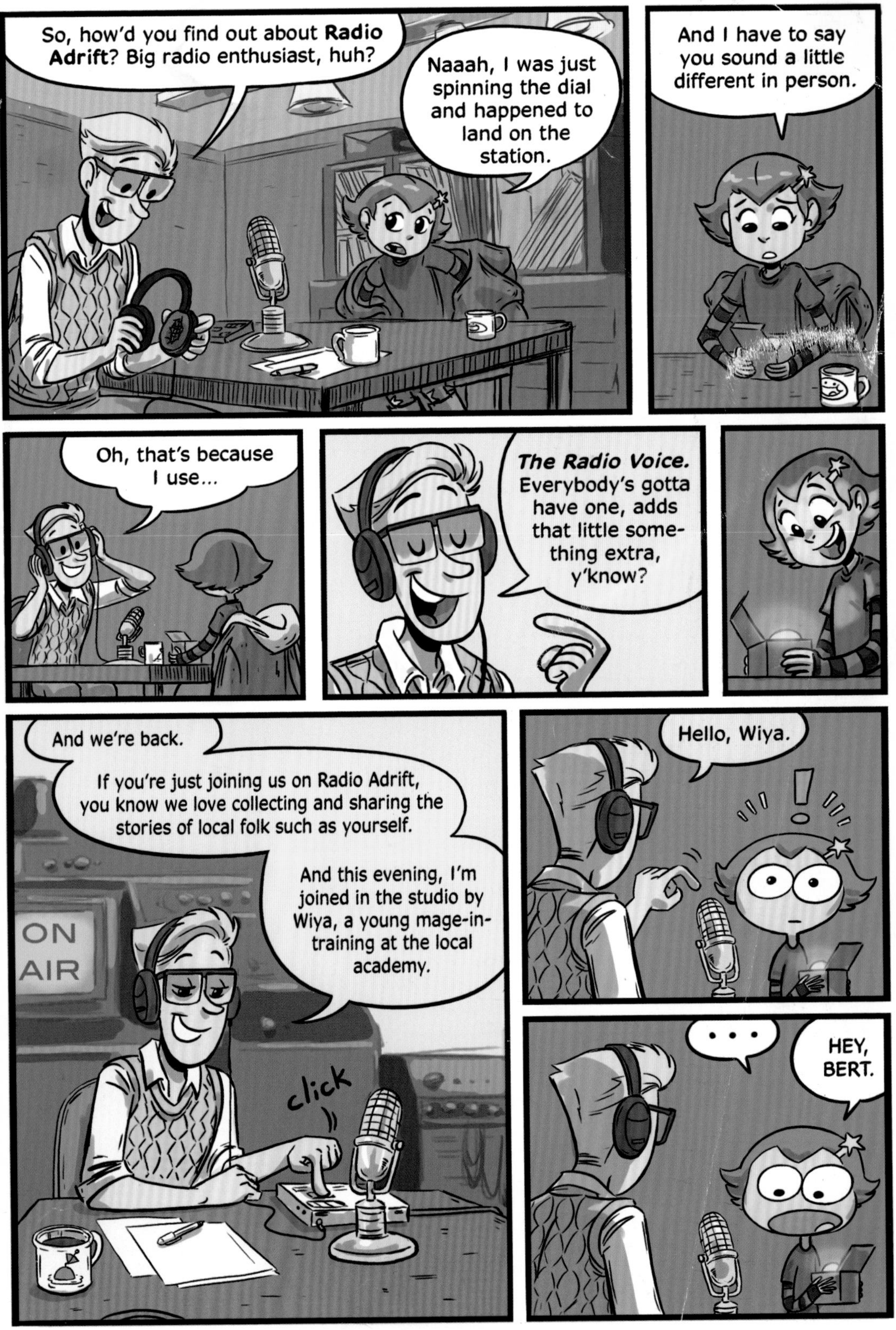
So, how'd you find out about **Radio Adrift**? Big radio enthusiast, huh?
Naaah, I was just spinning the dial and happened to land on the station.
And I have to say you sound a little different in person.
Oh, that's because I use...
The Radio Voice. Everybody's gotta have one, adds that little something extra, y'know?
And we're back.
If you're just joining us on Radio Adrift, you know we love collecting and sharing the stories of local folk such as yourself.
And this evening, I'm joined in the studio by Wiya, a young mage-in-training at the local academy.
ON AIR
click
Hello, Wiya.
!
. . .
HEY, BERT.

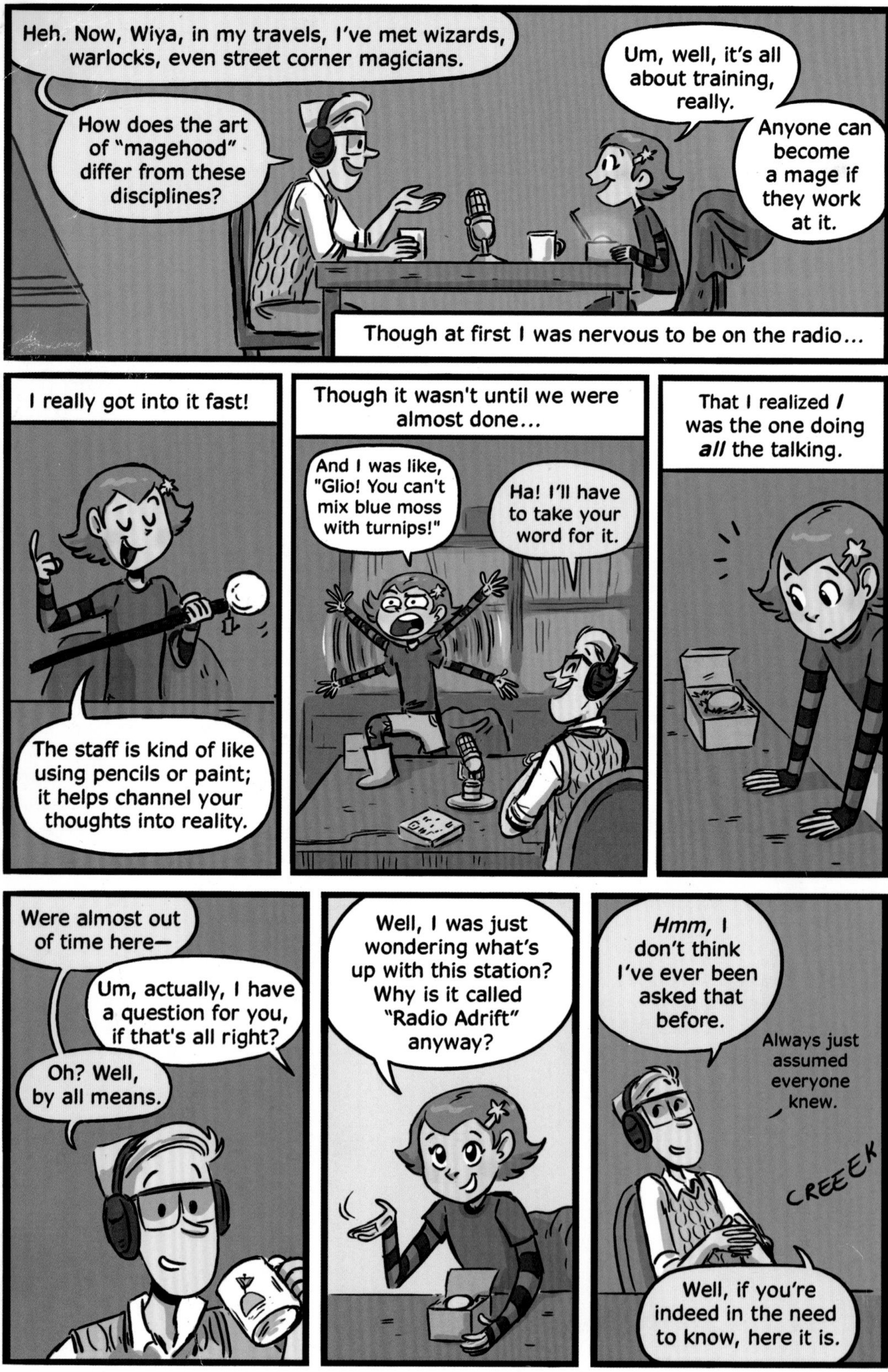
Heh. Now, Wiya, in my travels, I've met wizards, warlocks, even street corner magicians.
How does the art of "magehood" differ from these disciplines?
Um, well, it's all about training, really.
Anyone can become a mage if they work at it.
Though at first I was nervous to be on the radio...
I really got into it fast!
The staff is kind of like using pencils or paint; it helps channel your thoughts into reality.
Though it wasn't until we were almost done...
And I was like, "Glio! You can't mix blue moss with turnips!"
Ha! I'll have to take your word for it.
That I realized *I* was the one doing *all* the talking.
Were almost out of time here—
Um, actually, I have a question for you, if that's all right?
Oh? Well, by all means.
Well, I was just wondering what's up with this station? Why is it called "Radio Adrift" anyway?
Hmm, I don't think I've ever been asked that before.
Always just assumed everyone knew.
CREEEK
Well, if you're indeed in the need to know, here it is.

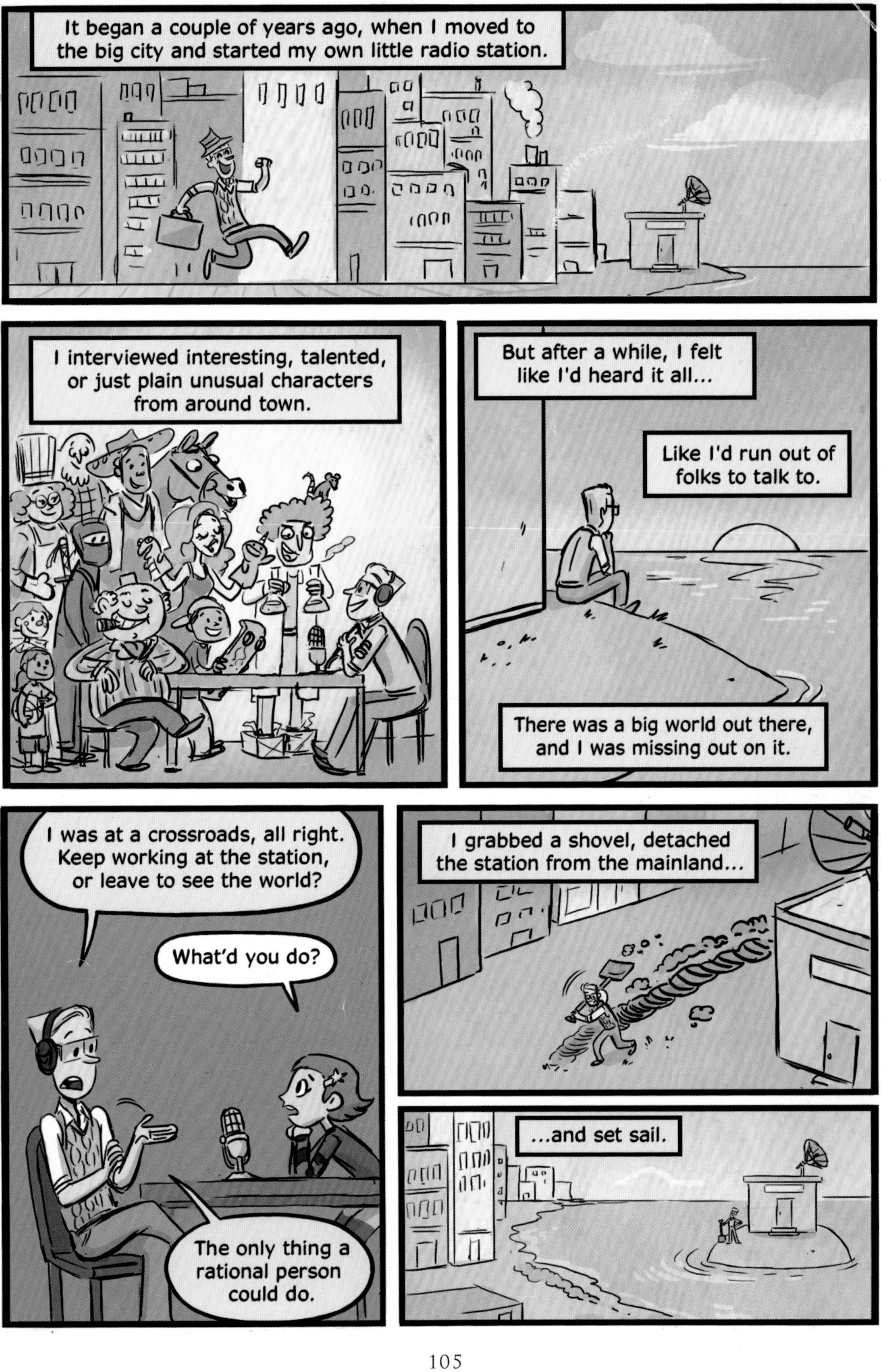

It began a couple of years ago, when I moved to the big city and started my own little radio station.
I interviewed interesting, talented, or just plain unusual characters from around town.
But after a while, I felt like I'd heard it all...
Like I'd run out of folks to talk to.
There was a big world out there, and I was missing out on it.
I was at a crossroads, all right. Keep working at the station, or leave to see the world?
What'd you do?
The only thing a rational person could do.
I grabbed a shovel, detached the station from the mainland...
...and set sail.

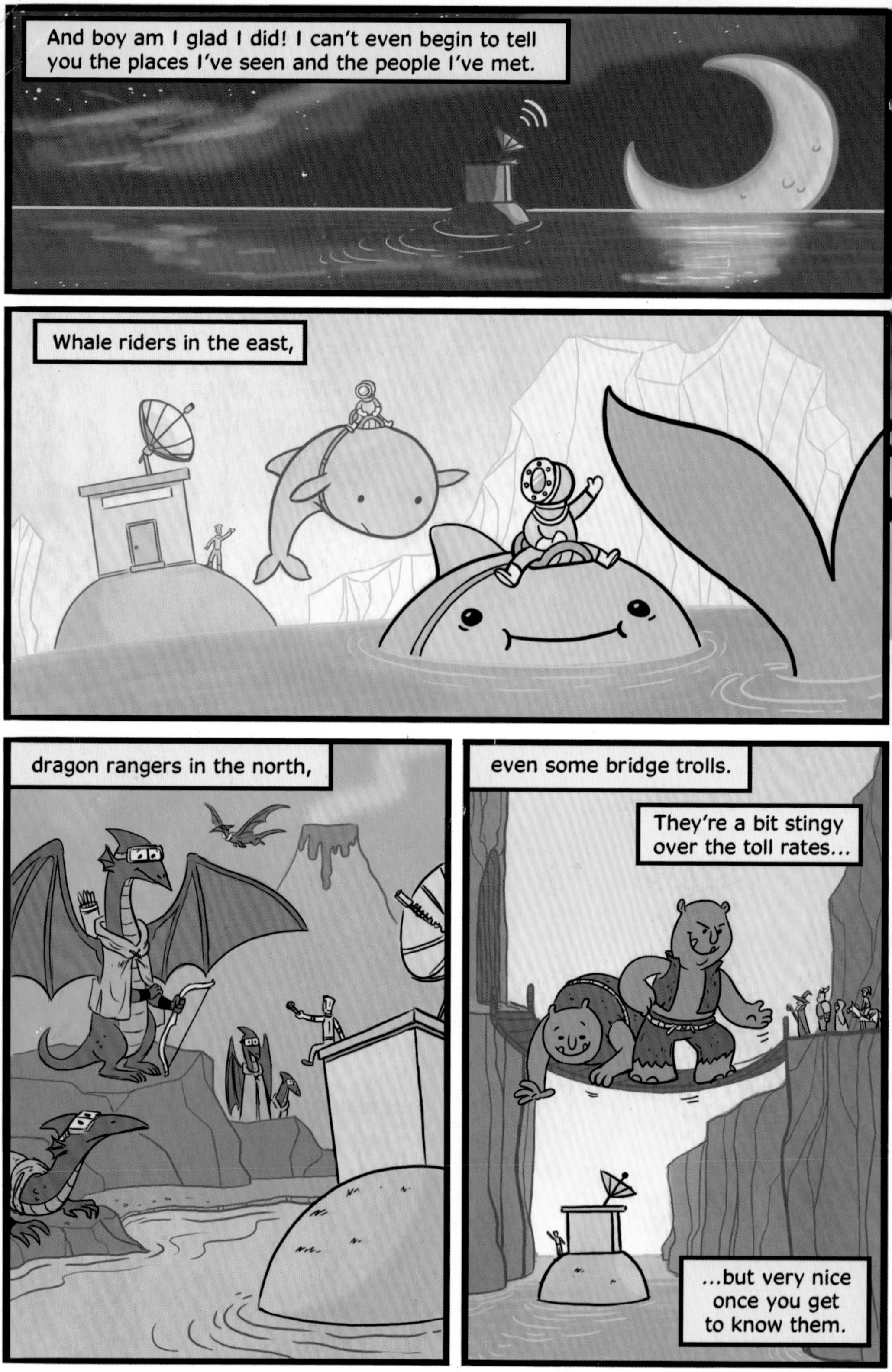
And boy am I glad I did! I can't even begin to tell you the places I've seen and the people I've met.
Whale riders in the east,
dragon rangers in the north,
even some bridge trolls.
They're a bit stingy over the toll rates...
...but very nice once you get to know them.

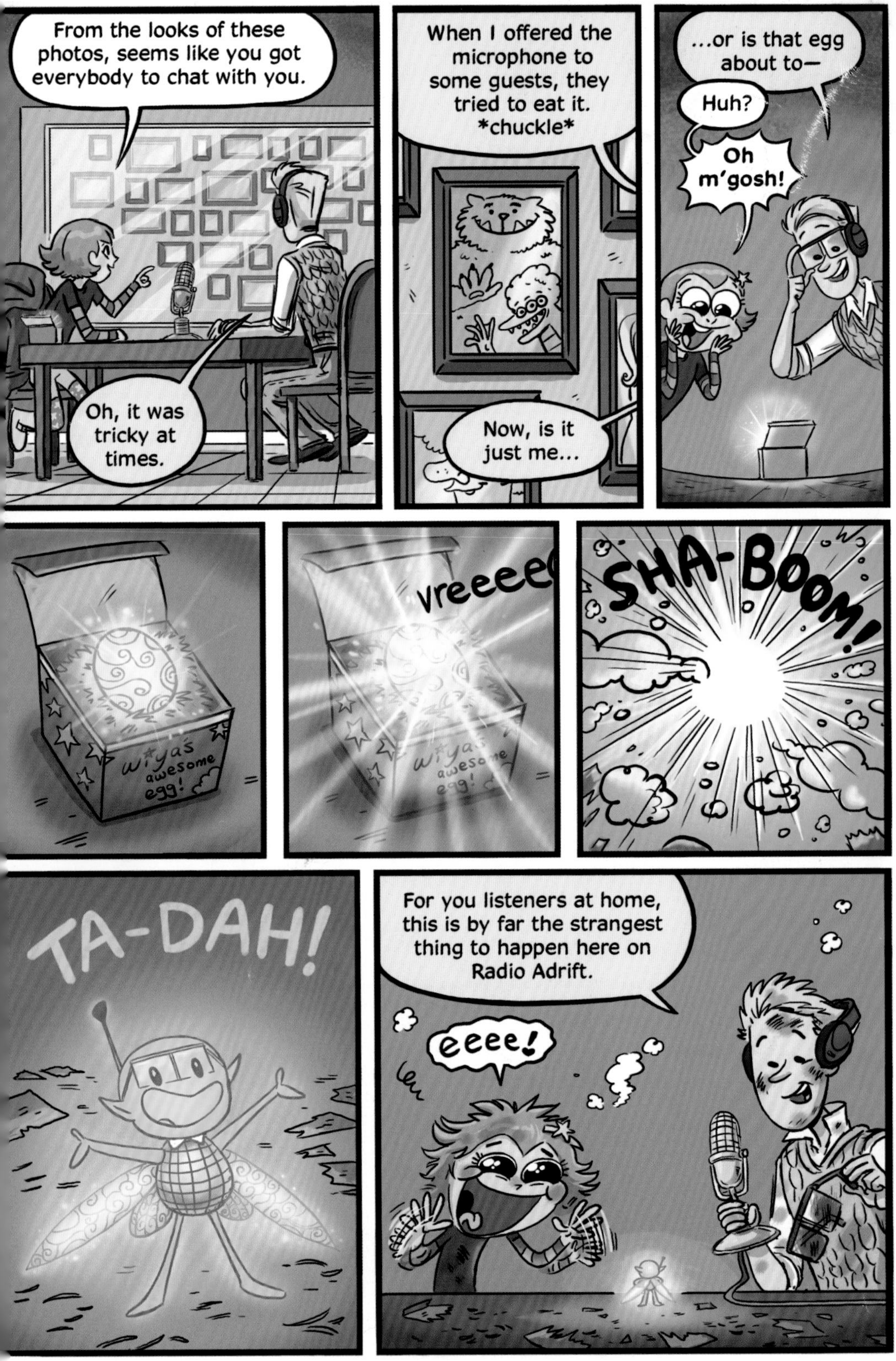

From the looks of these photos, seems like you got everybody to chat with you.
Oh, it was tricky at times.
When I offered the microphone to some guests, they tried to eat it. *chuckle*
Now, is it just me...
...or is that egg about to—
Huh?
Oh m'gosh!
w☆ya's awesome egg!
vreeeee
SHA-BOOM!
TA-DAH!
For you listeners at home, this is by far the strangest thing to happen here on Radio Adrift.
eeee!

That's all for tonight's broadcast.

Thank you for tuning in...

...as we begin our trip crossing the seas to hear from yobzzzzzzzz zzzzzzzzzffzzfz zffzzzzz...

Heh. Out of range.

It'll be a long time before we hear from him again, won't it?

bzzz

I wonder what else is on?

CLICK

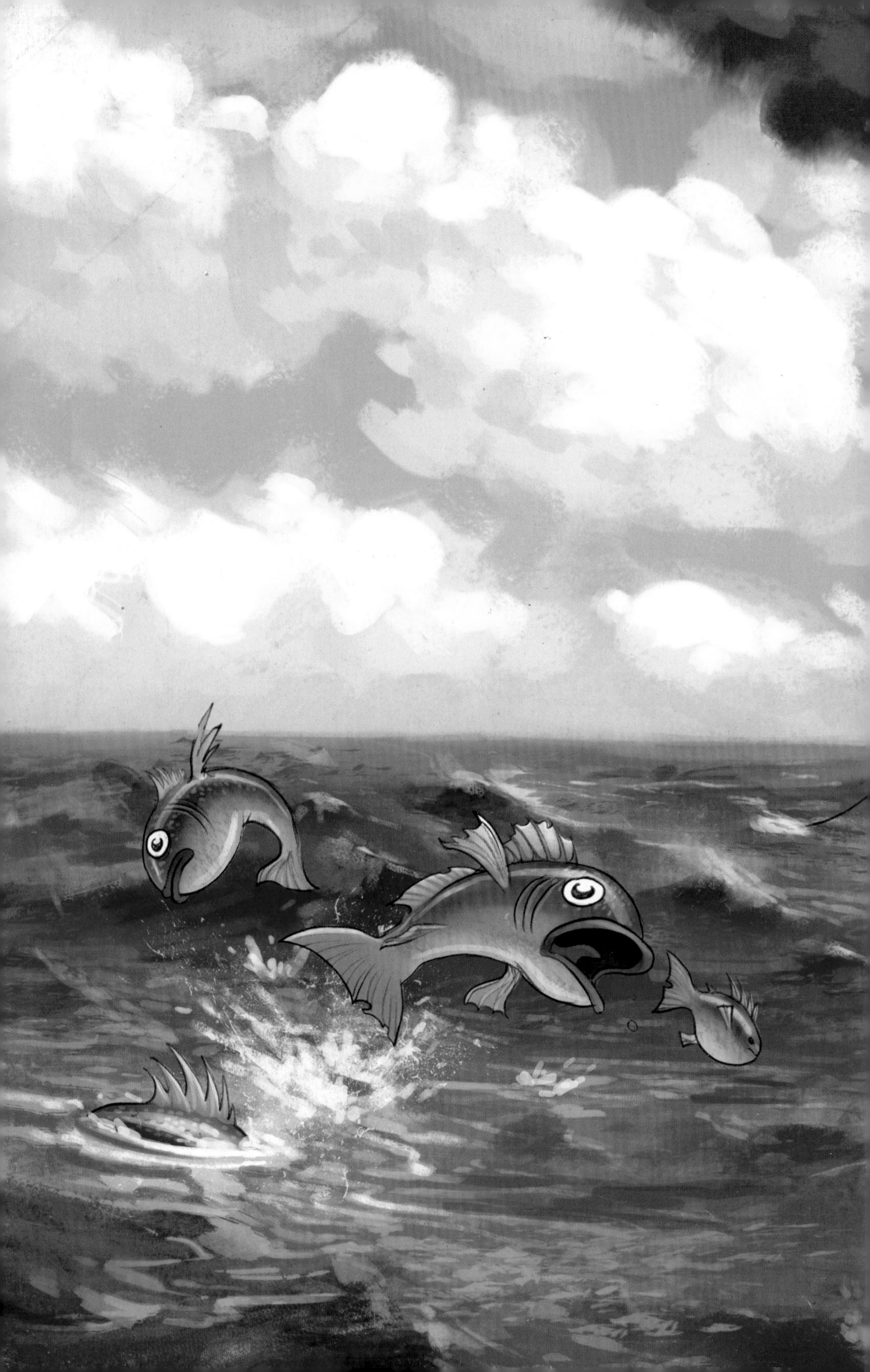

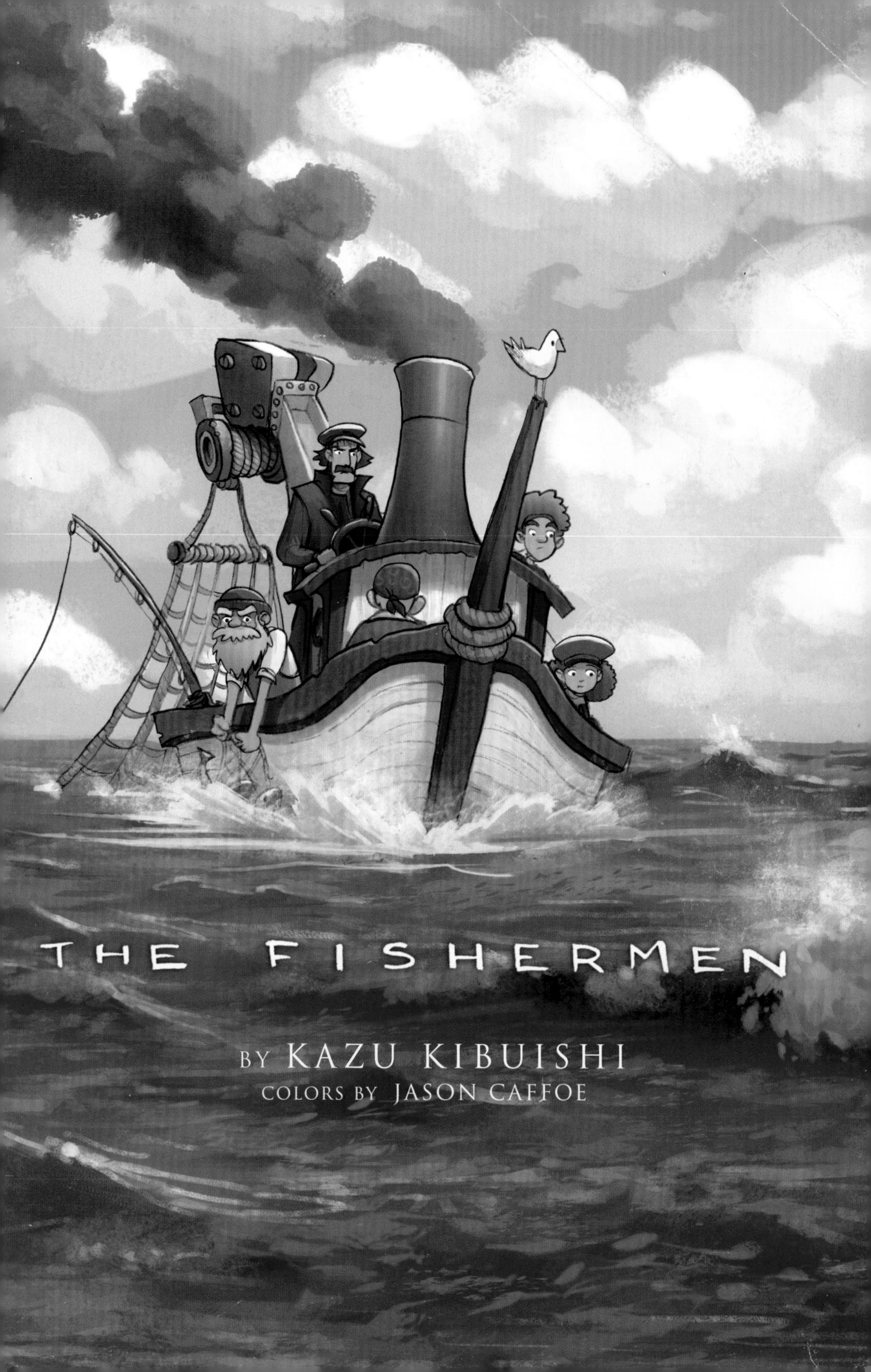

THE FISHERMEN

BY KAZU KIBUISHI

COLORS BY JASON CAFFOE

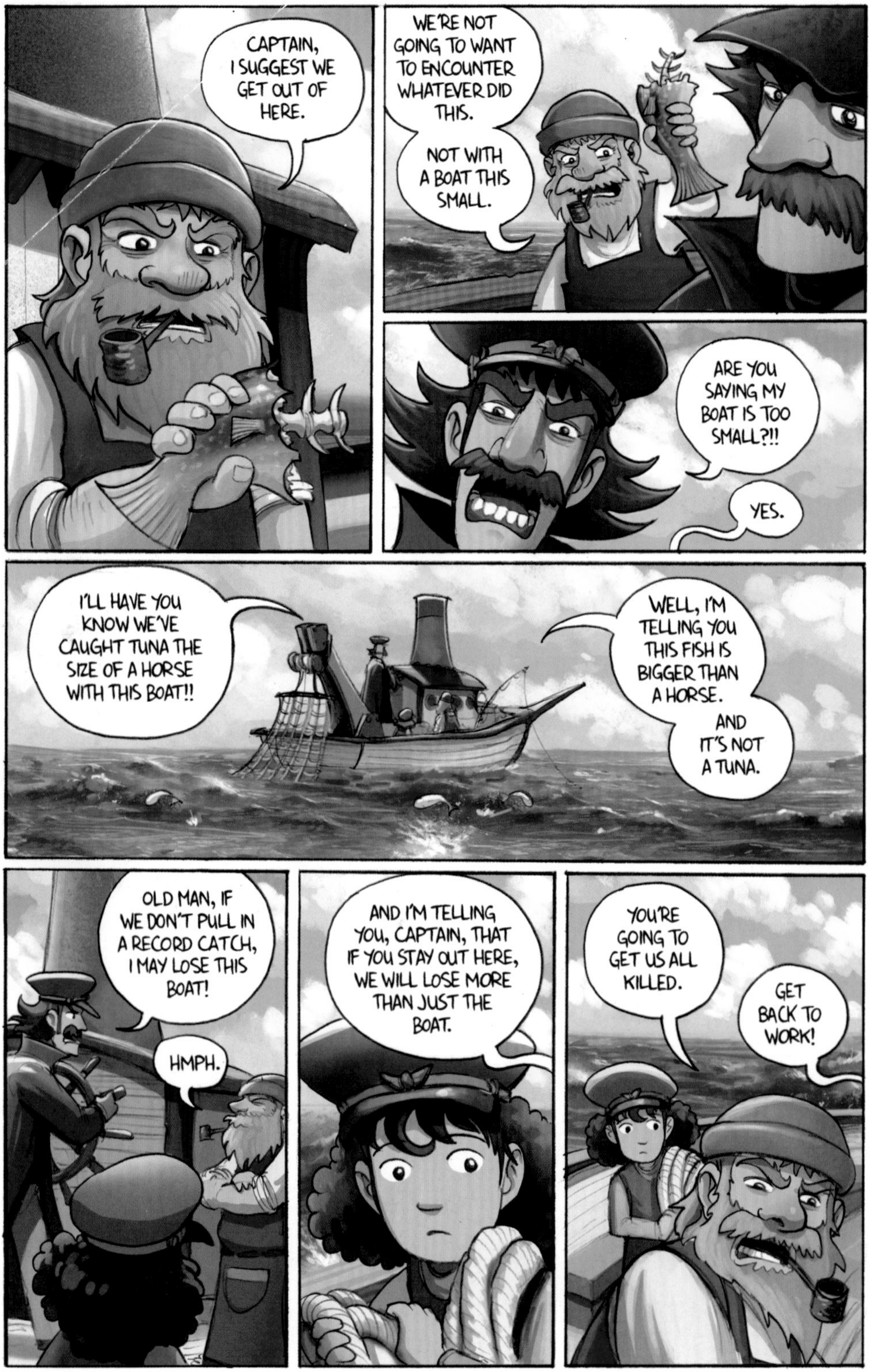
CAPTAIN, I SUGGEST WE GET OUT OF HERE.
WE'RE NOT GOING TO WANT TO ENCOUNTER WHATEVER DID THIS.
NOT WITH A BOAT THIS SMALL.
ARE YOU SAYING MY BOAT IS TOO SMALL?!!
YES.
I'LL HAVE YOU KNOW WE'VE CAUGHT TUNA THE SIZE OF A HORSE WITH THIS BOAT!!
WELL, I'M TELLING YOU THIS FISH IS BIGGER THAN A HORSE.
AND IT'S NOT A TUNA.
OLD MAN, IF WE DON'T PULL IN A RECORD CATCH, I MAY LOSE THIS BOAT!
HMPH.
AND I'M TELLING YOU, CAPTAIN, THAT IF YOU STAY OUT HERE, WE WILL LOSE MORE THAN JUST THE BOAT.
YOU'RE GOING TO GET US ALL KILLED.
GET BACK TO WORK!

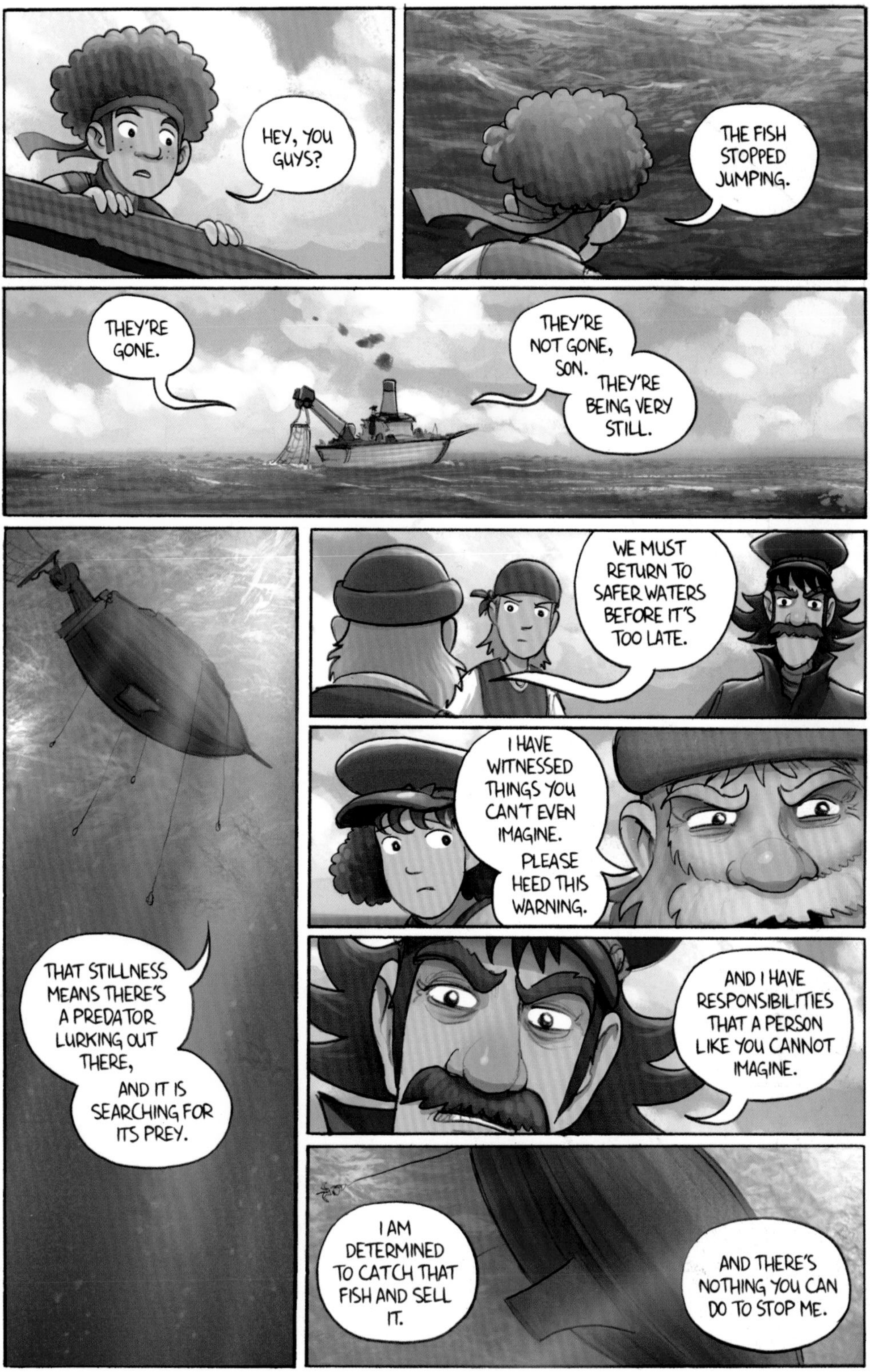

HEY, YOU GUYS?
THE FISH STOPPED JUMPING.
THEY'RE GONE.
THEY'RE NOT GONE, SON.
THEY'RE BEING VERY STILL.
THAT STILLNESS MEANS THERE'S A PREDATOR LURKING OUT THERE,
AND IT IS SEARCHING FOR ITS PREY.
WE MUST RETURN TO SAFER WATERS BEFORE IT'S TOO LATE.
I HAVE WITNESSED THINGS YOU CAN'T EVEN IMAGINE.
PLEASE HEED THIS WARNING.
AND I HAVE RESPONSIBILITIES THAT A PERSON LIKE YOU CANNOT IMAGINE.
I AM DETERMINED TO CATCH THAT FISH AND SELL IT.
AND THERE'S NOTHING YOU CAN DO TO STOP ME.

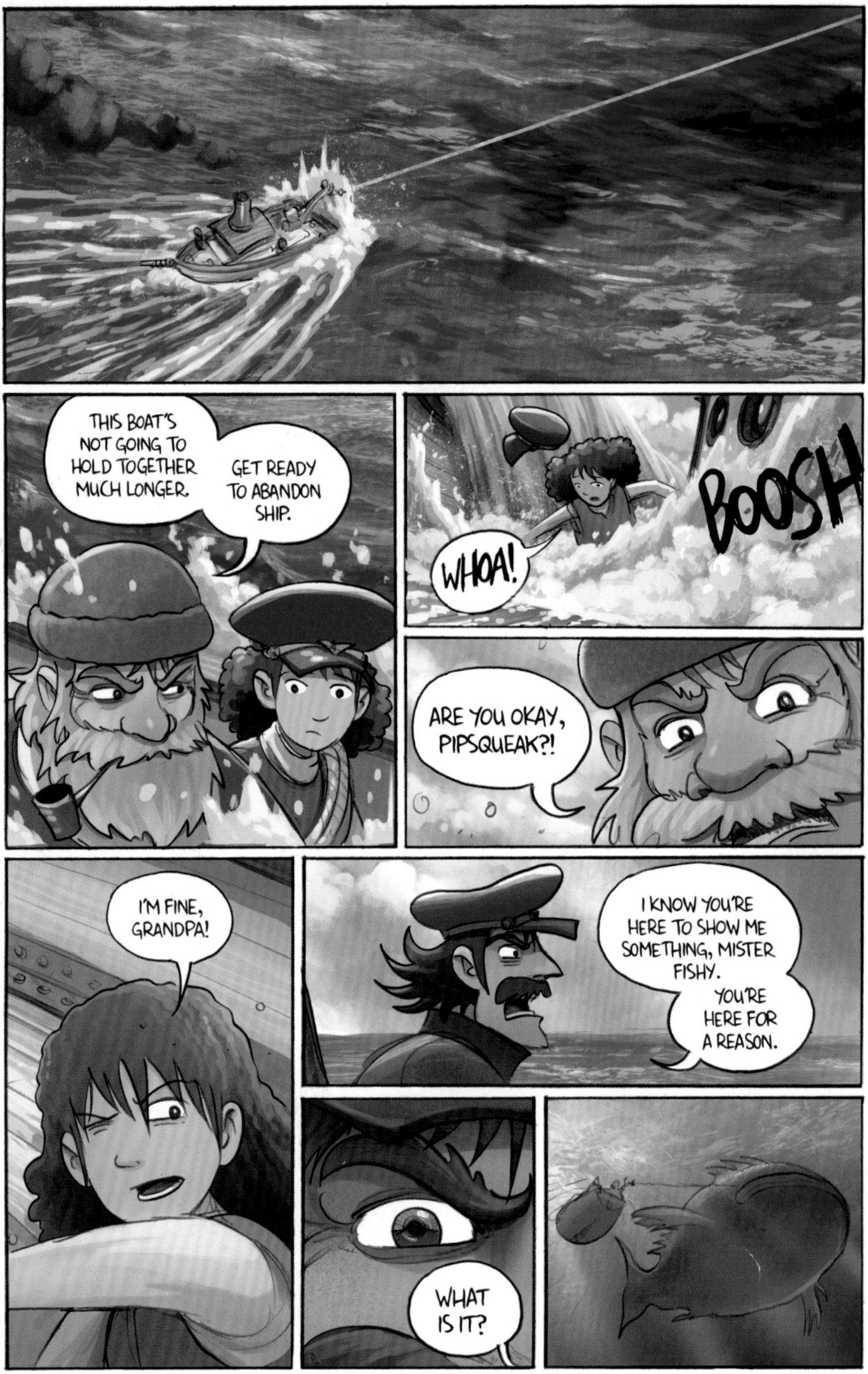
THIS BOAT'S NOT GOING TO HOLD TOGETHER MUCH LONGER.
GET READY TO ABANDON SHIP.
BOOSH
WHOA!
ARE YOU OKAY, PIPSQUEAK?!
I'M FINE, GRANDPA!
I KNOW YOU'RE HERE TO SHOW ME SOMETHING, MISTER FISHY.
YOU'RE HERE FOR A REASON.
WHAT IS IT?

COME ON. I'LL CATCH YOU.

DO YOU REMEMBER THE STORY I TOLD YOU ABOUT UNCLE ROY?

YOU MEAN THE ONE ABOUT HIM DISAPPEARING OUT AT SEA?

YES, THAT'S THE ONE.

IT WAS IN THESE WATERS WHERE HE WAS LAST SEEN.

I THINK THERE'S A REASON THESE ISLANDS DON'T SHOW UP ON THE MAP.

I BELIEVE THIS PLACE IS CURSED.

THIS PLACE IS GOING TO MAKE US RICH!

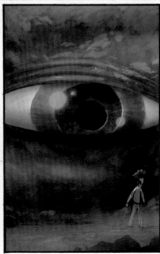

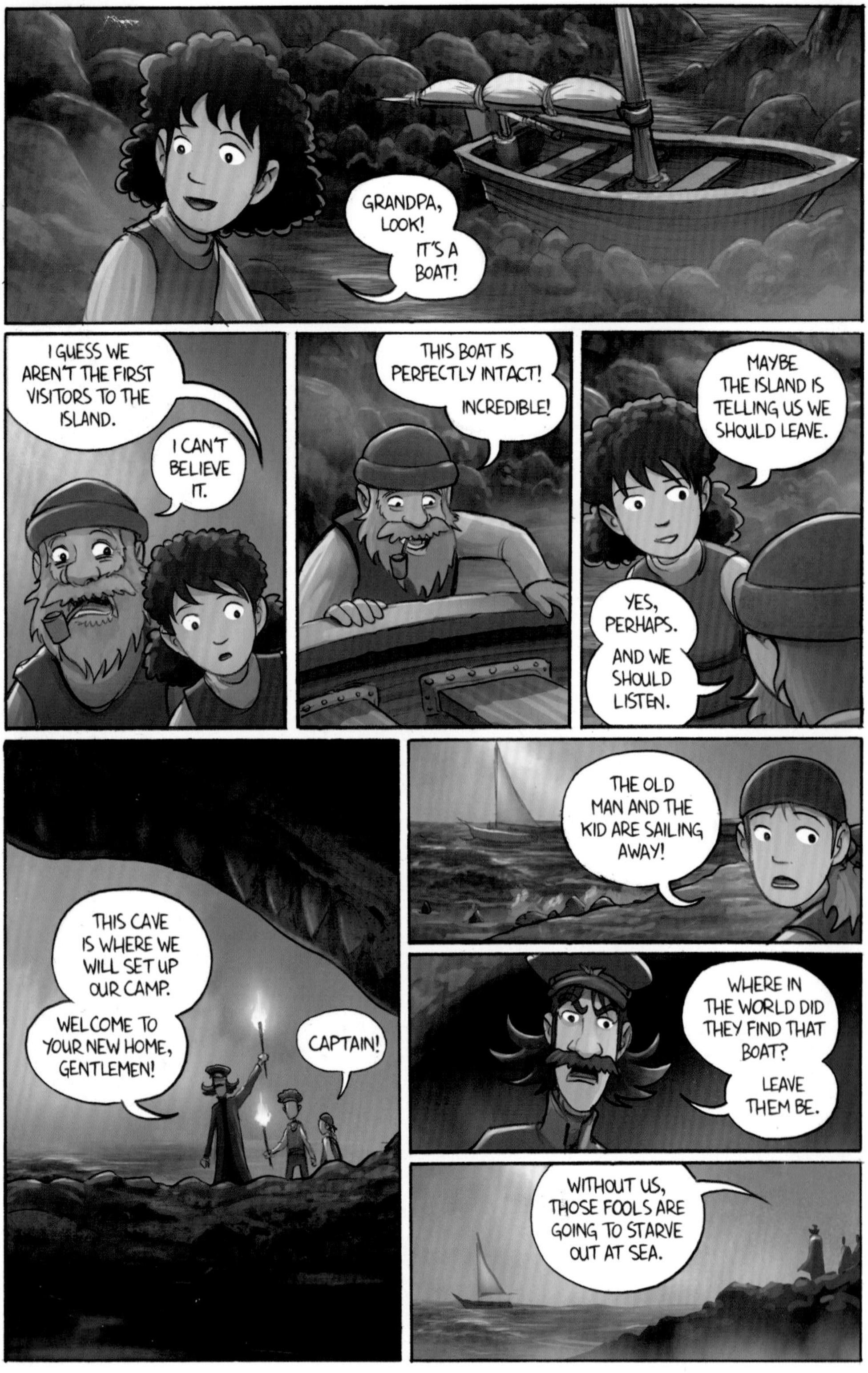
GRANDPA, LOOK!
IT'S A BOAT!
I GUESS WE AREN'T THE FIRST VISITORS TO THE ISLAND.
I CAN'T BELIEVE IT.
THIS BOAT IS PERFECTLY INTACT!
INCREDIBLE!
MAYBE THE ISLAND IS TELLING US WE SHOULD LEAVE.
YES, PERHAPS.
AND WE SHOULD LISTEN.
THIS CAVE IS WHERE WE WILL SET UP OUR CAMP.
WELCOME TO YOUR NEW HOME, GENTLEMEN!
CAPTAIN!
THE OLD MAN AND THE KID ARE SAILING AWAY!
WHERE IN THE WORLD DID THEY FIND THAT BOAT?
LEAVE THEM BE.
WITHOUT US, THOSE FOOLS ARE GOING TO STARVE OUT AT SEA.

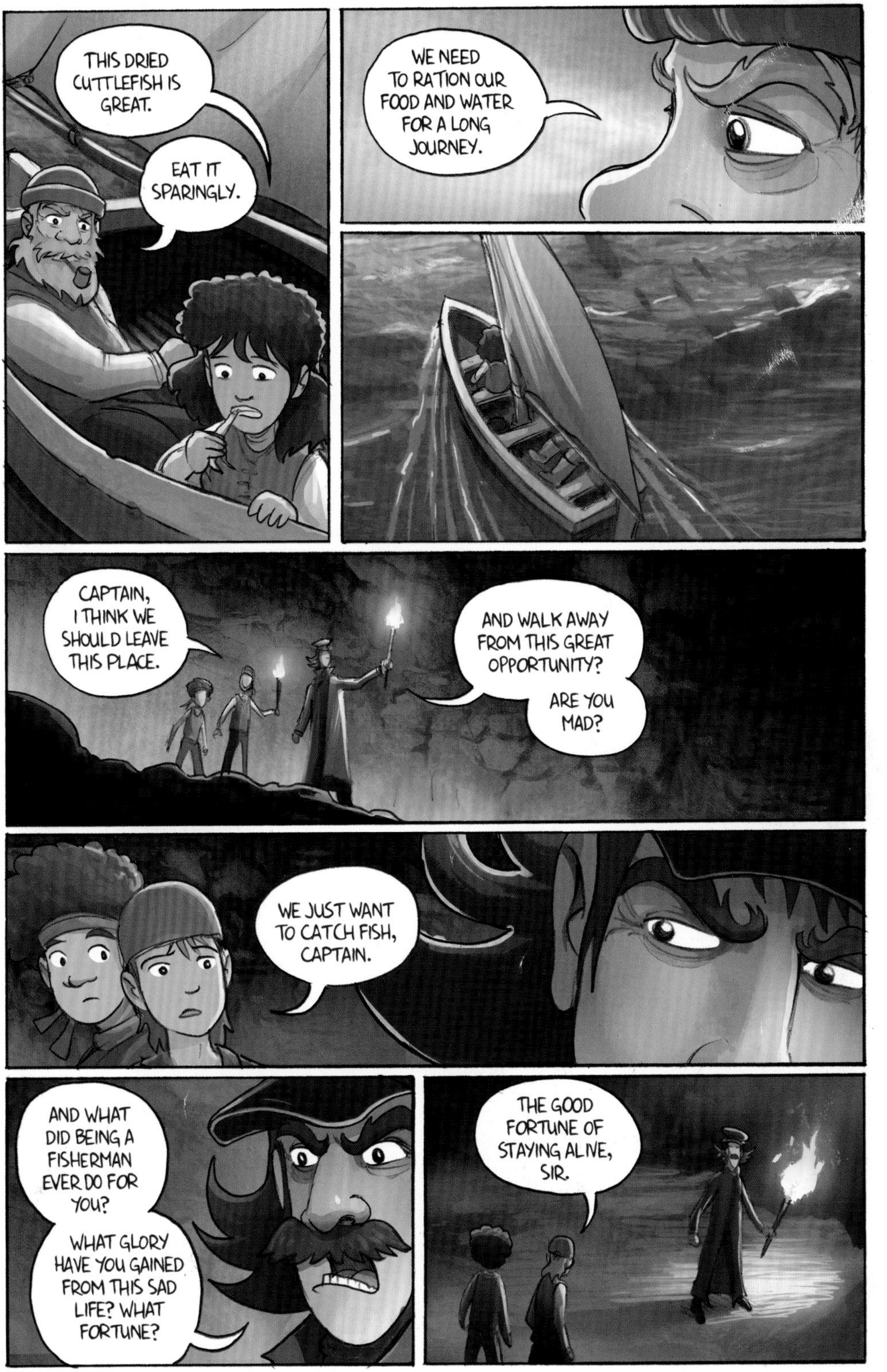
THIS DRIED CUTTLEFISH IS GREAT.
EAT IT SPARINGLY.
WE NEED TO RATION OUR FOOD AND WATER FOR A LONG JOURNEY.
CAPTAIN, I THINK WE SHOULD LEAVE THIS PLACE.
AND WALK AWAY FROM THIS GREAT OPPORTUNITY?
ARE YOU MAD?
WE JUST WANT TO CATCH FISH, CAPTAIN.
AND WHAT DID BEING A FISHERMAN EVER DO FOR YOU?
WHAT GLORY HAVE YOU GAINED FROM THIS SAD LIFE? WHAT FORTUNE?
THE GOOD FORTUNE OF STAYING ALIVE, SIR.

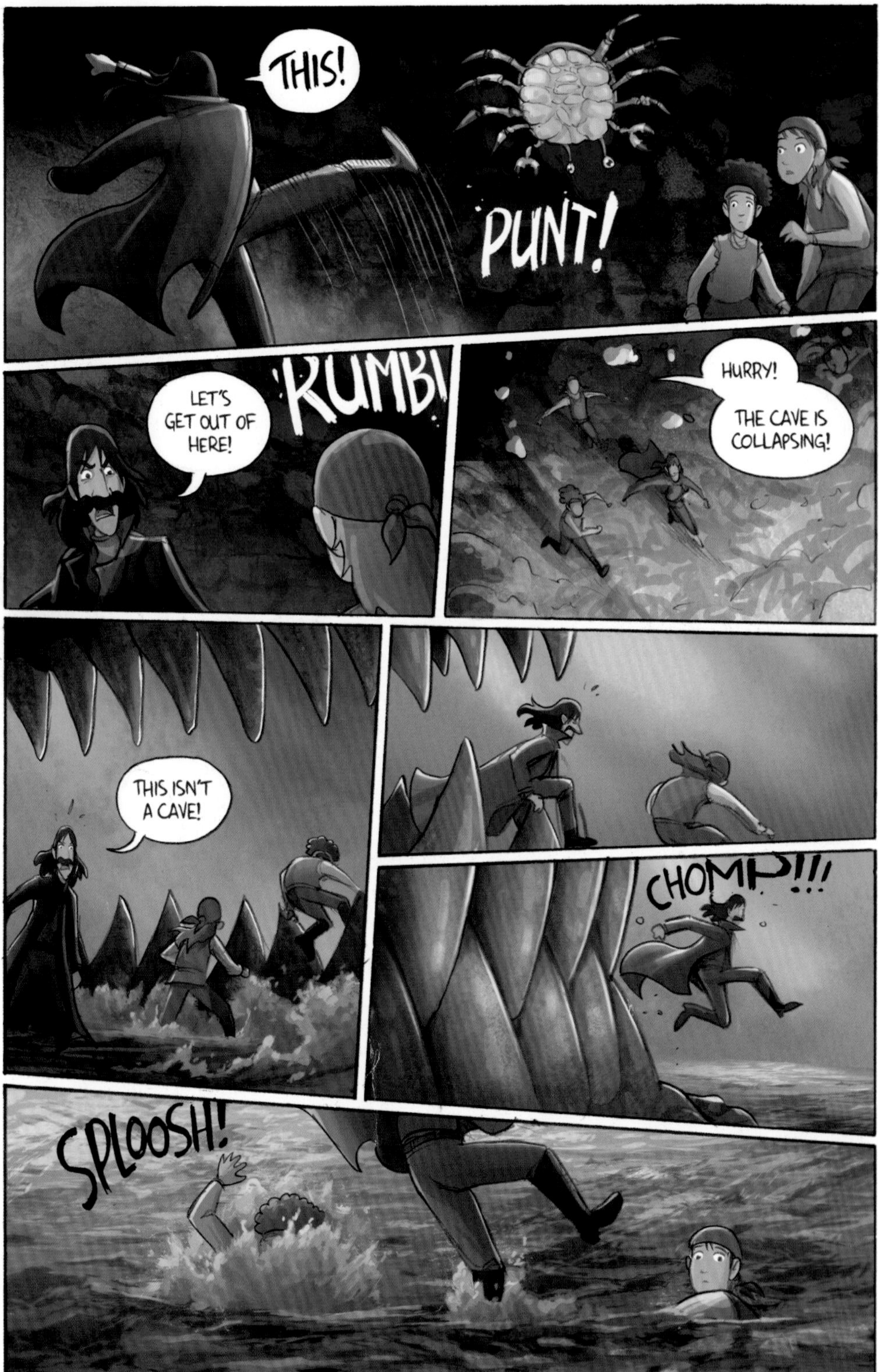
THIS!
PUNT!
LET'S GET OUT OF HERE!
RUMBL
HURRY!
THE CAVE IS COLLAPSING!
THIS ISN'T A CAVE!
CHOMP!!!
SPLOOSH!

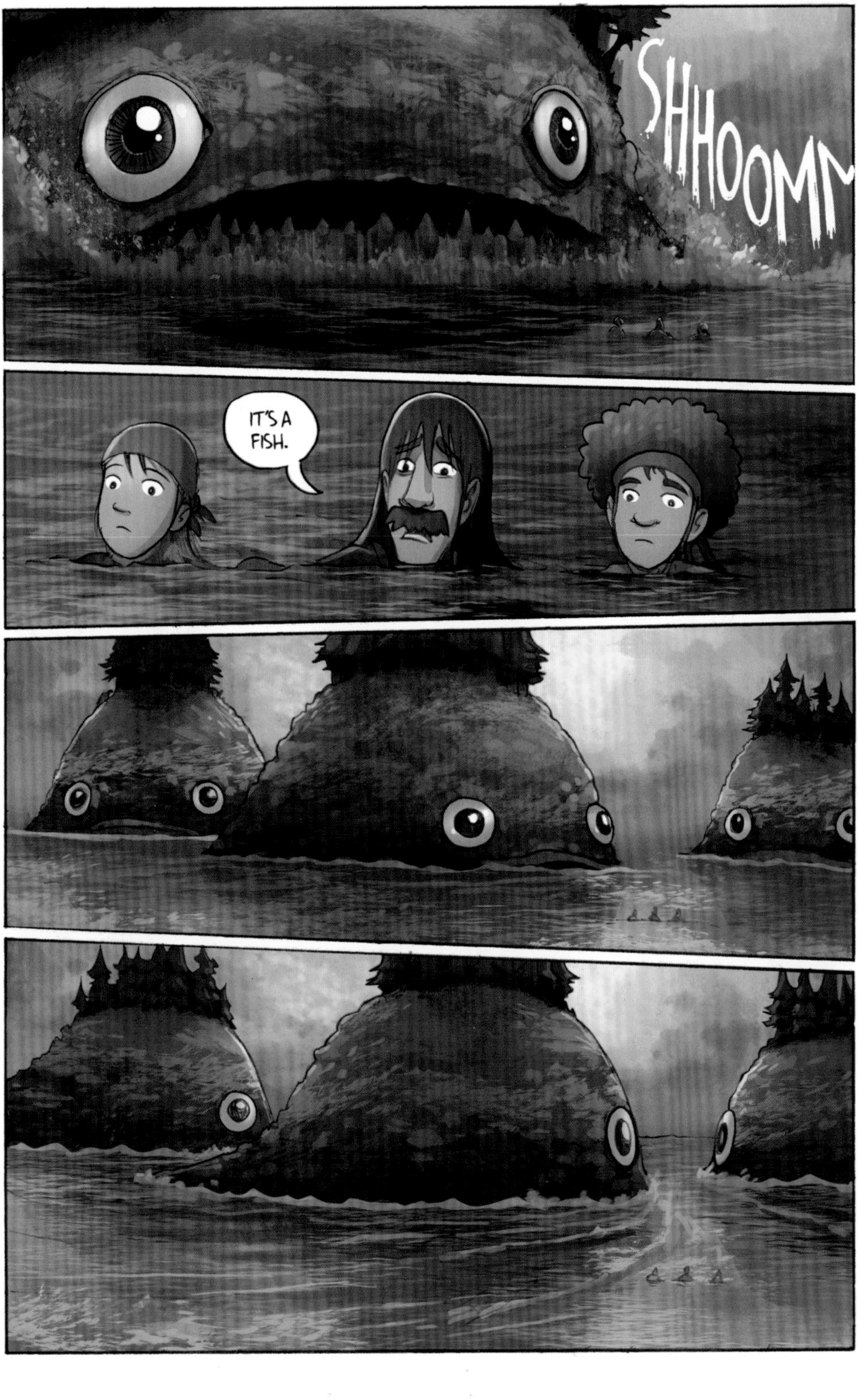
SHHOOMM
IT'S A FISH.

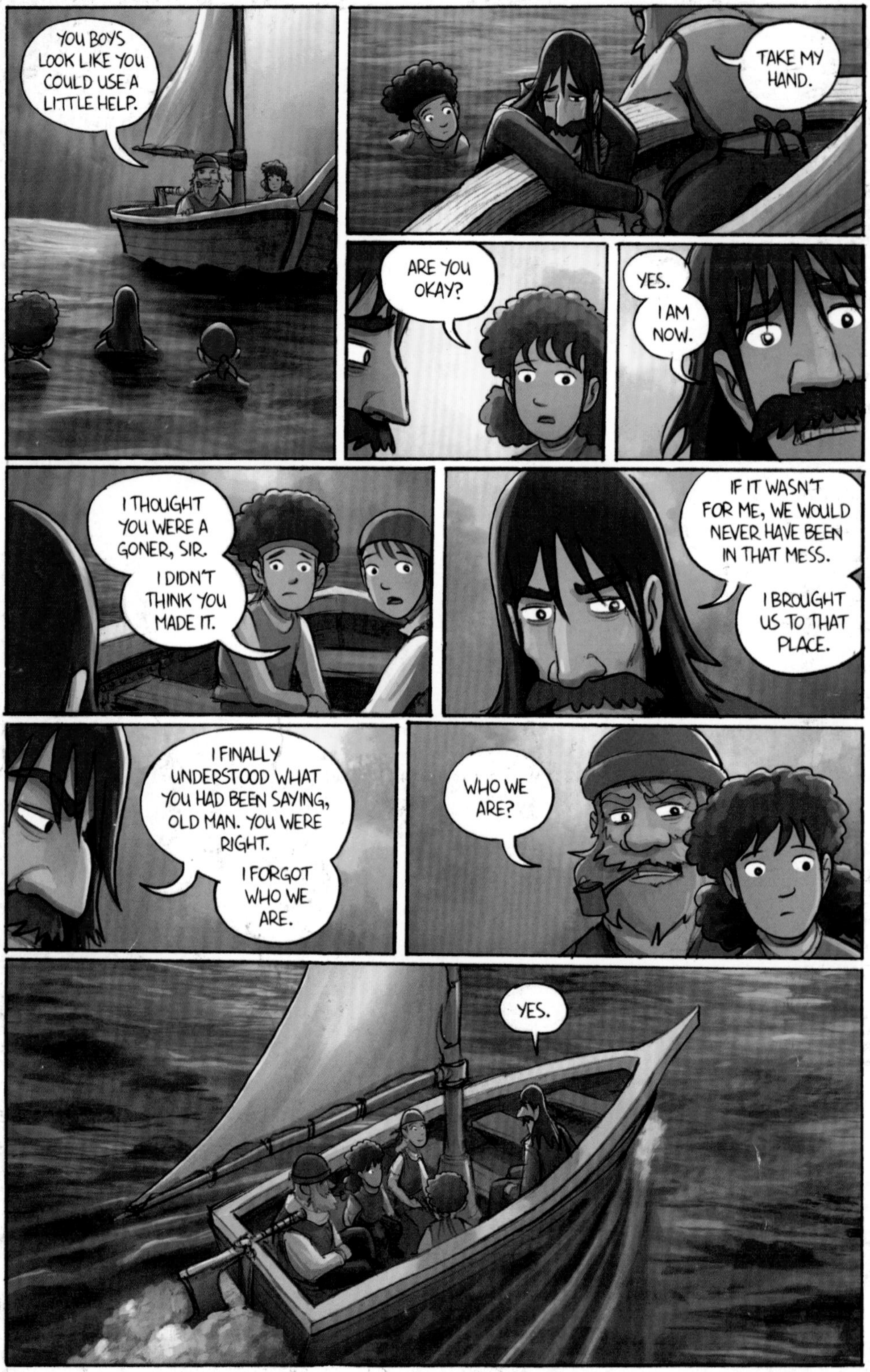
YOU BOYS LOOK LIKE YOU COULD USE A LITTLE HELP.
TAKE MY HAND.
ARE YOU OKAY?
YES.
I AM NOW.
I THOUGHT YOU WERE A GONER, SIR.
I DIDN'T THINK YOU MADE IT.
IF IT WASN'T FOR ME, WE WOULD NEVER HAVE BEEN IN THAT MESS.
I BROUGHT US TO THAT PLACE.
I FINALLY UNDERSTOOD WHAT YOU HAD BEEN SAYING, OLD MAN. YOU WERE RIGHT.
I FORGOT WHO WE ARE.
WHO WE ARE?
YES.